OLD SCORES

Also by Will Thomas

Some Danger Involved

To Kingdom Come

The Limehouse Text

The Hellfire Conspiracy

The Black Hand

Fatal Enquiry

Anatomy of Evil

Hell Bay

OLD SCORES

WILL THOMAS

MINOTAUR BOOKS ❦ NEW YORK

OLD SCORES. Copyright © 2017 by Will Thomas. All rights reserved. Printed in the United States of America. For information, address St. Martin's Press, 175 Fifth Avenue, New York, N.Y. 10010.

www.minotaurbooks.com

"An Awkward Way to Die" copyright © 2017 by Will Thomas

The Library of Congress has cataloged the hardcover edition as follows:

Names: Thomas, Will, 1958– author.
Title: Old scores : a Barker & Llewelyn novel / Will Thomas.
Description: First edition. | New York : Minotaur Books, 2017.
Identifiers: LCCN 2017018848 | ISBN 9781250077967 (hardcover) |
    ISBN 9781466890299 (ebook)
Subjects: LCSH: Barker, Cyrus (Fictitious character)—Fiction. |
    Private investigators—England—London—Fiction. | Great
    Britain—History—Victoria, 1837–1901—Fiction. | GSAFD: Mystery
    fiction.
Classification: LCC PS3620.H644 O43 2017 | DDC 813/.6—dc23
LC record available at https://lccn.loc.gov/2017018848

ISBN 978-1-250-19796-2 (trade paperback)

Our books may be purchased in bulk for promotional, educational, or business use. Please contact your local bookseller or the Macmillan Corporate and Premium Sales Department at 1-800-221-7945, extension 5442, or by email at MacmillanSpecialMarkets@macmillan.com.

First Minotaur Books Paperback Edition: October 2018

10 9 8 7 6 5 4 3 2 1

ACKNOWLEDGMENTS

As always, this novel could never have been written without my wife, Julia. She is the rock I cling to during life's tempests, my number one cheerleader, the practical one, and my best friend. She is also in charge of Barker's integrity, which makes for some lively discussions during the writing process.

I would like to thank my editor, Keith Kahla, for believing in a couple of private enquiry agents, and my agent, Maria Carvainis, for her willingness to go to bat for me, time after time. My manuscripts (yes, the kind written on actual paper) could not be in better hands.

CHAPTER ONE

I suppose it all began with the garden. Cyrus Barker's garden, I mean. It was a particularly good year for some reason. Everything came together perfectly. The gardeners were working, hard-pressed to keep the growth from getting out of hand, and anything attempted for the first time grew and flourished. It was too perfect, if you know what I mean. One cannot have the ointment without the fly, the yang without the yin. I should have expected something to happen to balance all that beauty, but I didn't. Ah, man, the eternal optimist.

The spring had been variable that year, blowing hot and cold, eventually giving way to a long, drowsy summer. My monastic room was too hot and stuffy to read in after breakfast, so I went outside to sit in the shade of the pagodalike gazebo. Barker puttered with his jacket off, raking the stones into swirl patterns. The garden was only ten years old, but it appeared as solid and ancient as Stonehenge, albeit a Chinese one.

"What are you reading so avidly?" Barker called from under a young Japanese maple he was trimming. The sun glinted from the black-lensed spectacles he wore.

"Herman Melville. American sea stories."

"Is life not exciting enough for you that you must find relief in adventure fiction?"

"It is getting rather dull. No one has tried to cut my throat in nearly a week."

"Ha!" Barker said.

"Are you ready for the tour?" I asked.

"Almost."

Kew was coming, or rather the director of Kew Gardens, William Thiselton-Dyer, along with a special delegation of envoys from the Japanese government. The latter were interested in establishing an embassy in London. Everything had a Japanese motif that summer in arts and fashion. English roses were doing their best to recast themselves as Asian cherry blossoms.

"Is there anything I can do?" I asked, feeling called to say something. "I could help with the penjing trees . . ."

"No, no, lad, you just go ahead and read."

Very well, so I'm not an expert gardener. Some wag, probably our butler, Mac, expressed the belief that bonsai (to give them the Japanese name) scream at the mention of my name. England has been called a nation of gardeners, but no one said anything about Wales. The only thing I ever grew in the garden was weary of the long list of names I was forced to set down in a notebook for the Guv, since even he could not read his terrible scribble. My attempts to plant or grow anything had ended in failure, and now just getting near a bushel of plants made our Chinese gardeners shuffle quickly in my direction to head me off.

"So," I said, "the Japanese have finally left their sequestered isle, and are taking a world tour. I assumed the Americans had the treaties there sewn up. The Foreign Office lads must be champing at the bit."

"I thought you were reading."

"I was. I left off in the middle of a sermon."

"Left off? You generally nod off."

"It's not my fault that the Metropolitan Tabernacle can no longer find a preacher the caliber of Charles Haddon Spurgeon."

"Pastors change, but the Word stays the same."

"Is that to be the text of the day?"

Barker believes me to be his own personal mission field. Scratch a Welshman and you'll find a pagan, or something like that. I am a professing Christian, but it wasn't my fault if some pastors like the sound of their own voices too much.

One of the gardeners passed by with the wheelbarrow, and eyed me critically. This was not a place to read at the moment, yet the purpose of such a garden is to bring peace to those who dwelt there, rather than provide a place where overly industrious men can find more work. My bookmark hovered over Melville's novel, ready for me to pack it in.

"How much more has to be done before it is perfect?" I asked, but it was a rhetorical question. The gardeners would work until the last second, then hurry out the back gate as our guests came in the front.

I prefer the garden in the fall. The maples turn red and send their seedpods spiraling slowly to the ground like tiny ballerinas. The koi grow sleek and fat, preparing for winter, and squirrels gather acorns for their nest. The willow loses its leaves and looks gaunt and skeletal. In such a garden at such a time a man could think or possibly write great things. That is, as long as he does not have to tend it.

I heard voices in the hall. I dropped the leather strap into the book in the middle of the sermon and stood. I held up Barker's morning coat and after he had put in his cuff links he slipped into it. He is impressive in a morning coat. He gave a nod and the gardeners began to disperse. It was a magic trick. This garden had suddenly appeared out of nowhere or dropped from the sky, yet it looked as if it had been here since Caesar first camped on the Thames. Cyrus Barker and I crossed the bridge to the back door and entered just as our guests came in the front.

"Konnichi wa," the Guv began, and went off on some long-winded and polite greeting in their native tongue.

There were half a dozen men in the hall, including the Kew representative and a gentleman from the Foreign Office, if I may be willing to stretch the term that far. The rest were mostly Japanese. I am able now by dress, manner, and feature to tell a Japanese from the Chinese, but then I had never met any of the former before. One wore traditional garb, but the others were in Western clothing. Most had black, European-cut suits and bowler hats, and the last two fellows wore coats and trousers of a military cut. The one in the kimono, the leader, came forward eagerly.

"Mr. Barker, thank you for inviting us to your lovely home," he said.

Barker bowed. "I do not expect my humble garden to reach your exacting standards, sir, but I am glad you thought coming worth your while."

Our guest bowed as well. He was a small man with gray hair cut in a Western fashion. I liked the ambassador right away. For one thing, he was probably under five feet tall, so even I towered over him. He wore an outer kimono of gray gulls in a white sky. His inner kimono, which just peeked through at his collar, was white, with some sort of embroidered pattern across it. By contrast, his obi sash was a deep red. On his feet, he wore wooden geta clogs, which clicked as he walked in our hall.

It wasn't just his appearance I liked, but his manner. As good as Barker's garden was, and really, it was excellent, he had probably seen every one in Japan, and yet he appeared to be awestruck by the work done here, and questioned the Guv closely on every decision he had made. Who would have thought to put the willow by the Japanese maple? How stark the standing rocks are against the red brick wall. The koi fish seemed to be peering up at us from under the lily pads.

Later, I heard that he had been a Shinto monk. That must have been it. He seemed more like a holy man than a politician or envoy. But then, who could resist such a man when he asked something of you or your country?

The military men were of a piece. One wore jodhpur trousers and tall boots, with only gold braid on his peaked cap to highlight the unrelieved black. He had a gray mustache. The other wore a long military coat decorated in gold scrollwork, with red collar and cuffs. He, too, appeared to be in his sixties, though his hair was black. Both frowned, as if coming here were a kind of punishment. Perhaps it was.

The director from Kew Gardens came forward, looking rather put out. William Thiselton-Dyer had a bulbous bald head as if overpacked with gray matter, and a soft beard that grew down over his tie. His nostrils were arched. Obviously he had hoped to be the one to give a proper introduction to all parties present, but he had been confounded by the eagerness of the envoy.

"Mr. Barker, may I present His Excellency Toda Ichigo, General Mononobe, and Admiral Edami of the Japanese delegation. These gentlemen are their bodyguards. I understand you are already acquainted with Mr. Campbell-Ffinch of the Foreign Office."

Just then, I saw Barker stiffen. Standing behind him I could see the muscles of his back tighten beneath his long coat. I noticed it, but no one else did. The Foreign Office man, Trelawney Campbell-Ffinch, was too busy stepping forward to greet my employer. Campbell-Ffinch was a noted boxer and had a reputation for getting results and not caring how he got them. By the time he shook the Guv's hand there was no sign that anything had occurred. One could in fact say that nothing had occurred, but if one knew Barker as well as I did, he would know better.

"Barker," Trelawney Campbell-Ffinch said with oil in his voice. "Good to see you, as always. These gentlemen are impressed with your daisies."

In fact, the Guv had no daisies, nor any other flower. An Asian garden is known for its austerity. Ours held standing rocks and a brook and lily pads, a bathhouse and garden shed and a gazebo.

Campbell-Ffinch was baiting him, somehow under the impression that the two of them were equals, anxious someday to get in the ring with him. To my employer he was no more than a gadfly, a midge, of not even enough importance to swat.

"Shall we see this corner of the garden, gentlemen?"

As they moved through his garden, Mr. Toda went first, followed by the general, Campbell-Ffinch, the admiral, Thiselton-Dyer, and the two bodyguards. The envoy was unarmed. The general carried a Western sword in his belt. Campbell-Ffinch had a bulge in his pocket from some sort of revolver.

"Ah!" the ambassador cried. "Wonderful!"

I forget what it is like to see this garden for the first time. It is magnificent; not large, perhaps, for this was a private residence in London, but very nearly perfect. The ambassador looked like a child stepping into a sweetshop. The Kew director hurried forward and led him to the left, skirting the koi pond. The other guests stood and took in the view.

General Mononobe, the one in the long coat, was an impressive sight, a stern man with a square jaw, black hair, and strong features. Campbell-Ffinch, in contrast, was younger, taller, blond-haired, and red-faced, with a light mustache. The admiral had gray hair under his cap and lesions from a bout with smallpox.

The bodyguards were a contrast as well. One was barely five feet six, with a large mustache, carefully waxed. He moved from side to side, rolling his shoulders as if he imagined himself much larger than he was. The other was well over six feet and close to eighteen stone, an elephant in a suit jacket. He was clean-shaven and his nose had been badly broken once and was still pushed to the side. When he lifted his bowler I noticed that he still wore the traditional Japanese topknot.

Barker had joined Thiselton-Dyer and the ambassador and was discussing the garden with them. I couldn't exactly say whether the tour was intended to be in English or Japanese, but they careened haphazardly from one language to the other.

"How's Barker's terrier these days?" Campbell-Ffinch asked in my ear.

"Woof," I replied. I didn't hate him, exactly, but we wouldn't be going out for a pint anytime soon. The Foreign Office had a reputation for doing whatever the government told them to without scruple.

Campbell-Ffinch looked bored. The garden couldn't even grow daisies. The general seemed to approve of the garden, but he kept a keen eye on everything in front of him. He had an intensity that was alarming. Once he flashed it upon me, but I pretended to be interested in the penjing tree at my side. Looking harmless is what I do best. Only reluctantly will I show the skills I have learned from my employer in six years of training.

Ambassador Toda seemed delighted with everything, but it could have been as much show as good manners. He was a diplomat, after all. If he found fault, he would not reveal it. What were they in England for? I wondered. Was it to start an embassy, or was there some other reason?

I am naturally inclined to take impressions. Luckily, that is also my duty. I noticed that the taller bodyguard was left-handed. The smaller one was well muscled under his topcoat, but the taller one was sleek and fat. The general watched the wind blow through the maple leaves as if he wanted to slash them with his sword. The admiral looked as stern a man as I have ever seen. I suspected Campbell-Ffinch considered himself in every way superior to these foreigners by the way he was behaving.

Our butler, Jacob Maccabee, came out then with a tray of tea, an iron teapot, and small cups. He carried it as if it weighed nothing, gliding along the narrow walkway that led to the gazebo. He cuts an elegant figure, our Mac, and would do his level best to try to impress our guests even if I wouldn't.

We all knelt and took tea in the pagoda-roofed gazebo. The Japanese delegation was sitting on the floor, legs folded. Thistelton-Dyer and Campbell-Ffinch found the position awkward. The tea tasted like little more than water. I'd have preferred strong coffee. The general looked as though he would agree. He kept looking at the Guv, either out of curiosity or something else. The ambassador and Thiselton-Dyer were the only talkative ones among us, though I filled the gap in conversation once or twice. Barker seemed preoccupied. I wanted to know what he was thinking, but understood that I could question him later. I have a problem with patience, or so the Guv tells me. The problem is, I haven't any.

Everyone seemed to be enjoying themselves and I didn't believe any of them. This was a political event. Everyone was politely following a ritual or protocol that was half English and half Japanese. It was possible that the ambassador had no interest in gardens at all and it was merely assumed by Thiselton-Dyer that a Japanese delegation must like Asian gardens. After this, perhaps they might visit the British Museum or even go to Buckingham Palace. We had worked for three weeks for a half-hour tour that seemed to have little or no meaning. Mr. Toda spoke enthusiastically about the garden afterward, but that was no doubt expected of him. Had there been any criticism, he would have kept it to himself.

"I fear we must keep to our schedule," Thistelton-Dyer said, rising from his seat. Western suits are not designed for kneeling.

The ambassador seemed reluctant to leave, but I assumed even that was expected. Politeness might be mistaken for enthusiasm. I'm not slighting the garden or our guests, but really, given limited time in London, wouldn't a Japanese envoy want to see something different? Take him to a pub for a few pints of good English ale, or to one of London's best coffeehouses, of which there are several. Better still, take him to Hampstead Heath and let him see a natural English garden. That might actually impress him.

We all stood and the protocol for leaving began. It was even more drawn out than the arrival, which had been cut short by the ambassador. One would have declared us the best of friends instead of total strangers. We hoped to meet again. We wished each other a good journey and a fine summer. We kept bowing until my back began to hurt.

Our guests passed through the house again to the front door and through it. In Lion Street, the cortège climbed into official-looking broughams and soon they bowled off into Newington Causeway.

I waited to see what Barker would say afterward, but he turned and went back out to the garden and sat in the gazebo.

That was our morning, the sort for which one prepares for weeks, and then it is over and one forgets it. The delegation went on to their next destination, and the one after that. Barker and I soon went to our offices and there was an end on it. Everyone forgot about the event. Everyone except for me. I couldn't forget the way that Barker froze when the envoys arrived.

CHAPTER TWO

We went to our offices in Whitehall, and nothing pertaining to the morning's visit occurred for the rest of the afternoon. We shut down our offices at six and were home again and dining within the half hour. My duties for the day were at an end. I took a cab and met a friend in the City, returning shortly after nine.

Inside I changed into a nightshirt, brushed my teeth, and read until about ten-thirty. When my eyelids began to grow heavy, I switched off the electric lamp on my side table and called out a good night to my employer.

There was no answer. Perhaps he had already fallen asleep. All the tension involved in preparing the tour must have worn him out. Generally, he reads until eleven o'clock or so.

"Sir?" I called, hoping my voice would travel up the stairwell to his rooms in the garret of the house.

I lay half asleep for perhaps five minutes before moving, but eventually, I rose and went out into the hall. Climbing the narrow staircase to the Guv's aerie, I expected to find him asleep. The thought occurred to me that, having broken his nose several times, when he sleeps one can hear him snore from several houses away. When I reached the top floor of the house, I discovered his bed undisturbed. Where was he, I wondered, and what was he doing?

"Mac!" I called down the stairs.

"Yes, Mr. Llewelyn?" our butler's voice carried upward toward me. There was no pause between my call and his response, as if he were waiting for it. I padded downstairs in my bare feet.

Mac was fully dressed and holding a candle in his hand in the hallway. He was looking out into the street through the narrow strips of glass on either side of the door. Beside him, Harm, Barker's prized Pekingese, circled the hall warily.

"Where has he gone?" I asked.

"He didn't say. He left not long after you."

"Did he receive a telephone call or a message?"

"No, he just left."

"What did he tell you?"

"Nothing. By the time I asked when he would return, he was gone."

I looked at the Swedish standing clock in our hall.

"He's been gone for hours, then."

"Yes," Mac replied.

"He can generally take care of himself."

"Generally, yes."

I considered the matter. "Surely he would have called if he knew he would be overlong."

"Of course. You know how considerate he is," Mac said.

"Should I go look for him?" I asked. "It's only been a few hours, but still . . ."

"Where would you begin? He could be anywhere. He could be in Paris or Amsterdam by now. And if not, he's out there among millions of people."

"So, what do we do?"

"I am a butler. I keep house. It is my duty. Tracking down our employer is yours."

"Right," I answered. "I just wondered if you had any suggestions."

"I don't."

"What was his mood when he left?" I asked.

"He looked preoccupied."

"Did you notice that he hesitated before greeting the delegation this morning?"

"No, I didn't notice. You think it significant?"

"It might be. You said he left not long after I did?"

"Half an hour or so."

"On the one hand, he could have been waiting for me to leave. On the other, he might have thought of something and left on the spur of the moment."

"Does that particularly matter?"

"Perhaps."

I might have said I didn't have the slightest idea but that wouldn't give Mac any confidence in my abilities. Not that he had any, mind you.

"I can't just traipse all over town, but I might pass by the embassy and see if the Guv is there."

Mac raised an eyebrow, but didn't reply.

"If I don't seem likely to return before midnight, I'll call. I hope he'll simply come home ahead of me."

"I'm sure he will," Mac said, though neither one of us believed it.

"To your knowledge, has he disappeared like this before?"

"It happened frequently after he first opened the agency. He was arrested often and had to acquaint himself with the Metropolitan Police and other local agencies. Now most would not dare arrest him."

"You think he was arrested?" I asked.

"I didn't say that. Stop making me do your work for you."

"I was questioning a witness. I'm not certain how reliable he is, though."

Mac rolled his eyes. He can roll them far back in his head. It was his standard method for suggesting that I'm an idiot who had somehow wandered in off the street one day and been taken in. Mac doesn't like to admit he was also a stray rescued by Barker. A Welshman and a Jew, rescued by a Scotsman, a household of outsiders in this mad country called England.

I thought about taking my pistol; thought long and hard, in fact, but decided against it. If I did attempt to enter the embassy, I would be hindered and possibly detained if I carried a firearm. I did carry a stout stick, however. London can be a dangerous place at night. The good citizens go indoors while the ones lurking in shadows all day come out to either find a way to make money or to spend it. They were not especially particular how to do either.

I had the address and it was a good one, fortunately. The temporary embassy was in the private home of Lord Arthur Diosy, *The Times* had reported. Diosy was a gentleman, the kind with a good deal of money, as well as an Orientalist who spoke fluent Japanese, so it seemed logical that he would host the delegation in his mansion, where he could both practice his Japanese and keep an eye on the entourage.

I had no idea whether I would even be able to see anyone, but then I wasn't sure I would need to. I would go there and then see. The address was in Bermondsey, a nice row of residences each of whose owner could have probably fed the entire population of Cwmbran, where I was raised. As far as I could tell in the twilight, the house was a white marble structure with pillars on either side of the door and twelve windows facing the street. It was all lit up, in spite of the late hour. I listened carefully to hear if there was a party going on inside. I had been introduced before. Perhaps I could get invited inside long enough to ask if Barker had come by.

The front door was guarded, however. A constable stood in front of each pillar and two of the bodyguards were sitting on the steps beside each other, watching and talking together. The place looked impenetrable. I doubted Barker would be up late attending an embassy party. For one thing, it was not the Baptist thing to do.

I had just about decided to go back home, when a heavy hand landed on my shoulder. I almost flicked my fist over my shoulder according to my training, breaking the assailant's nose. Luckily, I controlled myself. Constables take exception to being assaulted.

"Pardon me, sir," he said. "What is your name and your business here?"

"Thomas Llewelyn. I'm a private enquiry agent. I work for Cyrus Barker. I'm looking for him."

Then the constable took me by the elbow with his other hand. It's a strange thing about daily training in antagonistics. It tends to make one shy of being manhandled. The mind automatically goes to how to free oneself, and how to counter whatever might come next. My instinct told me to pull my hand away sharply and smack the edge of it under his chin strap. Logic told me not to get myself into trouble. Barker might need me.

"Come along with me, sir," he said, and began to march me forward toward the house, the very house I was trying to get into. Now that I was heading exactly where I wanted to be going, I wasn't sure I wanted to go any longer.

Once inside, I took off my bowler out of habit and continued moving forward. There did not appear to be a party, as I thought. The house seemed silent, but then the Japanese, from what I had observed, are a quiet race.

The mansion was sumptuous, but rather typical, with a large staircase in the middle, leading to a landing above and rooms on either side of a large hall. There were Persian carpets underfoot, and a display of ivory carvings from Japan, some a trifle ribald. In place of the usual baronial portraits, there were paintings of Japanese landscapes, and a feudal suit of armor. Mr. Diosy needed something on which to waste his money, I supposed. He could spend it as he liked.

I was herded into the bowels of the house. I suspected where we were going before we arrived. An inspector and two constables were in the kitchen with the cook. Cups and saucers were on the table, along with the remains of a cake studded with sultanas.

"Who have you got there, Wilkes?" the inspector asked.

"I caught this fellow lurking about outside, sir. He admits to being an accomplice."

"Oh, he does, does he?"

"I admit nothing of the kind. I arrived less than five minutes ago, looking for my employer, who has been missing for several hours. The cabman who let me off was license number 718. What has happened here? Why are you in the embassy?"

"Wilkes, search his pockets."

A skill inspectors acquire over their long years in the Metropolitan Police is the ability to ask questions without answering them. I might as well have been a sheep bleating for all that he paid attention to me. I supposed that facts were a commodity too rare to be passed about wantonly.

Wilkes, an eager, bumptious fellow, searched my pockets none too gently and finally slapped down Barker's wallet on the table. The inspector, still nameless, gave it a whistle and picked it up.

"Thick," he said.

"I'll expect a receipt."

The inspector read Barker's business card.

> ### CYRUS BARKER
> *Private Enquiry Agent*
> *Whitehall 112 7 Craig's Court, CE*
> *"Trust but be careful in whom."*

"Do you always carry another man's wallet in your pocket?"

"I do, actually. Mr. Barker does not like to pay for anything himself."

"Don't see why not. He's got plenty of the ready. Constable

Gore, quit swilling tea and count this money. The gent wants a bloody receipt."

"May I have your name, Inspector?" I asked.

"Dunn. 'H' Division."

Dunn was a small-eyed, square-jawed fellow in his mid-thirties. He was already beginning to look jowly, as if he were half bull-dog. His hair was slicked to his head and he wore straight side whiskers down to his jawline, in the manner of General Gordon. He was the kind that had risen up through the ranks, had seen everything, and was surprised by nothing.

"Inspector Dunn, has Mr. Barker been here this evening? As I said, I'm looking for him."

The inspector glanced at my business card, which was retrieved from my own wallet.

"He was. He's gone now. Some johnnies from the Foreign Office came and collected him. He wasn't here long, just long enough to shoot the Japanese ambassador."

"What?" I cried. "Are you serious?"

"Oh, no, I always tell little jokes like that. Tell me, were you sent to shoot someone else?"

"Of course not. I don't even have a pistol with me!"

"No, but I recognize a fighting cane when I see one. Did you plan to beat the man to death?"

"I only came here because I was looking for my employer. The delegation toured his garden this morning. I thought he might have come here."

"That's nice," Dunn said. "Did the ambassador criticize his roses, by chance?"

I was getting decidedly frustrated now. "Where did the Foreign Office take him?"

"Them Foreign Office fellows don't reveal their plans to lowly inspectors, Mr. Llewelyn. Your guess is probably as good as mine. Maybe better. Constable Wilkes, go out and track down cabman number 718 and get the particulars of how this gentleman arrived. And hop it. We don't have all night."

Dunn had just watched Wilkes pour tea into a mug and add cream and sugar. The constable was just in the act of bringing the mug to his lips for the first time when the order came. Wilkes made a dark face, put down his mug, and left the room. The inspector had the ability to irritate several people at once.

"So," I said. "You fellows caught Mr. Barker in the act or shortly afterward, and were questioning him when the Foreign Office swooped in and snatched up your suspect without a by-your-leave."

"Summat like that."

"Typical," I said. "And they're questioning him while you are forced to guard the premises and to look for clues."

Dunn raised a brow.

"And they'll probably take credit for the collar, as well, I have no doubt."

"Standard procedure."

"So, you're left with nothing."

"Not nothing, Mr. Llewelyn. We have you. Slap the darbies on him, Constable Gore."

I should have seen that coming.

"Am I under arrest, Inspector?"

"No, sir. You shall be questioned."

"Why not question me here and now, then? It will save time."

"I'm going off my shift. I've been up three days straight. Besides, if and when you're finally released from Scotland Yard, you'll be right there by your offices in Craig's Court. So you could say the Yard is paying your cab fare. Not that you'd have any trouble there, with your boss's wallet in your pocket."

"Much obliged."

"Tell me, Mr. Llewelyn, what was your Mr. Barker a-doing here at this time o' night? Was he hoping to be asked to dance?"

"That's what I'm trying to tell you. I don't know why he came here. I wasn't even certain that he had come here. It was an educated guess, I suppose."

"From an educated man, no doubt. In what college, sir, did you matriculate?"

I was slightly impressed that Dunn even knew what "matriculate" meant. These were deep waters. Men such as the inspector did not care for educated men, whom they considered posh. It was no good explaining that I had won a scholarship and that my father was a collier. To him, I ate my jam on a silver spoon.

"Magdalen."

"Cambridge?"

"Oxford. It's a common error. Both universities have a Magdalen college, but ours is pronounced with a silent *g*. Well, never mind."

My head is stuffed with too many facts. One never knows when one might pop out, such as in front of an inspector.

"Oh, no, Mr. Llewelyn. This is very illuminating. I never knew there were two colleges named for Mary Magdalene, the fallen woman."

"Actually, that's a misconception. Mary, the sister of Martha and Lazarus, was the fallen woman. Mary Magdalene was probably a—"

Dunn thumped me one in the stomach. Hard. Over the years in Barker's antagonistics classes, I had learned how to tighten my stomach, but only when I knew the punch was coming. Dunn's blow knocked the wind right out of me. I rolled on the floor in agony.

"Clumsy," Dunn said. "Sorry about that, young fella. I tripped. You all saw me trip, didn't you, lads?"

All of the men in the room agreed. Terrible how clumsy the inspector was, always having to apologize. He really must work on that.

Meanwhile, the air was slowly working its way back into my lungs, and my stomach chose, against expectations, to unwrap itself from my spinal column. Too soon, Dunn pulled me up roughly and set me on my pins.

"What were we a-talkin' about, Mr. Llewelyn?"

I coughed, not certain if I could speak.

"I don't recall, sir," I mustered.

He smiled. "Too bad. And there I was learning so many interesting things. Gore! Hail a cab and take this man to 'A' Division. No, better make it the CID. Keep an eye on him. I've heard of the Barker Agency. They are supposed to be slippery coves. If somehow he manages to escape, you'll be lugging floaters and flogging sewer duty until you're old and gray. Got it?"

Gore concentrated his gaze on me as if I had just insulted his mother. I smiled helpfully. I had been arrested or detained several times. Normally, I gave everyone as much chaff as I dared get away with, but now I needed to find Barker. The CID seemed like a good place to start. I had been on my best behavior, but it had still led to my being arrested.

"Come along, you," he said, gritting his teeth.

I sighed. "Whatever you say, PC Gore."

CHAPTER THREE

W e passed Barker's offices on the way to Scotland Yard and I craned my neck to see if anything was going on there. It was impossible to see from Whitehall Street, since the bow window mainly faced businesses on the other side of Craig's Court. The street is so narrow that once during the Regency period a carriage containing the speaker of the House stuck fast between two buildings and the man had to be cut out. Anyway, I saw nothing, for there was nothing to see unless someone was actually entering or leaving the premises.

We passed through the gate in Great Scotland Yard and slowed in front of "A" Division, where we alighted. A year before I had actually been in uniform, a special constable during the Ripper investigation, but that was water under the bridge. The Charing Cross Railway and Footbridge, to be exact. We went inside the offices of New Scotland Yard, where I strolled up to the desk sergeant and showed him my lovely new bracelets.

"Very nice," the sergeant said. "Good to see you again, Mr. Llewelyn."

"Likewise, Sergeant Kirkwood. What are you doing here so late in the evening?"

"I'm filling in for an officer who was ill."

There was no question about why I was in darbies or how Mr. Barker was or what the commissioner was up to these days, the rascal. He took my arrest as a matter of course.

"This way, Mr. Llewelyn," Constable Gore said.

"Thank you," I replied.

I didn't know the PC and had no wish to become better acquainted with his truncheon. Being perfect strangers was just fine by me. He led me up the stair and down a few corridors and then took me into a room where a man was seated behind a desk.

"Loiterer up Bermondsey way, sir. Has no alibi. Says he came there to find his master, Mr. Barker."

"Did he, now?" the man said. Actually, he was a detective chief inspector.

"I have an alibi, actually," I replied. "But it has not yet been verified."

A rough hand seized my shoulder and the constable was so close to my ear that his helmet strap brushed against it.

"Shut your gob, you," he said, as if by my correction we were now both in trouble.

"Leave the suspect with me, Constable," the DCI said. "That will be all."

"Yes, sir," Gore answered, tugging on the brim of his helmet. He left me alone with the inspector.

We stared at each other for a moment, sizing each other up.

"Hello, Thomas," he finally said. "It's been a while."

"It has, Terry. Congratulations on the new promotion, by the way. What has become of your dundrearies?"

"It has become policy at the Met that side whiskers and beards are to be avoided. Not smart enough," Terence Poole explained.

"You are back at 'A' Division, I see."

"Yes, no thanks to the two of you."

Detective Chief Inspector Poole had been transferred a few years ago when Commissioner Warren got the impression that he and Barker were working together too closely. Now Warren was gone, and Poole brought back into the fold of the Criminal Investigation Department. There was little going on in London that he didn't know about.

"Cyrus is in hot water again," he said.

"I think he prefers it that way," I answered. "What has happened now?"

"This evening, shortly after eight o'clock, the Japanese ambassador, Eechee—"

"Toda Ichigo."

"Toda Ichigo was shot dead. He was standing in an open window at the Diosy residence. Your guv'nor was found just outside the grounds, facing the building. A shot was fired, and when he was arrested, there was one spent casing in his Colt revolver."

"Was anyone in the room?"

"No, Toda was alone. There were no witnesses."

"Could Ichigo's killer and Barker have been firing at each other?"

"If so, Cyrus was the most likely shooter, even by accident."

I nodded. It didn't look well for my employer.

"What has he said?"

"I don't know," Poole admitted. "We don't have him."

"Who does? Special Branch?"

"Yes, and that Foreign Office man. What's his name? Something-about-a-bird."

"Trelawney Campbell-Ffinch."

"The very man."

"So, Barker is at the Foreign Office," I said.

Poole rolled his eyes. I'd made a tyro mistake. Unfortunately, I didn't know what it was.

"Very well," I said cautiously. "He's not at the Foreign Office. Why, exactly?"

"They don't take suspects back to their office. It is too obvious."

I didn't like the sound of that. "Where, then?" I demanded.

"A constabulary of some sort. The Special Branch has the right to commandeer an interrogation room if it is needed."

"But which one? There are at least forty."

"More if you count the City Police."

"Would they take a suspect to the City?"

"They might. You won't be able to deduce where by logic. They won't tell us and we cannot compel them."

The Special Branch had only recently stopped calling itself the Special Irish Branch, since their work often involved more than just Fenians. These days, there were Russian anarchists and Italian secret society members, German spies, and American confidence men. The Irish seemed almost law-abiding by comparison.

"What do I do, then?" I asked. "Wait?"

"There isn't much else you can do."

"What about you? Can you do something?"

"Not directly. If I send one message with his name on it, the new commissioner will hear of it and I'll be called in. I owe Cyrus, but I cannot risk my reputation to help him just yet."

"Can you ask someone else to do it?"

Poole's lips creased in a rare smile. His face was having trouble deciding what to do with it.

"Thomas, you're not as green as you once were. I'll see what I can do if and only if you tell me everything you know about this incident. If we're going to get on top of this, we must know more than Campbell-Ffinch."

"That shouldn't be hard."

I made Poole smile twice in one day. "Don't sell him short."

Poole scribbled on a sheet of paper and handed it to a constable.

I told him everything from the moment the director of Kew approached us and asked Barker to open his gardens for a tour of foreign dignitaries. Of course, Poole knew our garden. He had stood in it on several occasions. If Barker had close friends I could not name more than three. There was a Chinaman named Ho, a Scotsman with no obvious occupation named Pollock Forbes, and Terence Poole. One could add Mac or Etienne Dummolard, or Jenkins, our clerk. In fact, one might even add me, but all of us were employed by him. That is, except for Etienne, who acts as our cook but is unpaid. But he's a special case.

I explained up to and including walking in the door and finding Detective Chief Inspector Terence Poole.

"How many ambassadors, ministers, what have you, came to Cyrus's garden?"

"There were three of them."

"And how many bodyguards?"

"Two."

"Big fellows?" he asked.

"One was very large. The other, not as much."

"Were they armed?"

"How should I know?"

"Oh, come along, I know you better than that. You know how to tell if a man is heeled. Were they or weren't they?"

"They weren't. Nothing in any of their pockets that I could see."

"No swords, or whatever the Japanese use?"

"The general and the admiral each carried one, but I'm certain they were ceremonial. They might not even be sharpened."

"Top of the class, Tommy, my boy. The ambassadors were armed and the bodyguards weren't? We've fallen down the rabbit hole."

"You're saying they do have pistols, then."

"Of course. But they'd have to be well hidden," Poole said. "So, one of the bodyguards is big."

"He's massive. He's built like one of the standing stones in Barker's garden."

Poole had pulled out his notebook and was taking casual notes in it with a short pencil. "What about the other one? Would you say he was as tall as you?"

"A little taller."

"Distinguishing characteristics."

"Oh, yes. He had an elaborate black mustache curled at the ends."

"Did you have any other impressions of him?"

"He was very grave. Every time I looked at him, he was frowning. The other one, well, he wasn't genial, but looked rather bored, or was just being wary in case something should happen."

"Bit of a fanatic, was he, the chap with the mustache?"

I snapped my fingers. "Exactly. That was the impression I had. Like a watch spring wound too tightly. Jittery."

"Those are always the most interesting, don't you think?" Poole asked.

"What happened from your side?" I asked. "About the ambassador being shot, I mean."

"The Met was summoned by telephone to Diosy House around nine o'clock. Inspector Dunn was dispatched. He found the Japanese ambassador or envoy or whatever the hell he's called dead by the window. Shot in the upper chest. One entry, no exit. Some blood on the floor, not much. The window he may have been facing was open. Not long after, Barker was arrested across the street."

"Why?"

"Why was he arrested? He was carrying a pistol."

"Barker always carries a pistol if he suspects his life is in danger. I meant, why was he still hanging about? If you shoot someone, your best recourse is to get out of there."

"Perhaps he was confused or unsure."

"Barker hasn't been either of those things for as long as I have known him. He comes to a decision almost instantly and is convinced it's God given and not to be refused."

"Amen," Poole said, putting his palms together. "Where were you tonight?"

"I was out with a friend. I got back to Lion Street shortly after nine."

Poole stared at me again. If I listened carefully I could have heard the wheels clanking in his head. He got up and moved to a window that overlooked the Embankment.

"You were with a friend and you got back by nine."

"That's what I said."

"Will you give me her name?"

"How do you know it is a woman?"

"If it were your friend Zangwill, you would have told me, and you would have just been starting at nine. Barker tells me you often stay out past midnight. Also, you're acting strangely."

"You seem to know an awful lot about my private affairs."

"Yes, well, that's why I am a detective chief inspector. Now will you give me her name? I do have to establish your location this evening in order to eliminate you as a suspect."

"I thought Special Branch has their man. Let them handle it."

"They think they do. Perhaps they're wrong. I need to have your alibi for the evening."

"No."

He leaned forward across his desk as if he'd never heard that word before.

"Did you just tell me no?" he demanded.

"Yes, sir, I did."

"Let's try it again. Where did you go this evening?"

"I can't tell you that. If you question the staff there they shall recognize her and it might damage her reputation."

"I could toss you in the cells."

"Of course you could. You've done it before."

"We don't like being told 'no' at the Met."

"I don't believe anyone much cares for it, but we all must get used to it sometime or other."

"We're going to find out. You know that, don't you?"

"Perfectly, but by then she'll have been warned."

"Not by you."

"I'm not giving up her name. You can forget that."

"Fine, be Perceval, the gallant knight. See if it gets you anywhere."

"Are you going to arrest me?"

"I'm considering it."

"So, what is the scenario? I shot the victim with my Webley from across the street, a distance of hundreds of yards, then after Barker is arrested, I show up looking innocent. Just happened to be in the area?"

"Certainly," Poole said, lighting up a small cigar. "I like it fine."

A constable came strolling in and laid a folded slip of paper on his desk blotter. Terence Poole opened it, looked at it, and set it down again.

"Well, at least I know where he's been taken," the inspector said.

"Where?" I asked.

"Why should I tell you? You won't give me anything."

"You get a twisted pleasure out of this, don't you?"

"I do. Penge."

"Penge? That's practically in Kent! What's down there?"

"A constabulary of sorts. I gather the Irish boys wanted some time alone with your employer."

"I need to get him."

"You're still under suspicion."

"You've got both of us jugged at once this time, don't you? You're enjoying this far more than you should."

"I am, aren't I? Oh, very well. I'm pulling your leg. Get out. Go rescue your boss. I know where to find you if I need you."

"Can I have these removed, please?" I asked, holding up my shackled wrists.

He dug around in his desk, came up with a key and released me. I stood up immediately.

"Give my best to Cyrus," Poole said. "Tell him to keep his nose clean for once."

"I will," I said. "Provided I can find him."

CHAPTER FOUR

Penge is—well, it's Penge, isn't it? The name explains it well. It's a suburb of London that barely has enough population to warrant a constabulary that qualifies as part of the Met. It is a bucolic town, the kind Londoners like myself tend to make fun of. Nobody thinks for themselves and its newspaper is as likely to discuss what is happening in nearby Croydon as London, something a respectable Fleet Street rag would never do.

The next morning I stepped off the train at the station and looked about. The constabulary across the street was reassuringly square and boxlike, built in a dazzling white brick. It looked like it had only been open a few years and the town must be proud of it. There was barely enough horse traffic to make the bricks dusty.

Before hopping the train I had alerted Bram Cusp by telephone of Barker's situation. He is our solicitor and a very good one he is, too, but he's not much of a conversationalist. He'll usually be speaking to several clients within an hour's time. I have never seen a man make so many telephone calls. He's got an office hard by the Middle Temple, and if one is to believe his cuff links, he is a Freemason like Barker. When I called him, he grunted at the news that my employer was in jail and promised to get back to me. He is good at providing bail quickly.

I'll say this for Penge, the peelers looked no different than the London variety. The sergeant behind the desk was not especially impressed by a private enquiry agent's assistant from London.

"I wish to know if my employer, Mr. Cyrus Barker, is in the building," I said. "I heard he was brought here for questioning by the Special Branch."

The desk sergeant pointed to a bench and promised to return. I waited half an hour. I'm no scientist but I believe the molecular structure of constabulary benches is the hardest substance known to man.

"I'm sorry, young fellow," he told me upon his return. "A warrant has been issued. He cannot be released without standing before the bench."

"Mr. Bram Cusp is on his way," I said. I didn't know that for certain, but I thought it at least possible he was coming.

"Oh, good. We'll be glad to have a celebrity in town. I'll have someone sweep the streets."

He left me to my worries. About half an hour later, Cusp blew in from the street. He is a stocky, short, bandy-legged fellow with a squarish head and a short beard. There is nothing much physically to recommend him, nor is his voice particularly pleasant. Booming, I would call it. But he had something. Assumed confidence, perhaps, or a refusal to take no for an answer.

Entering, he clapped a hand on my shoulder and looked about the Penge Constabulary waiting room as if it were the British Museum.

"Where is he?" he asked.

"Inside somewhere," I said. "They won't let him go."

"Nonsense! You, there, Sergeant! I must speak with my client. I suspect he has not been treated properly."

"You'll have to sign here, sir."

I had been stopped as if by a brick wall, but everything opens to Bram Cusp. One gets the feeling that he has important friends at his beck and call, friends that would not be glad that you were thwarting whatever it was he wanted. I was feeling guilty for having wasted his time over something as trivial as getting the Guv released.

"I would be glad to sign the book, Sergeant," he said as if bestowing a favor on him. "Your station is beautiful, sir. A credit to the Metropolitan."

He turned and tipped me a sly wink after signing the book. In a pig's eye.

"Now, come let us find Mr. Barker," he said.

Cusp made a gesture, telling me to stay where I was until they returned. Reluctantly, I nodded. I was relieved to see him, but I was more worried about Barker than ever. He had been gone for over twelve hours.

For five minutes, I was alone in the waiting room, but no one entered during the entire time the sergeant was gone. I felt I had spent the entire morning waiting when our solicitor returned. When he did, he sat on the other side of the bench and spoke to me in a low voice.

"Apparently, the Foreign Office lads have administered quite a beating. Cyrus claims he is well, but I know when a client is in pain. He'll try to avoid it, but I need you to take him to a doctor. Don't accept no for an answer, do you hear? You know how stubborn he can be. I'm holding you to it."

"Yes, sir. Will he be released?"

"You leave that to me. I'll raise such a stink as will make the Thames smell like a mountain stream by comparison. This Campbell-Ffinch person has overstepped his bounds. The Foreign Office will close ranks around him, of course. Brotherhood and all that. Standard practice. I'll have to apply the heat evenly under the entire pan."

"Is he badly hurt? Can he walk?"

"You'll have to see for yourself. I'm about to call down the wrath of God in a minute or two. He needs treatment right away, I suspect. I'll distract them while you get him out of the building."

"What do you mean? Can we go with a case pending over him?"

"Leave that to me. They won't be happy, but they'll swallow it. They are responsible for what the Foreign Office does to a prisoner while in custody. There are laws about that."

"Right," I said, though I did not fully believe it.

Cusp bustled toward the front desk. He was a bustling sort of fellow. Just then a door opened and two men stepped out. One was a constable in the act of unlocking the Guv's darbies. My employer turned and looked at me, raising his chin as if to say hello. His face was red in that way that raw beef is red. Any skin that wasn't red looked pale. Normally, he is rather sallow.

"You, there, Sergeant," Cusp said. "Where is your courthouse?"

"Right behind the station," he answered, pointing a thumb over his shoulder.

Cusp was gesturing to me as he spoke to the sergeant, waving me to go.

"And what, pray, is your name?"

"Flynn."

I stood and walked over to Barker. He was standing, but slumped over. He looked knackered. Having brought him out, the guard returned to the bowels of the station.

I slid a hand under his arm. Then I stepped back, forcing the Guv to come with me. I took another step backward, looking very innocent. Meanwhile, Cusp was engaging in a conversation at the top of his lungs, punctuated by bombast. Sometimes I suspect he might be losing his hearing.

Another step, and then out the door. I dragged my nearly unconscious employer with me. He was twice my weight, wheezing and wincing from the pain. I hoped Cusp grilled them like a salmon, the Foreign Office, Special Branch, and the Penge Police.

"Come, sir. We'll find a cab."

He patted my wrist, something he's never done before. When

a cab finally stopped before us, he slumped into the seat and fell asleep almost immediately.

I was expecting a hue and cry, and then both of us arrested, but it never happened. Perhaps there was not much crime in Penge, and they didn't know how to go about apprehending a pair of fugitives. The possibility that they were embarrassed by what had happened in their constabulary and wanted us gone as much as we wanted to go never occurred to me.

We alighted at the station, and went into first class. The Guv could afford it, and anyway, no one would look for us there. Barker shuffled forward and eased down into a plush chair. Again, he slept. Once I was certain we were away and safe, so did I. I had been awake for thirty-six hours.

Of course, I didn't exactly say, even to myself, that this was the Guv's fault. If he wanted to go shooting ambassadors, that was his concern, but there are consequences to our actions, such as having the Special Branch turn him into a side of beef. Even I knew that, not that I actually thought he killed the ambassador, of course. Any minute and I expected the doors to burst open and constables would belch forth and surround us.

We got off the train at Victoria Station. I hailed the first cab that came clopping along, pulled by an ancient mare, and came to a stop at my frantic waving. It was no small feat getting Barker up into it. I suspected they had injured his ribs.

I did not want to pester him with questions at a time like this, but there was one thing I had to ask.

"Where are we going, sir?"

"Home," he replied.

"You need to go to hospital, if I may say so."

"Home."

"Let me be clear," I insisted. "We are going to the hospital."

He turned his head and regarded me. "Or?"

"Or I get off at the next stop. I'll clear out my room in a day or two."

He stared at me for a moment, then his mustache bowed the

slightest bit. "Brag and bounce. You wouldn't resign over such a trifling matter."

"You think not? You're going to that hospital if I have to assemble Ho, Mack, Jenkins, and everyone you know to carry you there. I won't hear any argument."

"I don't need a doctor."

"I suspect you need several. Was it Campbell-Ffinch himself who beat you so severely?"

"He tried to get information on my whereabouts on the night in question. After he left, the officers of the Special Branch each had a turn. They became angry when I wouldn't tell them anything. They also had several questions about past cases with which I was not forthcoming."

The last part of the sentence came out roughly and his face twitched in pain.

"Hospital, sir."

"We could call Dr. Applegate to come to the house."

"Hospital."

"Blast. Very well. Hospital."

At Charing Cross, they covered his face with sticking plasters and wrapped his ribs in gauze to cover the abrasions on his chest. His nose had been broken (for the sixth time, he told me later), along with a few cracked ribs, the physician suspected. The Special Branch were quite accomplished at beating a subject without killing him. Normally, they elicited a confession, but not this time. Barker is made of sterner stuff. I never thought I'd see the day he was bruised and battered to this extent, but I hadn't imagined a time when he would be handcuffed and manacled to a chair and unable to defend himself. All I can say is it must have been a stout chair. I've seen him reduce one to kindling. Anyway, the surgeon gave Barker a bottle of opiates I knew he would never use, and we left.

"I could have had Mac put a plaster on my face at home," he grumbled.

"It's wiser to be cautious than hasty," I told him. It sounded priggish even when I said it.

I got him home eventually and he would not accept help from either Mac or myself to climb both sets of stairs. Mac gave me the evil eye for allowing our employer to somehow get into trouble while I was out. Everyone thinks I'm responsible for keeping him safe, but suggesting the safest decision in any situation only made the Guv do the opposite. Heaven help him if his assistant were ever right about anything.

After dinner, Jacob Maccabee heated the water in the bathhouse to molten levels, but Barker was in no condition to try it. He went to bed and I availed myself of it alone. After bathing under a sluice, I soaked for a quarter hour, then pulled myself up on the boards and used the bathhouse as a sauna. By the time I was done, I was drowsy. It felt as if the soaking had detached each bone from its neighbor and it seemed at least a mile from there to my bed.

Harm waddled up, sniffed my bare toe suspiciously, and looked up at me. I'd done it wrong. I was supposed to either share the bath with the Master, where he offered me insights or orders involving a case, or he went first. This going by myself was totally unacceptable.

"Not my fault," I told him. "He got himself beat up by some Special Irish chaps."

He stared at me with those goggly eyes of his. There were standards to be met. One cannot have assistants using the Master's bath indiscriminately, or the empire would go to ruin.

"You've become as bad as Mac," I told him as we entered through the back door.

"I heard that," Mac called from down the hall.

"Good! I'm for bed. Good night."

I went up the stairs, noticing how very steep they were. Eventually, I climbed between the cool, crisp sheets and picked up a book. Home. A funny kind of home, perhaps, but my own. I would not trade it for another.

We did not go to our offices the next morning. As is often the case, his wounds were more painful the following day, not that he would admit it. His face was ruddy and swollen. I made a telephone call from our set in the hall to the one in our offices, hard by the telephone exchange, telling our clerk, Jeremy Jenkins, that we would not be in. Toward noon, Barker attempted to get dressed to go to our chambers, but I talked him out of going. At his request, I called Jenkins again to see if anyone had come round to arrest us. Despite our being well known to Scotland Yard and having offices less than a hundred yards away, there had been none. I assumed Cusp had provided bail and stood for us in court. I do not recall what else I did that day. It slipped by the way some days do, and was gone in a wink, never to be remembered.

Of course, Barker was up all the earlier the next day, before the sun in fact. The skin under his sticking plaster had turned purple, and he stirred with an economy of movement that told me he was still in pain, though the Guv is never one to complain. I knew better than to think I could get by with two days off together, so I dressed and went down to breakfast.

The kitchen was cold and dark. Our chef, Etienne Dummolard, is a temperamental fellow who sometimes goes off in a sulk. I pressed my own coffee and cut off a slice of bread to toast over the Aga. From the kitchen window I watched my employer in his garden consulting with his Asian gardeners. I was down in the hall waiting by seven o'clock, when he came in the back door.

"Ready, lad?"

"Yes, sir."

We had been using the new Underground station nearby to take us to the river each day, but the electric traction engines owned by the City and South London Railway with their brutally upright carriages was no place for a man recovering from a beating. Instead, we rode to Whitehall in a hansom cab, and a smooth ride it was, too. Sometimes the old way is best.

We were settled in our offices with fresh newspapers in our hands and a cup of tea at our elbows by eight o'clock, the third day since the showing in our garden, just in time to hear the door open and the sound of several boots rattling in our outer office. I assumed Scotland Yard had finally beaten a path to our door, but I was mistaken. Two Asian bodyguards in matching suits entered and looked about with concern. A moment later, General Mononobe entered. Barker rose to his feet and the two men bowed. My employer lifted the palm of his hand in the direction of the visitor's chair and our visitor sat. The guards stood behind the general at either shoulder.

Again, I found Mononobe impressive. His manner was calm, but I imagined he could be fierce when the mood took him. He wore a tall collar like a plinth on which his square jaw was set. His clean-cut features were strong, his brow dark, and his hair gleaming and plastered to his head with macassar. Not a hair was out of place.

"Mr. Barker," he said in a low, rough voice. "I wish to hire your services."

CHAPTER FIVE

How can I help you, General?" Cyrus Barker asked.

"Mr. Campbell-Ffinch has explained to me what a private enquiry agent does. I would like you to find the man who shot my old friend."

"But cannot Campbell-Ffinch do that himself? He has the resources. And then there is Scotland Yard."

"I do not trust organizations, Mr. Barker, not even my own. But individuals, one man, I feel I can trust."

"Why, we are almost strangers, General," the Guv said. There was something in the way he said it. Silky, perhaps. He is not a silky kind of person.

"Yes, almost, whereas everyone else in London is a complete stranger. You seem trustworthy, or so is my impression of you. Mr. Campbell-Ffinch has made several remarks to your detriment, but I do not trust him. Therefore, I choose to believe the opposite is true. Besides, I understand you are one of only a dozen or so men in London who speak Japanese. Some of the men that work in the embassy do not speak English as well as I."

Mononobe spoke English well, of a kind. He had an American accent, but then the United States had forced itself upon the isolated islands of Japan for trade concessions almost half a century before. I doubted there were many in that far-off land who spoke the Queen's English.

Barker seemed cautious, if not reluctant. I would have thought he would be champing at the bit to get his nose into this particular feedbag. The general sensed his reluctance.

"If the work is not palatable," he said, bowing humbly, "there is no need for you to undertake it. I merely wished to extend a favor since you honored us by showing us your beautiful garden."

What could one say after such an offer without sounding churlish? Barker sat back in the recesses of his tall desk chair and his face took on a stoic, masklike expression.

"It is not necessary," he said. "I accept your request."

"That is most satisfactory," Mononobe crooned. "I shall tell my aides to expect you at your leisure."

"You do realize Scotland Yard considers me the chief suspect in the ambassador's murder."

"I do, but I am a good judge of character."

"Tell me, General," Barker asked. "Now that Mr. Toda has died, who is in charge of the delegation?"

"That honor has fallen to me."

"No doubt you will be up to the task."

General Mononobe rose to his feet and bowed. Barker did as well. "I have duties to perform, as I'm sure you do. I look forward to seeing you."

"You may expect me within the hour," Barker said.

The two men with Mononobe moved to the front door and stepped out, scrutinizing Craig's Court for the ambassador's safety. The general passed my desk with no more attention than he gave to his own subordinates. I heard some sort of carriage roll off into the traffic of Whitehall.

Things were trundling along smoothly now. I am not an en-quiry agent for nothing, you know. I might even have learned a thing or two.

The first item of interest was that there was Cyrus Barker with his face damaged and puffy with a sticking plaster on it, yet the general said nothing. There is politeness, of course, but I thought it likely that even Japanese decorum might extend sympathy to such a visible wound. Being a general he would know that it might heal quickly, but some word would be given. More likely, the gen-eral had been informed that morning over his tea and rice.

The second was that Barker did not rush out. Normally, he is a hound on the scent. No injury or discomfort would stop him. He would contemplate and strategize for a while, but after half an hour he'd bounce out of his chair. He said he'd be there within the hour. Now, I was worried.

Barker sat in the chair and did not move for the longest time. He did not even choose a pipe and begin to smoke, which was often his first move after being hired for a case, the planning stage. I decided to take a dare.

"Three days ago," I spoke up, "I could not help but notice you seemed disconcerted by the delegation. Was there something spe-cific bothering you?"

"I was scrutinizing their medals," Barker said. "The general and the admiral each had a chest full of them."

"And what made the general look particularly at you?"

"How the deuce should I know? You must ask him about that."

I raised an eyebrow, but he doesn't rise to such clues on even the best day. All questions must be well thought out and reasoned.

"You do not know him, then?"

"How could I know him? The man has obviously not set foot in England before."

I rose from my chair and walked to the window with my back toward his desk, thinking furiously. It seemed that he was correct about this being Mononobe's first trip to the West. However, Barker had knocked about the East for many years before coming to England. He'd been in China, Hong Kong, Sumatra, and Shanghai. He'd even been to Japan aboard his ship, the *Osprey*. He never talked about his time there. In fact, even Mrs. Philippa Ashleigh, with whom he had a long-term relationship, admitted she knew little of it.

"Don't ever ask him about his time there," she warned me. "The slightest mention puts him off for the entire day."

I knew when to keep my mouth shut. This was one of those times. But when have I ever listened to advice from anyone but myself?

"Japan must be beautiful," I said. "Of course, all I have ever seen are stereoscopic cards. I understand you lived there."

"Aye," Barker said, but something in his voice told me his thoughts were thousands of miles away and he was barely listening.

Belatedly he rose, went to his smoking cabinet and chose one of his meerschaum pipes. It featured an Asian rice-grower in a conical hat. The art of meerschaum carving has degraded since that time. Now they barely look presentable, but in 1890 they were nearly works of art. The Asian face of this one was very lifelike, as if he would suddenly open his eyes and begin to move. The pipe had been smoked enough to lose its whiteness and the face had a golden glow to it, as smoke rose from the top of the little fellow's hat.

Baiting him would not work, but the Guv had taught me a whole range of tricks. I cautioned myself to be patient. As he so often said, all would be revealed in the fullness of time. Secrets had a way of being stripped bare all by themselves in his presence. All I had to do was be there and wait.

"I'm going to get a newspaper," I said, to no one in particular. "There might still be some mention of the shooting in the *Gazette* or the *Daily Mail*."

I received no response from the green leather chair behind the Guv's desk, which at the moment was wreathed in smoke. Stepping into the waiting room and out the front door, I headed north toward the statue of Charles I and Nelson's Column, tall and white behind it. It was a good summer day and a few leaves tumbled across the cobblestones in the wind, though there were no visible trees in the area. I turned into Northumberland Avenue and headed east toward the Embankment. I considered strolling along there and looking at Cleopatra's Needle, which is guarded by a pair of sphinxes. There was a rumor going about London that the sphinxes faced toward the ancient obelisk, rather than away from it, because they are in fact protecting London from the Egyptian curse the monument contained, but that was the sort of nonsense thought up in public houses after ten o'clock in the evening by enterprising journalists.

I stopped at a kiosk and picked up a copy of the *Gazette*. The death of Toda Ichigo was on the fifth page, though there was no news to report that we hadn't heard already. I turned and passed by the window of the Turkish bath. As I walked, I glanced into the window. Someone was matching my gait. That's not enough to prove one is being followed, even in the current circumstances, but it should give one pause. I'd have to keep a suspicious eye out for the fellow again.

Who would be following me? Surely, it wasn't any of the embassy bodyguards. I stopped and turned back. There was no one obvious. There were two possible groups that might have someone shadow me. The first belonged to Inspector Dunn. He had no plainclothes detectives of his own, but there was a squad of them at Scotland Yard. They had solved a few cases, but the Yard preferred not to advertise their presence to the press. The average Englishman still has trouble with the need for a police force at all, let alone one that walked among us, so to speak. The other likely candidate was Special Branch. They all wore plainclothes and they were a rough lot. They did not mix with the other departments, and the Met avoided them as a rule. Barker told me they were a close-knit bunch and that they treated each other like brothers.

I turned south, following Northumberland Parade. I swung my cane as I walked. It was that kind of day. A couple of young things ahead of me flashed their parasols and swayed like barges floating in the Thames, but I suspected it was more for practice than interest. I lifted my bowler and passed them.

I studiously ignored the east side of Northumberland Street. They had built a monstrosity there, the Edison House, named for the enterprising American who had filled our offices with electric lighting. It was a slab of white stone without adornment of any kind. Truly beautiful buildings had been built recently, such as the Savoy Hotel in the Strand, fashioned in the most beautiful Art Nouveau style. I imagined a city of the future made up of nothing but blocks, all squares and rectangles. What would future architects do with all their free time? I wondered. I blamed the Americans.

I caught another glimpse of him in a window. Dashed considerate of everyone to have windows facing east. I had played this game myself a time or two and was good at it. It helps to be unremarkable, so that even if someone sees you, you slip away, out of his consciousness.

Finally, I turned west and passed under the arch at the back of Great Scotland Yard. I sauntered by the Rising Sun public house, where our clerk Jenkins held court after five o'clock, then passed through the gate into Whitehall Street. I traded looks with the constable on duty who knew me. He didn't seem interested in arresting me for helping a suspect in a recent murder case to escape. I turned north again, past the blue light informing the public that the police division was here. Before I knew it, I was back in Craig's Court.

"Where the devil were you?" Barker demanded.

"I took a walk. I needed to clear my head."

"And did you?"

I knocked on my forehead. "Clean as a whistle."

"Here's the *Gazette*," I went on. "It has a bit about the murder. Very vague. Oh, and I picked up a shadow."

"Describe," he said.

"Under six feet, brown suit and a matching bowler, low crowned. Mustache."

"Scotland Yard?"

"Or Special Branch," I replied.

"I wish I'd seen him. I've become well acquainted with Special Branch, lately."

"It's probably best for his sake that he didn't run into you. Anyway, you're healing. Try to avoid fights, if possible."

"Come then. Let us visit the scene of the murder."

There is always a cab to be had in Whitehall Street. I raised my stick and within a minute a sleek-looking gray gelding pulled up with a pristine hansom cab. We clambered aboard, Barker more slowly than I, and sat back as the jarvey cracked a whip over the horse's head and carried us away.

CHAPTER SIX

One would think that places in which someone was murdered would have an air of tragedy about them. The opposite is true. No one in the nineteenth century was ever killed in a crypt or a dungeon; the eighteenth, perhaps. Most murder scenes were just an ordinary room five minutes before: a dull office, a fussy bedchamber, a book-lined study.

Also, once the body is removed, there is little sign that anything had occurred. Usually, there are no gouts of blood splashed across a wall, no hint of the killer's initials scratched in the wooden floor by the deceased. There is often a pool of blood, but a bucket of soapy water and a little dedication will get most of it out. One might conceivably need to buy a new rug, I'll admit.

We were shown into Ambassador Toda's room, which was both an office and a bedchamber in one. My own room was much the same, with a library thrown in, but it was less than a quarter of the size and not nearly so opulent. A glance informed me that I was being shortchanged. Barker had plenty of money. The least he could do is to provide his assistant, who risked life and limb every day, a few little creature comforts. Some bookcases, so I'm no longer knee-deep in tomes. A new bed, so we can give my old one back to whatever monastery it came from. Well. Some of us were never meant to sit in a Chippendale chair.

The room was long and narrow. We inspected every corner and opened the wardrobe, which contained only clothing, luggage, and the odd wooden crate tucked in a corner. No weapons were left by the killer, and if anything, the room looked bright and cheery, in addition to being opulent. I wondered how a former Shinto monk would feel about all this. He probably slept on the floor. Still, the carpet was softer than any bed in the East End.

Cyrus Barker had opened the window and put his hands on the sill, looking out.

"Over there is where I stood, by those bushes near the gate. Had I shot from there, the bullet would have pierced his chest, passed upward through his body, and exited through his shoulder. I suspect he was shot straight through. A bullet does not suddenly change trajectory from an upward angle to a horizontal level. Besides, it's ridiculous to think that a man can shoot a pistol two hundred yards and hit a target he is aiming at in the dark."

"What about the spent cartridge?" I asked.

"Oh, you believe the Special Branch, as well?"

"Of course not! But what about the spent cartridge?"

"I shot my Colt down in the basement before I left. I suspected I might potentially be going into a dangerous situation and I wanted to be ready. You have seen me do that before, have you not?"

"I have," I said. "You know, we were just talking to the ambassador three days ago. He was walking around in our garden, marveling over what you've done. Now he's dead."

"Is there a question in that statement?"

"Don't you feel anything?"

"Of course I do, but if I contemplated the deaths of the people

I have investigated over the years, I'd never finish a case. One must develop a thick hide."

"I don't think I can do that, sir. Or want to."

Barker shrugged his shoulders.

"Suit yourself, Thomas, but you chose the more difficult path."

He walked about the room until he came to the fireplace. It was a large and ornate Adam style, with classical medallions. It was too classical for my taste. He crouched down, perfectly balanced on the balls of his feet. At nearly half his weight, I cannot descend or ascend as easily as he.

"Lad," he said.

I came and looked over his shoulder.

"Footprints!"

"Shhh," he said, raising a finger to his thick mustache.

"He came down the chimney," I whispered.

"And returned in the same manner."

"He couldn't have been a large man, then, could he?"

"No."

"Let us tell someone! You'll be removed from suspicion."

"Let me carry it a few more days, I think."

"Why?"

The Guv didn't answer. He pretends not to hear questions which he doesn't wish to answer. Sometimes he provides me with all the clues to a case. Sometimes he doesn't, as if I am to infer the missing piece. One of these days I'm going to be fully trained, I told myself. I'm not sure I believed me.

We both bent and regarded the foot marks more closely. They were small and there were only two of them. The visitor did not move about. He landed and then crouched.

"A very small man, or one with small feet. A child, perhaps? You know they are used to make entrance to a building from a chimney, and then they open the door for their comrades. What are they called?"

"Snakesmen."

"Right. Well, suppose a lad came down the chimney, saw the

murder take place, and scampered up again. Then we'd have a witness."

Barker grunted. He obviously thought my scenario unlikely. The door opened then and the general entered. He bowed.

"Gentlemen, have you discovered our murderer?"

"No, sir, but we are progressing. Alas, this carpet does not leave impressions well. If I may ask a favor, it is that no one disturb this fireplace for a few days."

"Certainly," Mononobe said, and crossed to the fireplace. He saw the footprints and clapped his hands.

"Ah," he said. "Mr. Kito will see that the fireplace is neither cleaned nor lit."

I had not seen the bodyguard enter the room, Kito, of the curling mustache. He nodded his head.

"It will be so, sir."

"Do you require anything more?" the general asked.

"No. The blood spot can be cleaned if you wish."

"Thank you. It is disturbing. This has become my office. It was to be that of the minister of arts, who had no office, but he graciously offered it to me. Perhaps the thought that a man died here made him uncomfortable. He is not as robust as I."

"We have yet to meet him. Tell me, sir, where has the body of Toda Ichigo been taken?"

"Let me see . . ." He crossed to the desk and looked among some papers. He lifted one.

"J. H. Kenyon, Edgware Road."

"Ah, the best in London. Thank you."

"Not at all."

"We have met the late ambassador, the general, and the admiral. What other envoys are in the delegation?"

"Yes. We have the minister of trade, Mr. Akita, and the minister of arts, Mr. Tatsuya."

"Do they have bodyguards as well?"

"They do," the general said.

"Are any of them in the building at the moment?"

"No. Tatsuya is attending an event at the Grosvenor Gallery, Akita is in Sheffield, and the admiral is in Greenwich attending a naval demonstration."

"And His Lordship?" Barker asked.

"He is staying at his club, I believe."

"Which one?"

The general frowned. "Is there more than one? Forgive me, sir. I have no idea."

"It's not important. Please inform them that I wish to speak to them at their earliest convenience."

"Of course I shall, but I must warn you that their schedules allow little time for conversation. Each has twenty or more events in a day."

Barker crossed his arms and tilted his head to the side, still looking gravely at his host.

"Why so many? Now that the embassy is being established, haven't they plenty of time?"

Mononobe shook his head brusquely. "The ambassador was permanent, but the rest of us are gathering information and supplies in order to return to Tokyo. A complete staff of diplomats will be sent here after our return."

"Will you stay?" the Guv asked.

"Until my replacement arrives. I hope you will forgive me. I must perform the ambassador's duties as well as my own."

"Thank you for taking the time to answer our questions," the Guv said.

The general turned and left.

"You can be very polite when you need to be," I remarked to him.

"Diplomacy works better than putting the thumbscrews to a fellow."

"True, but it's not nearly enough fun."

"Come, Thomas."

We found a cab that took us to Edgware Road, and the squat, solid building of the J. H. Kenyon Funeral Services.

"Nothing but the best," I said.

"They prepare the royal family."

We entered and discovered that Mr. Kenyon was not in the building. We were handed to a subordinate, a recalcitrant one.

"Sir, we cannot merely show anyone in here. Do you have proof of your identity?"

Barker handed him our business card. He was a wizened-faced old man with a pallid complexion. He needed a day or two in the sun.

"This only vaguely proves who you are. The card could be manufactured. And how do I know you are working for the Japanese embassy?"

Barker reached into his coat pocket and removed a letter, handing it over.

"This is in Japanese," the officious assistant said.

"You need not inform me of the shortcomings of your education. There is the seal of the embassy. You are impeding the progress of our investigation."

"One final moment, sir."

Barker frowned and looked threatening. The assistant stepped back.

"The body is not ready to be viewed. It is being embalmed as we speak."

"I have seen the process. It does not affect me."

"Very well, sir. I have given my warning. This way, please."

He led us down several corridors into an open room lined in white tile. The Guv hadn't considered whether or not the process would affect me. The smell was sickly, almost sweet. There were tubes coming out of the body. Formaldehyde entering, bodily fluids exiting. There was a Y-shaped incision in the corpse's chest, and the final indignity, the ambassador's false teeth lay on the silver table by his head.

Barker crossed to the table and looked closely at the grayish-white figure.

"Has this wound been scrubbed?"

"A little, sir," the embalmer said. "We try to make all of them as presentable as possible."

"How did the wound first look?"

"Like he'd been burned with an open flame. But we'll sew up the fatal wound and cover it with some flesh-colored putty. No one will tell the difference."

Barker made a gesture, rubbing his finger and thumb together, as I pulled his wallet from my coat pocket and handed him a ten-pound note.

"Make him as presentable as possible. He was poorly treated here."

"Yes, sir," the embalmer said, pocketing the note so fast it looked as if it had evaporated.

We turned to leave.

"Sir," the man called out. "You forgot the envelope."

"Envelope?"

"It's there, sir."

We looked at a table off to the side, with a tin top. Barker came forward and picked up the envelope. It wasn't sealed. He weighed it in his hands and then opened it. He dug out a misshapen lump of metal.

"The bullet," I murmured.

Barker held it up to the lamp on the wall, revolving it in his hand.

"Smaller than my .45, and even your .44. It is misshapen because it struck something, presumably his spinal column. It would have drilled right through his heart, killing him instantly."

"That's a mercy, I suppose, but not much of one."

He dropped the bullet back in the envelope and held it up for the embalmer.

"I can't take this now. I'm not going back to Scotland Yard. A constable will be along shortly. When he does, send along my compliments to Inspector Dunn. My name is Barker."

"Yes, sir."

Barker left whistling, his hands in his pockets. He doesn't

believe in putting hands in pockets; it represents crassness in his eyes. It was his little way of celebrating.

"Why didn't you keep the bullet, sir?" I asked.

"It's not sporting. I'll give the Yard the same chance that I had. They cannot claim that I had the advantage."

"They'll say it, anyway."

"True, but they'll be wrong."

We turned at the corner and passed along Edgware Road. I was deep in thought, and I suppose I was silent for a time.

"What is occupying your thoughts, lad?"

"I am at a slight disadvantage," I admitted. "The Japanese are a closed book to me. Take their religion, for example. I know it is called Shinto, and they seem to like gardening, but I know nothing else about it."

"Then learn. Quickly, but don't read anything which appears lurid or exaggerated. Their manner is different, but they are human beings, after all."

"I'm sure Trelawney Campbell-Ffinch doesn't think so."

"The fellow does not trust anyone who is not an Englishman, including both of us." The Guv leaned on his stick as he walked along Edgware Road.

I hurried my step beside him. "That won't help him discover who killed the ambassador."

"It might be too much, even for me. Aside from a language barrier, which is not a concern for me, there are many phrases and references in their language which can only be learned in Japan itself."

"Of anyone in London, I would say you are the most qualified."

"Then I must limp along as best I can. There are two of us. If we can't work this out together, it is on our heads."

"Oh, good, then," I said. "I thought this would be difficult."

"That's the spirit," he said.

He doesn't understand sarcasm.

CHAPTER SEVEN

There is a certain narrow street in Limehouse which leads to a tunnel under the Reach, which in turn leads to a rather unusual restaurant on the other side. It is run by Ho, a rather rude Chinaman, who happens to be my employer's oldest friend. The food is Chinese, for which, against my better judgment, I have acquired a taste. When Barker said we were going to Limehouse, my first thought was garlic chicken and soybean patties in yellow saffron sauce.

More properly, the restaurant is a tearoom, and more properly still, it is a trap, a trap for information. The bland-faced waiters speak several languages and have the ability to remember conversations on the spot. These would be written down in Chinese and placed on Ho's desk to be considered that evening. Some information would go to Barker, some to Mr. K'ing, who is the undisputed leader of Limehouse, and some would be left to the discretion of Ho himself. Occasionally the odd tip would arrive at Scotland Yard, foretelling a jewelry store would be broken into or a charity about to be robbed. Other times he sympathized with the thief.

He is a muscular, dour, Macao-bred Chinese, shaved bald save for a long queue, with gold-ringed earlobes stretching to his shoulders. He generally speaks in Cantonese, and may feign being unable to speak English, but he can parse the language better than most Englishmen. Like Barker and Etienne Dummolard, he was a member of the crew of Barker's ship, the *Osprey*, first mate, in fact, and he came to England a rich man. This was how Ho chose to invest his money and time. The restaurant has a reputation for being clandestine, and many plans, including both bills on the floor of the House of Lords and plots to steal the crown jewels, were conceived here. Whatever the tearoom's exact purpose might be, it certainly wasn't boring.

We reached the tunnel entrance and stepped inside, as we had done weekly for years, and crossed under the river. As we entered the room, two dozen heads turned our way and Ho knew we had arrived before we even sat down. There was no way to know what reason the Guv had for coming, whether to trade information, have lunch, or to see his old friend. In any case, I was not going to ask. Observe and try not to be seen observing; that was the order of the day.

A waiter brought tea, and Barker visibly relaxed. The next I knew Ho came out of the kitchen in a stained apron and singlet. He crossed his burly arms and looked at us as if considering having us thrown out.

"Try the rice balls wrapped in tea leaves," he said.

"At your discretion," Barker replied.

"What brings you here?"

"Mononobe."

"Someone has redecorated your face."

"That was a gift from the Foreign Office and Special Branch. Trelawney Campbell-Ffinch and his boys."

"I prefer the Japanese to stay in Japan," Ho said.

"Either they are chafing under the restrictions placed upon

them by the Americans, or they hope to play us against one another."

"I would, in their situation," Ho admitted.

"We have been hired to investigate the matter of the Japanese ambassador's assassination."

The Chinaman actually burst into laughter. "Are you not the chief suspect?"

"You seem to know everything about it."

"I really must have a flutter over the matter."

"Only if you bet on the right man," the Guv rumbled.

Barker's cases generally became common knowledge among London's underground. Often wagers are made on the outcome of a case. Ho was an inveterate gambler of all sorts: fan-tan, dog racing, cards, mah-jongg, boxing. He rarely lost.

"Are you aware," Barker went on, "of some arrangement between Mr. K'ing and General Mononobe?"

"Why would you think that? Have you come across information I haven't?"

"I was merely asking if K'ing, being in charge of the Chinese sailors, and the most prosperous businessman in Limehouse, might wish to come to terms with the embassy."

"Of course not!" Ho said. "It's unthinkable. No self-respecting Han would have anything to do with an enemy of our people. Where would you get such an idea?"

"I was speculating," Barker stated, putting his feet up on the corner of the table in front of him.

"Stop it, then, at once. And kindly take your boots off my table."

Barker lowered the offending articles with something like a wry smile. At least for him it was. Anyone else would think it a grimace.

"Don't think the other side is eager to meet with us, either. Too much has occurred between us."

"I'm sure," I said, "the blame must be on the Japanese shoulders."

"Naturally," Ho answered. "We have been gracious to them for decades, even forbearing. What have they done in return? They have housed revolutionaries scheming to end the Qing dynasty, and tried to decide how best to dissect my country's carcass. I don't like them establishing an embassy in London. They're up to no good, mark my words."

I thought it more likely to be a result of native prejudice, but it is not likely one can convince a person through reason, after a lifetime of enmity. I did not see much difference between the two countries, but I supposed it was my own ignorance that was responsible for that. I felt the same suspicions about the English, but of course, that was their fault, not mine.

"Japan and China are natural enemies, of course," Ho said.

"China and the Blue Dragon are not the same thing," I stated.

Ho raised a finger to his lips. The Blue Dragon Triad was not to be named here. It was a so-called benevolent society whose nominal purpose was to tend to the financial needs of sailors plying their trade between Canton and London, but in reality, it was a secret society on the order of the Masons, save that occasionally a Dragon member was found floating in the river. I've heard tell if they peached, their tattoo would be branded off before they were thrown in the river. I've also heard the men were held underwater with poles until they drowned.

"Why do you say that?" Ho asked me, glancing at my employer.

"In order to find out," Barker replied.

"Is your ward involved?"

I looked back and forth at the two men, trying to read their faces. Bok Fu Ying was Barker's ward, a girl about my own age who had actually been given to the Guv by the Empress Dowager of China to look after his Pekingese, Harm, whom the empress had bred. The year before, Fu Ying had been wed to Mr. K'ing, for good or ill. I was not sure of all the particulars, but I heard later that Ho had hoped to marry her himself, though he was twice her age. At any rate, a cooling between him and her new husband was inevitable. Some of it splashed on Barker, but then there was always a certain amount of intrigue in Limehouse.

"I don't know yet."

"But you suspect."

Barker shrugged his wide shoulders, then winced. I suspected it was his ribs.

The food arrived and we ate. There was a table full of small dishes. Ho ate with us, but both he and my employer looked dissatisfied. They switched to Cantonese for a few minutes for privacy's sake. I ignored the slight and ate noodles flavored with prawns.

"I understand," Ho finally said, returning to English, "that the entire embassy was to be invited to the Inn of Double Happiness, but Toda's death postponed that."

"Had they met? Mr. K'ing and Ambassador Toda, I mean?"

"Not to my knowledge. They were to meet for the first time when the meeting was to occur."

"How was the offer made? By messenger? Who made the first overture?"

"I have not heard so far. I can ask for you."

Barker shook his head. "There is no need. I'll find out for myself."

"You will visit Fu Ying?"

"I have neglected her lately."

It was true, and not merely lately. Fu Ying was a young woman taken from everything she had known and forced to adopt a foreign country by her owner. She had problems adjusting, even though she tried especially hard to please him. She was also a source of interest among the Asian community, which was nearly all male. I heard she received several proposals of marriage from rough sailors, wealthy merchants, slumming aristocrats, and powerful mandarins. I even considered something in the line of a proposal myself, once. Fortunately, God doesn't permit every harebrained scheme we envision. At any rate, Barker and the girl had stopped talking, and before we knew it, she and K'ing had eloped. As far as Barker was concerned, she had done it to spite him, jumping from pan to flame, thumbing her nose all the while.

"Yes, you have," Ho said. No one else I knew could get away with such a remark. I'd have been kicked into a nearby dustbin. "And if she chose an unsuitable husband, whose fault is that? A girl has no business choosing a husband for herself. She lacks discernment, wisdom, caution. She could have married this one, and then look what a son-in-law you would have!"

I ignored the jibe at my expense, and bit into a spring roll. I had heard this conversation several times before.

"She was a slave and an orphan," Barker replied. "I gave her a home and trained her as best I could to face a cold and cruel world. She chose her partner and there is an end to it."

"She married too young."

"He is the most successful man in Limehouse," Barker pointed out.

"He is a drug addict."

"He was held against his will a couple of years ago. Perhaps she can wean him from the poppy."

"K'ing has lost some of his money and prestige. He takes risks."

"Often he is successful."

A servant brought Ho's pipe to him, a metal contraption like a watering can. He filled it with tobacco and lit it and sucked the smoke through a small reservoir of water.

"It will all fall on your head one day," he said in a high, rough voice, before spitting out the smoke. "You mark my words. It will end badly."

"That is her affair, not mine," Barker said. "If it happens, we shall be there to help her, the three of us."

Ho rose, spitting Cantonese under his breath before quitting the dining room for the safety of his office.

"What did he say?" I asked.

"He compared the sense of two *guailo*s to that of a mayfly during its one-day life span."

"Not a complimentary remark, then."

"Decidedly not."

"He's still bitter over her marriage."

"I didn't promise her to him, no matter what Ho thinks. I didn't promise her to anyone. It was her own decision whom to marry. She did not solicit my opinion."

"Would you have consented?" I asked.

"I would have warned her that K'ing is a complex individual. He is not bound by Western concepts of right and wrong, nor by the Eastern beliefs he left behind when he came to this country."

"What is his background?"

"No one knows save himself, as far as I can tell. K'ing is obviously an assumed name. I know not what his real name is nor where he is from. He started as a sailor for the Blue Funnel Line, and formed the Blue Dragon Triad, an offshoot of the Heaven and Earth Society. He had natural abilities and a desire to learn. He would have gone far. He still might if he can overcome his opium addiction. But one hears rumors."

"Rumors, sir?"

"Aye. He'll disappear for days at a time, but the reasons are often legitimate. He has a staff of employees willing to help him or lie for him. He doesn't make use of his own opium den ever, which is below his casino in Limehouse, but the rumor is that he frequents out-of-the-way dens on waterfronts all over the empire, and never the same one twice."

"What does he tell his wife?"

"He claims he has overcome the effects of his incarceration years ago by my old enemy, Sebastian Nightwine, but then, that is what one would expect a confirmed opium eater to say."

He stood and nodded toward the stairwell leading toward the tunnel. I looked about and noticed no fewer than three waiters nearby, wiping tables or arranging flowers. Silk flowers don't require arranging. I rose to my feet and casually followed the Guv from the room. More than once we had relied upon information gathered here, but I didn't care for supplying it myself.

We did not speak in the tunnel. Our voices carried too well there. I reached up and knocked on the ceiling overhead with a knuckle. The dull thump of the river above reverberated through the chamber. At the other end we climbed the stone stair and left through the door. Then, and only then, did we speak.

"Can you think of any reason why K'ing would want the new Japanese ambassador killed?" I asked.

"As we said earlier, there is no love lost between China and Japan."

"But K'ing is not a typical Chinaman."

"True. For example, he invited the ambassador to his establishment."

"Yes, but he could have invited him in order to kill him."

"Perhaps. We haven't all the facts. We have precious few, to be honest, but that is normal for this stage in the case."

"But any handle will do," I said, as we walked along a wicked-looking street named Ropemaker's Fields.

It was a phrase he used often in our antagonistics class. He'd seize a collar, an elbow, even a foot, and use it to take a man to the ground until he was helpless. What it basically meant was not to look or hope for something to come along. Use what you have at hand this very moment.

"Aye," he murmured.

"So, what do we do now? What handle have we got?"

"There was a person in the room with Ambassador Toda."

"How do you know that?"

"I saw them from across the street. They emerged from the chimney."

I stopped and stared at him. "You saw someone on the roof? Why didn't you say something to Scotland Yard?"

"Scotland Yard didn't ask. The Foreign Office and Special Branch asked, but not very politely. I was under no obligation to tell them, and their methods merely made me want to spit in their collective eye."

"So, was it someone dressed as a chimney sweep?"

"No, someone dressed as a burglar. Garbed in black, and heavily masked."

"How do you know he was in the room the ambassador used? He must have emerged from a common chimney."

"A man is murdered, and someone appears on the roof dressed in black. It is not difficult to make a connection."

"This burglar, which way did he go?"

"To the north end of the building, where I assume some sort of corbel or drainpipe led to the ground."

"He got away, and you got the blame. He could be anywhere right now. If only we knew who it was."

We turned into Three Colt Lane, where Barker had purchased a property for his ward, Bok Fu Ying.

"I know who it is, lad. I knew then. Our presumed assassin is a woman."

Raising his stick, he rapped on her door.

CHAPTER EIGHT

A small, plump maid met us at the door of Three Colt Lane. Barker had hired an elderly couple to watch over Bok Fu Ying while she was unwed, reasoning she might want to be with those who could speak her native tongue in Limehouse. When she wed, they had been replaced, but at whose insistence I was not certain. Now that she was a young married woman, we saw less of her than before.

"May I help you?" the girl asked.

"We wish to speak to Mrs. K'ing," the Guv said, removing his hat.

"Who is calling, sir?" she continued in a singsong voice.

"Mr. Cyrus Barker and Mr. Thomas Llewelyn," I supplied for my employer.

The girl frowned, shrugged her shoulders, and left us standing outside his own front door, bought and paid for. Very well, so he had given it to the couple as a wedding present, but it was no way to treat the closest thing to family. Or his assistant, for that matter.

She returned a few minutes later in no particular hurry, and led us up the staircase as if she felt leading us was beneath her dignity.

Fu Ying was seated at a table writing letters. She was dressed like an English lady, from her coiffed hair to her button shoes. Her dress was of pale gray with pink accents and she wore pearl earrings. Her face was powdered and her lips and cheeks lightly rouged. The Llewelyn eye misses nothing.

"Sir!" she cried, jumping to her feet.

"Fu Ying," he rumbled, stepping toward her.

She opened the door and barked orders in sharp Cantonese down the hall. Then, she took our hats and sticks and directed us to a couple of small chairs carved in China. Gingerly, we sat.

"Are you well? Sir's face is bruised. Is Damo well? I fear I have been neglecting him of late."

"Harm is fine. I am fine. We are all fine."

"What brings you to Limehouse?"

"Cannot a man come to see how his ward is finding married life?"

There was an awkward affection between them, but their relationship was very formal. It was too formal, in my opinion.

"Of course. And how is Mr. Llewelyn?"

"My father is quite well, thank you," I told her.

She bowed. "Thomas. Forgive me."

"Not at all," I said, dismissing the remark with a wave of my hand. There was no need to be formal around me. I work for my wages.

The door crashed open and the maid entered, laden with a tray. There was a pink palm print on her cheek, I could not help but notice. Fu Ying hadn't done it. There must be a housekeeper about the house who still knew what was going on. The girl poured tea in spite of the tears in her eyes. There was no more dawdling. She poured each of us some oolong, then left quickly. As soon as she was gone, I spoke.

"Mr. Barker was arrested by the Foreign Office. They consider him the chief suspect in Ambassador Toda's murder, and detained him overnight. They chained him and tried to beat a confession out of him. His solicitor had him released. This morning General Mononobe of the Japanese embassy has hired us to track down Toda's murderer."

So far, Fu Ying had betrayed no emotion at the harrowing tale, but she suddenly turned her head as I finished.

"He hired you?"

"Yes. Is there any reason why he shouldn't?"

The two exchanged a look. It's difficult to tell with Barker hiding behind those large discs, but I believed so.

"Not at all. I'm sorry Sir was detained."

"Would you be so good as to tell me why you were on the roof of the Japanese embassy?" Barker asked.

"I don't know what you mean," she replied.

"I am more than your benefactor, I am your teacher," he said, referring to her martial training under his tutelage. "I have trained you for ten years. I know your every move and could choose you out of a crowd in the dark. The way you moved along the ridge of the roof was unmistakable; I taught you to move like that. Only two people have been trained that way and both of you are in this room. Mr. Llewelyn, did you climb the chimney of the Japanese embassy?"

"No, sir, I did not. At the time I was dining in the City."

"There. You see? One accounted for. And where were you the night of Ambassader Toda's murder, my dear?"

"I was with my husband."

"No doubt. And precisely where was your husband?"

"He was working at the inn."

Barker shook his head. "I hope you avoid that den of iniquity as much as possible."

"But it is my husband's place of business. It's no longer the opium den it once was. Now it has a restaurant and tables for gambling. My husband intends to buy the old theater next door and renovate it for entertainment and meetings."

"I know for a fact that opium smoking still goes on in the basement."

Fu Ying now looked annoyed. She used to hang on every word my employer said. I suppose marriage can change people's opinions.

"Oh, that. Most of the addicts are old men. He would rather have them smoke under his care than at a less scrupulous establishment. He takes his responsibilities in Limehouse very seriously."

"Why did you go to the embassy that night? I presume K'ing had some business plot involving the Japanese delegation."

Fu Ying inhaled, trying to decide whether to confide in him. She exhaled, and shrugged her shoulders. "My husband asked me to. I have no more to say on the matter."

"Why were you there?" Barker asked.

"Please do not ask me that question now, sir," she pleaded, bowing her head in shame.

"You do understand that you have become my chief suspect. You climbed down into the room. Toda died. You climbed out again and left, notifying no one. In my eyes, you are the most likely suspect in the murder of Ambassador Toda Ichigo."

"I did not murder him, sir. You must believe me."

"Why must I believe you?" the Guv growled.

"Because I have promised another that I would say nothing. I am sorry that I could not tell you."

Barker opened his mouth to speak and shut it again. He began to pace about her carpet, his hands clasped behind his back. I understood what was agitating him. He had respect for anyone who keeps a vow. While he does not encourage secrets, when one has taken a vow, he or she is duty-bound to keep it.

"Did you not see me?" he asked.

"No, sir."

"I was across the street. I saw you very clearly. You have been trained to observe. Why didn't you see me?"

"I was preoccupied," Fu Ying replied. "A man had just died at my very feet. I was escaping."

"Excuses!"

Barker was sometimes a harsh teacher, in order to make us independent, knowing he cannot be there every time we were in trouble. A father disciplines his children.

"I will be more careful next time, sir," Bok Fu Ying said, a hiccup in her voice.

"Pray do. I could have been someone with a rifle. I could have been the police. I hope you will never do something like that again."

"I would like to do as you wish, but I belong to another now. I cannot always do your bidding."

My employer shook his head. I thought that would be all, but Barker suddenly went off in Cantonese, or perhaps it was Mandarin. He was from Foochow and she from Peking. Fu Ying responded in kind, and it went on for at least five minutes. Whatever language they were speaking was an excellent one for arguing.

As I understood Barker, he had chastised her for not seeing him, rather than to make her break her promise. I'm not saying the man is perfect. He can have a monumental rage at times, most often at himself. I have seen him punch a brick wall that he knew he could never break down.

Personally, I believe he loved Fu Ying, as only a father can. She had come to him a terrified fourteen-year-old girl. If the dog she cared for died, or if she displeased her owner, she could be killed. She was engaged for a time to the previous assistant to Cyrus Barker, but he had died in the line of duty. The Guv bought a house for her in Limehouse among her own people. If there was any drawback it was that he was an adult male who had no way to understand a female less than half his age.

The argument wound down. Barker stopped pacing and Fu Ying regained her composure. I admired her courage. Barker's Chinese name means "Stone Lion." He could roar with the best of them.

Barker sat and our hostess poured more tea, though by now it was lukewarm. We drank it, and pretended that nothing untoward had occurred. We were all civil again.

"If the vow should be lifted, I expect to be told," Barker said.

"I shall, sir," she replied.

"No. You *will*."

The Guv lifted his cup. "I will not ask why you were there. What happened in the room, as you recall?"

"I climbed the building to the roof," she answered, setting her cup on a table. "It was absurdly easy. Then I climbed down the largest chimney, which was still rather tight. I had no more set foot in the cold grate than a shot was fired very close to me in the room. I saw a man run past. Then I saw the ambassador fall. He saw me, too. He fell to the floor and reached out to me for help. Me, a stranger dressed in black, standing in the fireplace. I debated whether to help him, but he died just a few seconds later. Naturally, someone would be coming at the sound of the shot. As quickly as possible, I climbed the chimney walls and hurried away."

"You accomplished nothing," Barker stated.

"True, but I got away. I was not captured, as you were."

Another slight, I thought. How the mighty have fallen.

Barker threw back his head and laughed. "So I was. Have you heard since then what had been happening at the embassy?"

"There is no way to know. My husband tells me everything at the embassy is in turmoil. I understand General Mononobe has sent a telegram all the way to Tokyo as well as a courier. There is no telling how long either will take."

"I gather your husband sent you to find out when the delegation might go to the Inn of Double Happiness."

"Perhaps."

"The information must be very important to him."

"I cannot say."

Barker crossed an ankle across his knee and folded his arms.

"He has purchased a great deal of property in Limehouse and Poplar lately."

"He has. He is a successful businessman."

"Is he at the inn today?"

"No, he is busy at the docks."

Barker ran his finger along his nose. "Has he overspent, in your opinion?"

She shrugged.

"Sometimes it is necessary to invest. There is no way to know if it will profit."

"Are you taken care of here? Do you yourself need money?"

"Sir, I could not take another farthing."

Barker had settled a substantial dowry on Fu Ying, which still made her uncomfortable.

"Codswallop. If you need anything, you know how to ask. Is everything well?"

"It is," she responded.

Right, I thought. She wouldn't ask for help. She'd grit her teeth and hope for the best.

He rose from the chair and she did likewise. She put her hand on his arm and he patted it.

"Come, Thomas."

I nodded at Fu Ying and then turned and followed after my employer. We stepped out of the building into a stream of Chinese sailors, either coming from a ship or going to one. Barker towered over them all.

"She wouldn't tell me," he said, when we were out on the street. "She always has before."

"Do you still think as well of K'ing as you once did?"

"He is young. He will make mistakes. I hope he will be prudent overall."

"Do you worry about her?"

"I don't worry at all. Who by worrying increases his stature? I pray for her. I offer her help. What else can I do?"

"Yes, well, I worry for her, and she isn't even my responsibility."

"You still believe she married poorly. Do you think Ho the better man?"

"Ho? Good heavens, no. I mean, he might be a better man, but a husband for Fu Ying? Decidedly not," I said.

"I must admit there are activities about the tearoom that I find unsavory. I have spoken to him about it."

"Yet you allowed her to marry a man who owns an opium den."

"Opium dens are not illegal, lad. Not yet, anyway. And he has expanded."

"Yes," I said, as we walked around the docks. "Into a gambling hall and a public house, without getting rid of the den. It's the same old activities with a new layer of gilding."

"What would you have me do? Kick in the door, take Fu Ying by the wrist and drag her out of there?"

"It may come to that if worse comes to worst."

"You worry too much."

"There is too much to worry about."

"Are all Welshmen so gloomy?" he asked.

"We have to be. We are realists. Perhaps she didn't need a wealthy husband. She needed to work with one side by side, starve with him, strive with him, and ultimately succeed with him. She would have babies they couldn't afford and have been deliriously happy."

"You believe her marriage is loveless? You believe I have turned her into a bauble?"

I shrugged my shoulders. "She didn't look particularly happy. And I wouldn't want my wife climbing down chimneys, no matter how skilled she might be at it."

"Perhaps I made a mistake," he conceded. "And perhaps not. K'ing could grow sleek and fat and become the first MP for Limehouse. It's a gamble, really."

"Could you speculate about why she was there?"

"I could if I thought it would do any good. She could have been sent to kill someone, but I believe her conscience would be troubled by doing so. I doubt she would do that unless forced, or she would tell me if she were in trouble, even as independent as she is. That leaves three possibilities: she was sent to see something, to speak to someone, or to take something. If so, her mission failed. She barely had time to move before a man was shot."

"That's if we believe her story. She might have had more time in the room than she claims."

"True. I did not see her enter, only leave. The timing is suspicious in that she left immediately after the ambassador died. On the other hand, if you were dressed as a thief in a fireplace in a room where a man has just been killed, would you not beat a hasty retreat?"

"I would."

Limehouse was dank and oppressively warm. I wished I could remove my jacket, but the Guv has standards.

"What kind of object might be there?" I asked. "It might have to do with his business. The entire house is full of dozens of works of art. I wonder which is worth the most?"

"Probably the Buddha head with lapis lazuli eyes."

"Wait," I said, stopping under one of the few street lights in Poplar. "K'ing is a businessman. He is not a thief as a rule, though he might hire someone if whatever he needed was important. It might have to do with his business. He wouldn't scrutinize a piece of art without assessing its value."

"Agreed. Something to do with business and something to do with the Japanese, though since he is a Chinaman, one would expect him to despise the Japanese."

"Perhaps he has set aside the traditional prejudices of his forebears for business interests," I said. "By the way, thanks for informing me about Bok Fu Ying's visit to the embassy."

"As I recall, I didn't."

"Exactly," I said.

CHAPTER NINE

Private enquiry work is not the kind of employment that adheres closely to a schedule. Some things take longer than others, and when one is obliged to investigate something, there is traveling time and road conditions to consider as well. Barker claims that he would like nothing better than to sit on the private throne in his office and have all information come to him, but I knew better. A couple of hours in his green leather chair makes him anxious to be up and about again.

The following morning, Barker reached a long arm, snaring the telephone set on the edge of his desk, and growled a telephone number into the operator's ear.

"I would like to see you, sir," he said into the receiver when the call went through. Then after a few seconds, no more than five, he hung the earpiece back onto it.

There are protocols in place for using the telephone set. They were printed and given us along with the set when it was first installed in the office. It is polite to identify oneself to the operator

so the listener is not deceived into believing the speaker is someone else.

Barker rose and prepared to leave the office. I had a ledger book
in my lap. Sighing, I tossed it on my desk and hurried after him.
It had begun to rain. I hailed a cab just before he did and climbed
aboard with no idea of where to tell the driver to go. Barker
shouted, "Limehouse!" and offered a sovereign if he got us there
in twenty minutes. Then he sat back and watched the silver rain
coming down just inches away.

We were soon on our way to Limehouse and I sat there, wondering at his motives. Did he need to consult again with Ho or
were we to speak with his ward again?

We passed down that great artery of London, Commercial
Road, as we traveled through Whitechapel and Poplar before
reaching Limehouse. There we rolled right by the entrance to Ho's
and Three Colt Lane. That left only one possible destination, the
Inn of Double Happiness.

"You intend to speak to K'ing," I said.

"I do."

The street was nondescript, a warren of buildings facing in
every direction. It was easy to get lost here. I imagined that may
have been one reason this location was chosen. The inn itself was
something of a disappointment, for anyone expecting an Asian
fantasy. There were no standing arches, no scooped roofs or pa-
godas. Limehouse is as Asian-looking as Barnstable. The inn was
large, however, having once been a warehouse on the docks of
Limehouse Reach. There was plenty of room for gambling tables,
exotic food, and in the cellars below, an endless supply of opium
pipes.

"We are here to see Mr. K'ing," Barker announced to a young
Asian woman at the entrance, who appeared to be a sort of hostess. I raised a brow. There was a time when Fu Ying was practically the only Chinese girl in all of London. Now there were
several.

"Do you have an appointment?" she asked.

"We do. Tell him his father-in-law wishes to see him."

The young woman came from behind a standing desk. "Wait here. I will inform him at once, sir."

She hurried off.

"Father-in-law?" I asked, looking at my employer. "That's a term you haven't used before."

"It was expedient. It will get us in the door."

We looked about. Nearby, a group of men laughed over a game. At another table, there was an open bottle with a kanji label on it. I lifted it and sniffed. It was sweet and alcoholic, but I could not place the aroma.

"Plum wine," Barker murmured over my shoulder. "There are no grapes in China."

There were lavish carvings everywhere, and painted scenes of a romanticized countryside. Above the entrance through which we had passed was a small shrine with Oriental figures I could not recognize and in front of which joss sticks were burning.

The girl returned and bowed to us, as befitted the father-in-law of her employer. "Mr. K'ing will see you, sir. Please follow me."

We were led down a hallway. I'd been to the inn before, when the only decoration was netting and packing boxes. Now, it was almost sumptuous. K'ing had been investing a good deal of money.

We were led through a door into K'ing's office. He had spared no expense. There were jade and ivory carvings and hanging lamps. He sat behind a table that rivaled Barker's in size. There were thick carpets under our feet and a bearskin rug.

"Gentlemen," he purred. "Won't you come in and have some tea?"

Barker and I removed our hats, but retained them. I stared at K'ing intently. A few years had changed him physically. He shaved his head now, and had grown a mustache. He was still wearing his tortoiseshell spectacles. His face was gaunt, which made his brow and forehead more pronounced.

The girl poured tea for us, then as soon as we held our cups, she returned to her post.

"My dear father-in-law, to what do I owe this unexpected visit?"

"We have been retained to investigate the death of the Japanese ambassador."

K'ing sat back in his chair. "I see. You came because you have heard that I had dealings with the embassy. It is so. I have spoken with a General Mononobe. However, I was not fortunate enough to meet the ambassador before he was shot."

"I will not argue that fact," the Guv replied. "Under what conditions did you and the general speak?"

K'ing's eyes narrowed. I hazarded a guess that he had been having his own way for too long and was now unaccustomed to a challenge.

"He had lunch with me. We discussed having a party here for the embassy, but nothing was actually decided. Then the ambassador died, so our plans fell through."

"And yet you sent your wife to find out more about the embassy's plans in London."

K'ing smiled, as if the Guv were somehow quaint. "Mr. Barker, as usual, you are remarkably well informed. I assume my wife told you about my little request."

"Only after I confronted her," Barker replied. "You see, I was across the street when she left the building. I watched her do it. Her methods are unique. After all, I taught her."

"Fu Ying has grown sloppy. I should have expected it."

My face colored just then. No man should deliberately insult his wife in front of other men. However, I wasn't there to correct his lack of manners. I had my pencil and pad out, and was taking notes. I would leave Barker to do the correcting.

"She was unable to collect information for you regarding the general's plans, due to the sudden shooting. Did she tell you she saw anything?"

"She heard the shot, and the sound of footsteps," K'ing answered, "but by the time she bent and looked into the room, the ambassador was breathing his last. At least she had the presence of mind to climb back up the chimney."

"Her arrest would have been difficult to explain for either of you. Is there a particular reason you saw fit to use my ward on such a dangerous mission?"

"She asked to go. I told her I would send someone else, a thief whom I have employed on one or two occasions, but she insisted. Her skills were going unused, she said. She wanted to help me. She is my wife."

"And my ward."

K'ing shook his head. "No longer. She is of age, and she is now my wife, my property, according to both English and Chinese law. I am within my rights."

"Mr. K'ing," Barker rumbled, "do I look like the sort of person who gives a tinker's damn about rights? She may be your wife and your property, but her interests are still under my protection, and if I thought she were being taken advantage of and her liberty endangered, it would grieve me, sir."

K'ing held up a hand. "It is my intent neither to grieve you nor to endanger my wife," he said. "I care very deeply for her. I was reluctant to send her to the embassy, and I see that my fears were justified. It is not my fault, sir, but yours. You left her to languish in Limehouse with little to do. You trained her in no other occupation save that of a boxer. You dressed her like a perfect doll with no plan for what to do with her when she reached marriageable age. When I first met her, true, she was a beauty, and arguably the best fighter in Poplar, but she was adrift. When we wed she threw herself into good works among the poor population here. As she told me, she wanted to feel needed."

There was silence in the room then. K'ing actually looked over at me, as if he had said too much. Barker sat there in that immobile way he has, save that his index finger made abstract designs on the edge of the desk. Barker told me once that when someone criticizes you, you must take it to heart, and try to see yourself from his or her point of view. I wondered if he would follow his own advice. The Guv has a temper he bottles up most of the time, but I've seen it blow up as well.

"You are correct," he said. "I had never raised a young girl be-fore and I did it poorly. I dressed her well and gave her a house to live in, but I rarely saw her. I was establishing the agency. I thought she would fare best among her own people, but perhaps it would have been best had she stayed in Newington."

K'ing looked away uneasily. Barker is the still water that runs deep and just then he caught a glimpse below the surface.

· "Nothing dangerous happened to her anyway," he assured us. "Fu Ying escaped safely and came home. I regret sending her out, but she survived."

Barker nodded.

"I realize that I have no claim upon you or your wife now, but I ask that you refrain from involving her in the more dangerous aspects of your work."

K'ing gave a slight smile, as if at some private joke.

"I believe I can safely promise you that. Also, I acknowledge your claim upon Fu Ying. She loves you like a father. I would not stand between you. For one thing, as you yourself will understand, I am very busy, and any time you give her is appreciated."

"I will make time," Barker said.

"I am pleased to hear you say it."

"Pray tell me, what did you send my ward to do?" Barker asked.

K'ing shook his head. "So direct, yet you spent most of your life in China. It is a business matter. My business, sir. Not your business. It had nothing to do with the ambassador's death. The general and I had no chance to go beyond pleasantries, and at this point, I'm not certain that the matters we discussed shall be con-sidered again. Had I known the ambassador would be killed, I most certainly would not have sent my wife there. I would not hurt her for the world."

Barker nodded as if satisfied. "I am heartened to hear it. I care for her deeply. With all my power, I want to see her happy."

"As would I, Mr. Barker, but fate is not often kind."

There was that word again. I scribbled "fate" in shorthand and circled it. Mononobe had used it, and now K'ing. I wondered if that was an Eastern concept he had borrowed, or a Western one.

"Is there any other matter you'd like to discuss?" K'ing asked. "I am very busy, but stay for lunch if you wish. We are not as innovative as our old friend Ho, but you will find our food superior."

"I, too, am busy, sir. If you are able at some point to discuss the events which caused you to send your wife to the embassy, I would be most interested in the information."

"I will take that into consideration, Mr. Barker."

He and the Guv bowed to one another.

Three cultures bow to one another, I thought. The Chinese, the Japanese, and the English. The Scots normally do not, nor the Welsh, but we lived in this country and had picked up the custom. Russians don't bow when they meet, or Italians or Argentinians. It was not pertinent to the case, but it was interesting.

When we reached the lobby again, Barker asked for a chair. He looked tired, as if he were running on sheer will. The hostess saw that chairs were brought and faced the room. A cup of tea was placed at our elbows.

"Vice," he stated, staring at a table covered in pieces of paper. I recognized the game known as fan-tan.

"As I recall, you won your ship in a game of fan-tan," I said.

"I did," he admitted. "But only after having lost enough to pay for it twice. I was young and naïve."

"Why did we come, sir? If it was to learn what Fu Ying was doing on the roof, we failed."

Barker leaned back in the wooden chair and it protested under his weight.

"I wanted to see his eyes. He did not have pinpoint pupils. He has not been smoking opium lately."

"Perhaps he gave it up," I said.

"One does not simply give up opium, Thomas. It is like an octopus that slowly ingests you. One cannot get away from its tentacles. It will drag you down to the depths."

Barker frowned at the room. "And gambling is no better. Many of these men will return home with the news that they have lost their family's food money for the week. Children will go hungry. Men will lose their wives, their homes, their occupations. They will sell their work tools for one more game. This opulence, these fine green baize tables and carpeting, it is at the expense of hard-working families. Goodness only knows how K'ing has skipped around the laws to open this establishment."

"Does this change your mind about him?"

"I fear it does, but so far he has not broken any laws that I can see, just as before with his opium den. What he does is not illegal. It is merely unsavory."

"Even if the money goes to a benevolent society?" I asked.

Barker gave a sigh of exasperation. "I don't know how much of his receipts go to help the poor here. He would not show his balance book. So far, I see little change in the daily lives of the people here in Limehouse. This is my fault."

"How is it your fault?"

"I have thrown Fu Ying to the ravening wolves. Worse yet, I have been schooled in a harsh lesson by the very man to whom I gave her. It might have been better if I had married her to Ho."

Barker pushed himself up and out of the chair. He looked gray, as if he had aged a decade in an hour and a half.

"Come, Thomas," he said. "I need to get out of this perfumed house of sin."

CHAPTER TEN

Just because Cyrus Barker had just returned from somewhere didn't necessarily mean he wouldn't go right out again. He only had so many working hours before nightfall and didn't like to waste them. On the other hand, sitting and cogitating might be a better use of his time. It could be either one.

I liken waiting for Barker to decide what to do about a case with waiting for a brown trout to decide whether to bite down on a royal coachman. One had to be patient. Once back in our chambers, the Guv didn't settle in his chair. He gathered the post and ripped through it quickly with his stiletto letter opener. He stuffed a pipe with his own particular blend of tobacco and set it alight. Then he stood in front of the bow window facing nothing but the offices on the other side of Craig's Court, and blew smoke at it.

"Reporters," he muttered. "They are gathering near our door. It appears we arrived just in time."

When he was done fouling the window and reading the circulars in the post, he settled fitfully into his chair with a good deal of harrumphing. Meanwhile, I read the *Gazette,* and in particular the article about the shooting.

"You are not mentioned by name, merely that someone has been brought in for questioning," I said.

"No doubt that is due to Bram Cusp's influence. Don't expect it to continue. There are a half-dozen reporters in the alley hoping to get a statement. Jenkins!"

Our clerk appeared in the doorway. "Yes, Mr. B?"

"Make up a sign. State that I will not give interviews but that the agency has been retained by the Japanese delegation to investigate the murder of Ambassador Toda."

"Right," Jenkins said, and opened his desk drawer in the waiting room where he kept his pen, ink, and papers. Jeremy Jenkins was a former forger with superb orthography. He could have made a living as a calligrapher or scrivener if he wanted to. The only reason he didn't, save perhaps out of a sense of loyalty to Barker, was the fact that his favorite pub was one street away.

Barker picked up the telephone receiver from the candlestick set on his desk and spoke a number into the mouthpiece.

"Is he there yet? Where is he? When is he due to return?" There was a brief pause. "Nay, don't bother. Thank you."

He hung the receiver back in its cradle, then consulted his turnip watch. It was a battered old thing, much out of date, but it must give excellent time, for he was never without it.

"Call a cab, lad."

I was up and out in a few seconds. I passed by most of the reporters, but not all, and anyway, I had to come to a stop to hail the hansom.

"Come on, Thomas. Give us a statement. What's Push up to?"

"Mr. Llewelyn, is there any truth to the rumor—"

"Just a few questions, sir, that's all we ask."

"I suggest you be patient, gentlemen," I told them as the cab drew up, fresh from Scotland Yard. "Our clerk is making a sign even now that I believe you will find interesting."

A minute later my employer shot out of his chambers, taking

the stairs two at a time. Brusquely, he shrugged off the clamor of the questions and pulled aboard the vehicle. I followed suit.

"The City!" he called overhead.

We bowled past the statue of Charles I, which is considered the exact center of London, and Trafalgar Square, where pigeons perched on the hero of Waterloo. We slid into the Strand and Fleet Street and eventually into the City. The cab slowed by an oddly shaped building, or rather, two mismatched buildings connected together, one round, the other rectangular.

"The Temple Church," I read from a sign as my employer stepped down.

"Founded by the Knights Templar in 1185."

"What are we doing here?"

"We are trying to learn more about the ambassador's mission, and who sanctioned it."

"By talking to a priest?"

"Not a priest, Thomas. Pollock Forbes. There is an initiation going on there this morning. I hope to speak to him."

"Ah," I said.

Pollock Forbes is head of an order of the Knights Templar. Not the same order that originally fought in the Crusades and achieved wealth and power; that one was destroyed in the 1400s, or so it is said. The one Forbes led was an organization composed mostly of bankers, barristers, and Scotsmen, an order of Freemasonry. However, I've often reasoned, if the original Templars were still in existence, wouldn't they appear as a harmless group of Free-masons that met in the original church but claimed to have nothing to do with the group?

"This church is peculiar," Barker said to me in a low voice.

"It looks it," I replied. "For one thing, it's round."

Barker grunted. "I meant in the ecclesiastical sense."

"Ah," I said for the second time. "Not strictly run by the Church of England, then. Is it Her Majesty's?"

"No," the Guv responded. "It belongs to the Inner and Middle Temples."

"Barristers. Who else might belong to an organization which no longer officially exists?"

"Exactly."

"Barristers become members of Parliament, while others don't get reelected and become barristers again."

"Correct."

"And what do the Templars do, precisely?"

"They are a fraternal organization."

"Extremely powerful men who get together in secret in order to wear vestments and perform rituals no one would understand."

"If you wish to put it that way, yes."

"May I assume these fellows would never use their connections to accomplish anything on a large scale."

"Just charitable events."

"And they have no idea where the original Templars kept their fortune, which I understand was considerable."

"Sorry, lad." Barker shrugged his shoulders.

"Thought as much."

We arrived at the temple door and entered. The round nave was tiny. It was built of Purbeck marble with a circle of columns and was only about fifty feet in diameter. There were grotesque heads carved into the walls on small medallions, mostly of men making ludicrous faces. I thought to myself, you have the most beautiful marble and this is what you use to decorate a church? Churches are sober, spiritual places. One doesn't want to look to the heavens and see a face leering at you with his tongue lolling out. There are certain fashions in architecture that deserve to end and be seen no more.

The small chamber was packed with men, dozens of them squashed into this miniature nave. I began to see a similarity between the faces above and the ones below.

The men with Forbes eyed us suspiciously, as if they felt we might have spied on the ceremony. I very much suspected that Barker was already a member, but I had not been invited, and had little curiosity about the whole thing. If they wished to wear aprons and red crosses, that was their prerogative.

A man came forward and pressed my hand. It was our old friend Pollock Forbes. He is whip thin but always expensively dressed, favoring Liberty waistcoats in outrageous patterns. He had curly, light brown hair and a pale complexion. He looked like a young blade loitering about town, and that was how he wished to be thought. No one need know that, like Ho, he was one of Barker's "watchers," collecting information which, from time to time, helped in our investigations.

"To what do I owe the honor?"

"I have a new case and I would like your insight. Are you in a hurry to get back or can I buy you an early lunch?"

"I don't eat much these days," Forbes admitted, "but my doctor has recommended a half pint of stout every day to build up my stamina."

"Then I'll buy you one down the street."

Just then a priest entered and looked at us as if we were there to loot the silver. By mutual agreement, we exited the church. He could have it all to himself.

Forbes led us along the street and down an alley into one of the most iconic buildings in London: nothing less than Ye Olde Cheshire Cheese itself. I had always hoped to come here, where Charles Dickens liked to duck in for a quiet pint in his favorite public house. It is mentioned in *A Tale of Two Cities* and in Stevenson's *The Dynamiter*. I doubted that either wrote anything in the actual building unless he had the eyes of the Cheshire Cat, for it is the gloomiest building in a city famed for its gloom. One has to stand in the doorway for a while until one's eyes grow accustomed to the charcoal-gray atmosphere. The flames of candles, lanterns, and gaslights inside produced a nimbus glow around the patrons and henceforth gave up trying to light the rooms. So much for one candle being sufficient to pierce the darkness.

We sat and I tried to decipher a menu, but it was not necessary.

Any food in Britain can be found in Ye Olde Cheshire Cheese. One merely has to call out and it will be brought steaming hot and bubbling from the kitchen. There may be nothing exotic about the food, but it is traditional and wholesome and filling, and were one to somehow return a century after, the exact same recipe would be brought out, possibly on the same plate.

"Fried potatoes, your best game pie, and pints all around," Forbes ordered. "Oh, and bring some sprouts while you are at it."

"Thrilled" is not a word I throw around lightly. It sounds overly exuberant. However, I was thrilled to be there. It was as if Dickens himself would pass our table and ask to borrow the salt, or Dr. Johnson, who once lived nearby, would try to squeeze his girth between the chairs. Why had I not come here sooner? That's London for you. A place of great historical and literary significance slapped into an ordinary street with no signs and an entrance round the corner.

"I never expected to see you outside of the Café Royal, Pollock," I said.

"I often have meetings at the Temple. This place is convenient and while it's not a patch on the Royal, it's such a quaint old place I find I come here often."

Our seats were in the back row. Forbes looked comfortable here. His reputation as a dandy was bolstered by his often paying Oscar Wilde's tab at the Café Royal. One wouldn't think that the pockets of his velvet jacket were stuffed with memoranda and bills from the House of Commons. Nor would one understand that the Masonic Hall behind the restaurant was generally at his disposal. His reputation as a young man who had inherited a lairdship and was squandering it was deliberate, while what work he did through the Templars was anonymous. Those who knew, and precious few of us there were, did our best to keep his incognito a secret. Here I was, having an epiphany, while he and the Guv were looking almost bored.

"I'm going to assume, Cyrus," Forbes began, "since you are

not especially a social man, that there is a purpose to your coming to see me. Is there something I should know?"

"I have been retained to investigate the death of the Japanese ambassador."

"Really? With a case against you pending in the courts?"

"Apparently, General Mononobe wanted someone he could trust, and on the strength of seeing my garden, he decided that I am the man."

The pints arrived, large, frothy glass mugs of oatmeal stout which sloshed over the sides and left new rings among the many old ones. If I could have, I'd have purchased one of the ancient tables for my room. Could the *BJ* carved into the edge with a knife have been the work of Ben Jonson?

"How can I help with your investigation?"

"I don't need anything beyond facts or rumors that have been bounced around the Houses of Parliament. Did the Japanese make the initial offer for an embassy?"

"They did. The MPs are patting each other on the backs. The Foreign Office has tried for years to get under that Japanese shell but it was considered impregnable. Then, poof! It opened by itself."

"What did you know about the victim, Toda?"

"A Shinto scholar. He lived as a monk for a time until he was dragged into politics. His death is a severe loss to the country. He was much loved, I understand. There will be statues made of him. This death doesn't reflect well on the two countries' relationship."

"Will his death cause changes to the government?"

"Decidedly. He was a pacifist. Also, something of a referee between the general and Mr. Akita, the minister of trade, who is a businessman and espouses free trade. Japan is little more than barren rock and until now the government has been forced to accept the Americans' price on wood, coal, cotton, and just about everything else. Believe it or not, the Japanese are Anglophiles. While we are wearing dressing gowns with old Japanese woodcuts printed on them, they are trading tweed on the black market."

"And Mononobe?"

"Obviously, he's from the military side. The Japanese psyche desperately wants to prove it is the equal of the West. It won't be caught flat-footed again as it was in 1853 when the American, Admiral Perry, arrived and began dictating terms."

"So it is Mononobe against Akita?" Barker said. "And now the referee has been shot. Why was Mononobe made second in command?"

"He has the seniority. Apparently, he fought in the Boshin War on the imperial side. As I understand, he saw the writing on the wall early, switched sides to the emperor, and defeated his old samurai comrades. A real slash-and-burn general he is."

"How much power does he have now? Can he broker arrangements himself, or must he take the information back to Tokyo to be decided there?"

"Oh, he's got full power now, he and the admiral. Their arrival has the entire navy slathering. He'll want to order at least one destroyer."

The game pie arrived, swimming in its own fragrant gravy and accompanied by roasted potatoes, speckled with parsley and salt, and buttery brussels sprouts. We all set to.

"And what of Akita? Does he have power to make deals, as well?"

"He's already been up to Sheffield, placing orders. He'll want anything and everything we can offer him. He's trying to turn a feudal country into a modern civilization single-handed, and to make the best deals. He's as shrewd as a Scotsman, and this from a Scotsman."

"Would either have been able to accomplish this with Toda alive?"

I noticed Forbes took the thinnest slice for himself and began picking at it. Forbes had consumption. His lungs were swimming in liquid. His constant fight with the disease left him with little appetite. "He's a friend of yours," I told myself, "and he's going to die one of these days, and there isn't a damn thing you can do about it."

"I believe Toda would have exercised caution and restraint," he said, moving the food around on his plate.

"So, with him dead, there is no one to stop either group from making decisions. Is it possible they are each spending the same money?"

"That I couldn't tell you, but it's been done before."

"Does everyone in Parliament agree this is a good thing? The arrival of the Japanese, I mean?"

"No, not everyone. Lord Granville was quite outspoken on the floor of the House of Lords this week. He said you cannot put a savage in a Savile Row suit and expect him to behave like a gentleman. Granville is a xenophobe of the first order, but some of the decisions of their military, the punishment of prisoners, for example, have been barbaric by our standards. They have been in isolation for hundreds of years in feudal conditions, doing things the exact same way until it has become ingrained in their psyche. Now suddenly, they must act like Westerners or perish."

"What is the mood of Her Majesty's government regarding the Japanese?"

"They were cautiously optimistic until Toda's murder. Now the idea is, 'Well, what would you expect?' I'm sure the Palace wishes the delegates would have the good manners to go away now and put their house in order. Come back in a few years. However, both parties are full steam ahead, if you know what I mean."

"That's enough for me," I said, putting down my pint and pushing myself away from the table. My trouser band was pressing against my stomach. The Cheshire Cheese was dangerous. If I came here too often, I'd be as fat as old Samuel Johnson. I could just picture myself moribund, puffing after a suspect.

Barker stood. "Thank you, Pollock. Is there anything I can do for the organization?"

"Just grease the wheels, Cyrus."

"As always. You've given me much to think about."

Cyrus Barker and Pollock Forbes fought over the bill and Forbes won, but not without a struggle. Aside from being a barrister and the leader of the secret society, Forbes was also laird of his clan, and while Barker was not a member of it, he expected no nonsense about who pays what from a mere commoner. The Guv would be certain to pay next time and to overpay the tip while he was at it. I didn't actually see Forbes pay. I assumed he had some kind of account at the Cheshire Cheese.

We parted in the street and Forbes shook hands all around. I put my finger and thumb in my mouth and whistled for a cab. If the weather is good, one could hear me a dozen streets away. A couple of minutes later one came trundling around the corner and pulled up in front of us. We clambered aboard and sat back and were soon on our way.

CHAPTER ELEVEN

It must be fun dangling an assistant on a hook all the time. I gave my employer a look which meant "I want to know where we're going, but I'm damned if I'm going to ask." Finally, he took pity on me.

"We're going to the embassy again. Now that we know better how things stand there, I want to question the general more closely."

Lord Diosy's residence looked very different by day. The exterior of the building was the color of yellow cream, the roofing of red tile. The gate which had been so imposing the first time I had seen it was wide open now and there was nobody to stop us entering. I wondered if Dunn would still be there, ordering his subordinates about.

"Do you suppose His Lordship is charging the embassy rent on his fine home? And what do you think he is doing at his club in Pall Mall?"

"I doubt Diosy is charging them anything. He's wealthy by

anyone's standards. As I understand, he has been encouraging the Japanese to return here after their last European tour several years ago. He is forming a Japanese society here."

The door was answered by different bodyguards from the ones we had seen before, but all wore identical suits and low-crowned bowler hats as if it were a livery: cutaway coats over matching black waistcoats, high collars with blue ties, and checked trousers. Gaitered shoes completed their ensembles. With Toda gone, no one I saw was dressed in their country's traditional kimono and obi. They were trying very hard to fit in among these Western barbarians.

We were led to see the general. He was seated at a desk in a modern suit with a calligraphy brush in his hand, perhaps writing an account of the ambassador's death for the emperor. He looked up at Barker without speaking.

"I have some more questions for you, sir," the Guv said.

Mononobe lifted a palm toward the chairs in front of the desk. I had seen Barker make such a gesture earlier. We sat and I waited for the Guv to begin.

"Where were you at the time Ambassador Toda was killed, General?"

"We were downstairs in the dining hall," he answered. "We needed to decide what our individual itineraries would be. There was so little time and so much that commanded our attention."

"I see," Barker said.

"We decided to forgo some of the ceremonies. We saw no reason to attend sporting events, for example. There were better uses for our time."

"Were all the ministers present?"

The general looked at us, considering his answer. "They were. Most of the time, anyway. It was a formal meal, but we had much to discuss."

"What do you mean, most of the time, if I may ask, General?"

"We were receiving telephone calls from our various appoint-

ments, wishing to verify if we would come. We went and returned."

"So, at least once during the dinner, each of you left the room?"

"I did not. It was my meeting and I wanted all of us to decide
what to do."

"Why were you in charge? Where was the ambassador?"

"Upstairs. He was not feeling well. He was nearly seventy."

"Did you hear the shot?"

"No, Mr. Barker, I didn't. None of us did, or our bodyguards
would have defended us immediately."

"Was Mr. Kito with you?"

"Oh, yes. I go nowhere without him."

"Is he your personal servant or was he assigned to you for the
duration of the visit?"

"All of them were lent at the pleasure of the emperor, except
for Mr. Toda's guard, whom he brought along. Where are you
from, Mr. Barker? Your manner of speaking is most unusual."

"I am a Scot, sir."

"A Scot! The first I have met. Why do you not wear the kilt?"

"I own one, sir, but it would excite undue attention here in the
south were I to wear it."

"Were you in the army yourself, sir? You seem to have a military bearing."

"Here and there, General. Mostly in the East."

"Do you believe in reincarnation?"

"No, sir. As a matter of fact, I do not."

"Then perhaps you believe in fate."

"If by that you mean that our lives are not in our own hands
most of the time, then yes."

We had come to question the general, but instead he seemed to
be interviewing us.

"How came you to receive that scar, sir?"

Barker reached up and touched the old wound which bisected
his right brow and cut into his cheek. "A souvenir of your country."

"I recognize the cut that made it, a war sword. I have seen other men with such a wound."

"Tell me, General Mononobe," my employer said, turning the conversation back to his questions. "With Mr. Toda dead, do you plan to continue his policies here or your own? I understand you had different ideas of what your country's future should be."

"I would be roundly criticized back in Tokyo if I did not follow Toda's policies to the letter," he explained. "However, I am free to meet whom I choose and make alliances."

"Of course. You would be free to witness the demonstration of a weapon such as the heavy siege howitzer, for example, as long as you did not purchase one without your government's permission."

"You understand that perfectly, Mr. Barker."

"Or a cannon. Or a battleship."

"Oh, we have ordered a battleship from your Stepney Yards. That was already planned before we arrived, during Toda's tenure."

"But just the one."

"Just the one. So many countries now have modern weapons. We must be able to defend ourselves. We cannot expect the American navy to do it for us."

"I quite understand."

"Forgive my manners, sir!" Mononobe cried, and passed over a box of Dunhills. Barker and I declined, but the general helped himself to one and soon had it lit and drawing.

"Do you think you can find the man who killed my old friend?"

"I believe I can lay hands upon him shortly, yes. With your permission, I would like a list of every member of the delegation and all bodyguards and servants."

"You assume the killer is Japanese? How very British."

"I already know who might have an interest in your arrival, sir. I have no need for a list of Englishmen, since I have one of my own."

"Ah. Forgive me."

"Not at all. I—"

The general, still puffing on his cigar, raised a framed photograph from his desk and regarded it.

"My daughter, Mr. Barker," he said, with some degree of pride.

"Very pretty," the Guv said.

"Regrettably, she has passed. Our country was in upheaval."

"My condolences, General."

"Are you married, Mr. Barker?"

"No, sir. Mine is a dangerous profession. I should think twice before exposing a wife to such dangers."

"You are still young. I'm sure there is time."

Barker was in his early forties, but Mononobe must be approaching sixty. I supposed to the ambassador, my employer was young, though I might have a different view on the subject.

"Do you recall where the ambassador's bodyguard was at the time of Toda's death?"

"He was guarding the front door. We had no idea an attack would come from within. He has lost face and the blame will fall to him."

"Is he the large fellow we saw in the garden?"

"Yes, Mr. Barker."

"May I speak to him?"

"I'm afraid he has disappeared," Mononobe said. "He just walked off. Perhaps he is getting drunk in one of your public houses."

"Did anyone see him leave?"

"No."

"So, he may have been lured away."

"More likely he is contemplating jumping in the river."

"Was he at the door the entire time during the night of the ambassador's murder?"

"I have no idea, sir. I'm afraid I do not keep track of bodyguards. There was the matter of our itinerary to discuss."

"Who found the body?"

"Ohara. He completed his shift and went to Toda Ichigo's room."

I tried to put it all together. Barker was out in the bushes, Fu Ying was on the roof. The guards were changing, the ministers were coming and going. From the point of view of an enquiry agent, it was complete chaos.

"I shall make a list for you," Mononobe continued.

"Thank you. Is Mr. Akita in the building?"

"You shall have to ask at the front door. He comes and goes hourly. I believe he intends to visit every manufacturer in London. He is a very energetic man, but then, he is the youngest member of our party."

Barker rose. "Thank you for answering my questions, sir. Come, Thomas."

The ambassador put down the photograph he was contemplating and nodded solemnly. Barker led me out of the room. We asked one of the guards if Mr. Akita was in the building, and for once we were in luck. He had just returned and was working in his temporary office.

We knocked upon the door and were answered in Japanese. Barker walked in. A Japanese man with a Western haircut, a gray serge lounge suit, and pumps was sitting in a chair reading the *Financial Times,* with a cup of tea and a half-eaten napoleon at his elbow.

"Can I help you?" the man asked, switching to English. He was perhaps thirty-five or an athletic forty. No older, certainly. He rose and looked at us inquiringly, with none of the suspicion I saw on the faces of the other delegates.

"Sir, I am Cyrus Barker. I have been hired to investigate the murder of Ambassador Toda for the general."

He stood. "Gentlemen, have a seat. Such a tragedy. I can't believe the master has gone all this distance, merely to be shot by an insane person."

"You think him insane?"

Akita shrugged. "Of course. Toda was a man of peace. He didn't have an enemy in Japan, while your country is full of eccentrics and murderers, or so your literature informs me."

"I hardly think our literature indicts us in such a fashion," the Guv rumbled.

"Oh, no?" he replied. "I have never met a murderer to my knowledge. How many have you known?"

"Dozens," the Guv admitted, "but I am not a good example, since my occupation is the hunting down of criminals. Tell me, sir, why did you not come to my garden the other morning?"

He scrunched up his face, which made me smile.

"I'm not much for gardens or pastoral activities of antiquity. I prefer modern life, and my time in this country is precious. I must meet every important merchant that I can in the short time I am here. Japan needs cloth and fuel. We need food and steel, inventions and marvels of the modern age if we are ever to compete. We have been isolated so long, we are in danger of being left behind. The Industrial Revolution must reach my country and find a foothold."

"And you are the man to do it," I added.

Akita gave a satisfied smile.

"Of course. Toda, for all his wisdom, would not have done it. He always had one foot in heaven. The things of earth—trade treaties, business mergers, and global finance—had no allure for him. Nor for Mononobe. The world is a Go board for him. More than anything he wants to prove that the ways of old Japan still function well in this world of underwater telegraph cables and trains that can travel sixty miles in an hour."

"Do you suppose Ambassador Toda's pacifism may have angered some people?"

"No, not at all," Akita said, settling back in his chair and tenting his fingers. "He was a soft-spoken man, but highly inspirational. He could convince a wild horse to wear a saddle merely by talking to it. However, his position was highly debated before he was chosen, and some felt slighted."

"Are you among them, sir?"

Akita sat back in his seat and stared at the ceiling as he drew breath.

"Yes, that is so. I wrote in several journals before we left that Toda was not the proper man to lead the embassy. The government insisted, and suggested if I continued to stir up trouble I would not be invited as a delegate. I—what is the term? I bit my lip. My opinions were never in question."

"And Mononobe?"

"He claimed to be in favor of Toda leading, which of course was the popular opinion in the government and among the populace."

"I gather he has plans of his own, and people to see," Barker said, which of course, he knew.

"Oh, yes," Akita said. "He has been attending military demonstrations here and there since we arrived. Tours at Aldershot and Sandhurst. The horse guards on parade in their barracks and demonstrations here and there."

"Is he doing this with the government's blessing or against it?"

"Mr. Barker, my government's plans are secret, even from me. One goes ahead with one's plans and then one is either rewarded or censured when it is done. It's not a comfortable way to do business, but it is our way."

"Some would say Toda's death was convenient for you, as well, sir."

"That is so. I admit it. I was told to rein in my purchasing while he lived. Now I have funds at my disposal and a limited time in which to spend them."

He tapped the desk with the point of his finger. "But make no mistake, gentlemen. If I cut a man's throat, it is on the stock exchange. There are more ways to ruin a man than by simply pulling a trigger."

"How is your relationship with the general?"

"I must toe the line, as they say. Mononobe is a powerful man. He has backers, important families who are also manufacturers. Old samurai families. By their traditions, I am a peasant. My kind of people only exist in the modern world. The old aristocracy is fading away, but men like Mononobe do not realize it. He will fight on forever.

"Unless you have anything more for me, I'm afraid I must go.

I have another appointment. Several, in fact. I am one man doing the work of a dozen."

Barker stood.

"We shall leave you to your work, Mr. Akita. Thank you for taking the time to speak to us."

We turned, and Akita picked up the receiver on his telephone set. By the time we left the room, he was talking to a manufacturer in Durham.

"Hmmph," Barker rumbled.

"What is it?"

"Tradition versus modernity."

"It's a new age," I said. "Almost a new century."

"Did you notice Akita did not bow when we left? He did not even shake our hands. Sometimes I feel modernity is merely an excuse for a lack of manners."

"Are you feeling well, sir?" I asked. I had seen him grimace when he rose.

"My ribs are aching."

"Did we accomplish anything by coming here?"

"Perhaps. Facts accumulate like snowflakes."

"That sounds distinctly Japanese, sir," I said.

Barker used the bannister to descend the stairs, and he did so slowly. When he reached the front door he spoke to the two body-guards there.

"Is the admiral here?" he asked.

"Not here," a guard said.

"And the minister of arts?"

"Not here."

I wasn't certain how much English the man knew, but we took his words at face value.

CHAPTER TWELVE

When we returned, Jenkins looked at us pointedly, his eyebrows raised, then looked into our chambers. We had a visitor, obviously, an important one. One cannot leave this place for a second, I thought.

Barker entered, with me behind him. A man sat in the visitor's chair facing Barker's desk, an elegant man in an expensive suit, carrying a thin black walking stick which he held along with a pair of kid gloves. His hair was slicked back, his face aquiline in that way that only an aristocrat has. He looked like an advertisement for suits. I wondered if he had come to hire our services.

The gentleman stood and handed Barker his card, which the Guv examined before handing it to me. This was Lord Diosy, I realized, the embassy's host.

"Good day, Your Lordship," he said, shaking his hand.

I nodded deferentially, but the man came forward and shook my hand with a dry, firm grip.

"Mr. Llewelyn," he said, as he took his seat again.

"I came to discuss the ambassador's death," he began.

My employer sat back in his deep green leather chair and regarded the aristocrat. "Events have been slowed by activity in the East End and the inability of several key members of the delegation to tell the truth."

"The Japanese are like that, you know," Diosy said. "They'd rather tell you the lie one expects rather than tell the truth, which they consider ill-mannered."

"Pray, sir, what caused you to become so interested in the Japanese?"

"My father went there at the behest of the English government after Perry's conquest, to inform them that Britain did not want to be left out of the arrangements and would support the Japanese monarchy if necessary. He stayed for years and I was raised there. I spoke Japanese from a young age."

"I see," I said, scribbling shorthand as fast as I could.

"I fear this delegation had been doomed from the start. General Mononobe and Minister Akita represent key figures in two parties, the National and the Progressive. The nationalistic party is traditional, and the other is pro-Western. There has been a good deal of argument in the newspapers in Tokyo and ill feelings on both sides. The news of Toda's death has only recently reached Japan and I understand there is nationwide mourning. Both sides proclaim his death a catastrophe in order to curry favor with the crowd."

"If the election were today, who would win?" Barker asked.

"Probably the Progressives, but not by a wide margin. Their party represents the 'common man,' calling for an end to the feudal system and new occupations for everyone. The traditional party is funded by several wealthy Japanese families and manufacturers and does a lot of saber rattling. They are for kicking out the Americans and either returning to the old ways or beginning a new chapter."

Barker sat back until he was in the shadow of his green wing chair.

"What kind of chapter?" he asked.

"A military one. Any country that has ever insulted them in the past, any politician who offers another choice, any region which shows itself unenthusiastic, is held up for punishment or ridicule. Without going into detail, they have suggested that perhaps a small conquest or two would make Japan an empire."

"I see," I said.

"You may not believe me, gentlemen, but the Japanese are a very sensitive people. They are polite and diffident. A man might begin a long friendship with a woman which never progresses into marriage because he fears rejection. However, there is a historic tradition which represents the ideal of the warrior, so that this diffident chap I was speaking of may spend six hours a day practicing with a sword. Of course, the sword has been officially outlawed to stop any attempt at insurrection, but most former samurai, or sons of samurai, still own them in secret. The police know of this but do not arrest them unless someone is injured."

"Mononobe represents this party," Barker said.

"Yes," Diosy replied. "Frankly, I would prefer he had not come, especially since the heads of both parties are here in one building, but no one could keep them out."

"What of the admiral?"

"That is a good question. Edami began as a traditional samurai, fighting for the shogunate. Since then, he has become a member of the emperor's council. His purpose in Mononobe's plans is to draw members from the Progressive Party to their ranks, out of respect for him. There is a large part of the population that respects the military."

Cyrus Barker nodded. "I suspected as much. Has it destabilized the country?"

"More than that, it has destabilized Asia. China is quaking in their boots. The military could attack north into Korea or south into Hong Kong or Formosa. The Chinese army is large but poorly armed and trained, a mere paper tiger. After the nation's lightning defeat by the Americans, they want to bolster their own pride with a quick victory. It doesn't matter who or how."

The Guv nodded, contemplating what the aristocrat had said.

"I understand you speak Japanese, sir," Diosy continued. "Have you ever been there?"

"I have."

That's Barker, I thought. Loquacious to a fault.

"Where?"

"Hokkaido. Near Hakodate. During the Boshin War."

"Good Lord! On what side?"

"The losing one."

"My father took us to England until Japan and China both stabilized. I recall how strange this new country seemed. No cherry blossoms or temples. Strange food and stranger people."

"It is just as the delegation must feel now, alone in a strange land, cut off from the familiar," I remarked.

"No doubt."

Diosy paused for a moment. We were getting down to the reason His Lordship had come.

"Look here, Barker. Is there anything you need? Can I help in some way? The delegation, well, damn it; it is hemorrhaging. A few days ago, I thought the embassy might get a firm footing. Now I fear it has brought its own problems with it."

"I need nothing, sir, and I appreciate your concerns. Should I require anything I shall ask."

"Very well," Lord Diosy said, looking dissatisfied. "I hope you know what you are about."

"Understand, sir, that I can find the ambassador's killer," my employer said, tapping the desk. "But I cannot guarantee they won't attempt more mischief. They will be as they are, and I cannot watch every one of them all day long."

"That's fine. We've got Inspector Dunn for that. The man has practically taken up residence. I trust him to keep order in my house, but finding the murderer is another matter."

Barker stood. "Thank you for coming, Your Lordship. I'll keep you informed."

Diosy rose in that way one does if one has a perfect tailor. He brushed his leg with his gloves as if removing a speck of dust, and gave the chamber one more look before leaving.

"Very nice," he said. "Is that a real Ming vase?"

He indicated a vase that stood on a pedestal near the window.

"Yes," my employer replied.

"If you ever wish to sell it, pray let me know."

"I shall."

Lord Diosy showed himself out. Some people are too well bred to say good-bye.

We closed shop at six and made our way home. During dinner, both of us were preoccupied. Finally, I spoke.

"Sir, I must confess I am lost. I know nothing about Japanese history or culture. I've never been so out of my depth. It's like a closed book to me."

"Then you had better open it."

"I could speak to Liam Grant, at the Reading Room."

I consulted my watch. Grant wouldn't be leaving for a few hours, and I knew precisely how to while away those hours.

"Sir, I have an errand to run. Then I'll go see Mr. Grant."

Barker nodded. He was trying to put together the pieces of a complex puzzle. Behind him, Mac was fuming. Neither of us had done justice to the meal, although Harm didn't mind the scraps I fed him under the table.

Later that evening, I visited Mrs. Cowan, my intended. Normally a man calls within certain daylight hours, but I worked during that time. Our compromise was to sit in her garden in full view of the neighbors, her maid, and the Bevis Marks Synagogue. Still, I would take what I could get in order to see her.

Rebecca had a narrow, solemn face, dark eyes, and a quiet manner. She could be lively at times, but she had a gentle soul that was balm to me.

"What is Mr. Barker investigating this week?" she asked, as we settled ourselves on two comfortable chairs with a tea table in between us.

"The murder of the Japanese ambassador."

"Oh! I read about it in the *Chronicle*. Poor man, to come all this way around the globe only to die in Bermondsey."

"It is a terrible place to die," I said.

She swatted my wrist. "You're incorrigible. I don't know why your employer suffers you."

"Should I ever find out, you'll be the first to know." I leaned back in my seat. "How are your parents?"

"Well enough," she said. "They are visiting Edinburgh at the moment. My father is something of an itinerant rabbi, you know."

"Do they have synagogues in Edinburgh?"

"Of course. Jews are everywhere since the Diaspora. There have even been Jews in China for thousands of years."

"Imagine that! But not in Scotland."

"No, we're still considered a novelty in Scotland. Certainly no more than a couple of centuries."

"I see."

"Your Mr. Barker is Scottish and has lived in China. I should like to meet him sometime."

I hoped to delay such a meeting, to be honest. I wanted her all to myself.

The garden was warm, and birds were settling in for the night. Unfortunately, the garden wasn't mine, having been given to her and her late husband by her parents. I wasn't certain I could live in Asher Cowan's house after we were wed. As it was, I had little to offer her save a heart, and possibly some heartache. We sat in companionable silence for a minute or two.

"It's peaceful here," I remarked.

"It is," she agreed.

"No one shoots anyone here, or tries to attack them."

"Practically never."

"I could use a little bit of that in my life."

"And perhaps I could use a little excitement. I have been cloistered here. Nothing I do has any import."

"You'd be surprised."

"Now you're just flattering me."

"Is it working?"

"We shall have to see, Mr. Llewelyn."

She rose, with a rustle of fabric. "You must go."

"Already? I have only just arrived."

"We are being watched by scandalized eyes."

I stood, as well.

"Very well," I said. "I'm going. But I'm coming back."

She gave a hint of a smile. "I'm counting on it."

CHAPTER THIRTEEN

Technically, Liam Grant was not a librarian, but he could be found in the Reading Room all day every day, feeding on knowledge like a pilot fish feeds upon a shark. Being a gentleman, he had a private income, and this was how he preferred to spend his days. I seemed to recall that he had a particular interest in Asian studies. He sounded just the man.

My very first "watcher," Grant lived a very circumscribed life, according to a timetable. He "worked" at the museum until nine o'clock when it closed, walked across to the Alpha Inn on the other side of Montague Street for dinner, and then went home, which happened to be a flat on the same street. He rarely left that street from one week to the next. Oxford Street next door might as well be Borneo as far as the likelihood that he would visit it someday. But then, it was the knowledge he had ingested from those books he read that interested me. His eccentricities were his own concern.

My hansom pulled into Montague Street promptly at nine, and

I was just getting out of the cab when I saw Grant step out of the museum entrance and raise his umbrella. I hailed him.

"Mr. Llewelyn, is it not?" he asked, after placing me.

There was nothing remarkable about his appearance, a gray-haired man approaching sixty with a pair of pince-nez spectacles and a mild manner. He looked a typical Englishman. However, his mind was first-rate, and he used it on a number of esoteric subjects. I hoped Japanese history was one of them.

"May I join you at the Alpha?" I asked. "I had something I wanted to ask you about."

"One of Mr. Barker's cases?" he asked.

"Indeed."

Liam Grant considered Cyrus Barker an interesting specimen. I wasn't certain where he got his information, but there was a file in his brain with the Guv's name on it, and it was far from empty. I hazarded a guess that a brain like Grant's was always looking for stimulation, and I could safely say that Barker would provide it.

Ten minutes later we were snug in a corner of the inn with a pint of stout and a bacon sandwich in front of each of us while the rain buffeted the window nearby. A fog had set to in earnest, as well. There were worse places to be on an August evening.

"What subject are we discussing this time?" Grant asked. "As I recall, we talked about Tibet and Shambhala the last time we met."

"Japan," I informed him, as I took that first wonderful sip of stout after a long day and licked the foam from my lip. "And its recent history."

"Ah!" he said, in approval, as if the subject had merit. "I suppose it has to do with the death of the current ambassador."

"It does," I admitted. "We are investigating the case. Frankly, I am at a loss. I need insight. I hardly know where to start."

We bit into our sandwiches, hot, toasted, and full of bacon. I appreciate recipes full of spices and exotic ingredients, but sometimes the body cries out for a plain bit of bread and bacon, even when one has already dined earlier on turbot prepared by a great chef. Needless to say, I wouldn't inform Mac of this little indiscretion.

"Japan," he said, warming to the subject. "A fascinating little country!"

"I keep hearing how its society is a mirror image to our own, and that we have much in common."

"You would think that, wouldn't you? But nothing could be further from the truth. No, if you think that way, you're going to put your foot wrong every time."

"Excellent," I said, leaning forward. "That is what I've come to hear. So, how do I put my foot right?"

"Up until fifty years ago, the country was isolated. I mean completely isolated, as if it were located on the moon or the planet Mars. For all they knew, people in other countries had faces in their bellies and flew like storks."

"Then what happened?"

"In 1853, Commodore Perry of the United States arrived with his navy and demanded a trade agreement at gunpoint. It totally demoralized the country. They suddenly realized they weren't the center of the universe, but rather, a small backwater of little use to anyone."

I nodded, considering as well as I could the implications.

"Of particular concern were American firearms. Japan had brought the usage of swords to a high art form. Now they were rendered nearly useless, and with them the aristocracy that used them, the samurai. It precipitated a war between the samurai and the Imperial Army, the Boshin War, which the government army won. Since then the country has been on a self-improvement regimen, essentially inflicting the Industrial Age upon a feudal society."

"That sounds impossible," I said.

"It is. And yet they will do it. You have to understand the Japanese character. They can be fierce. But they'll just as easily destroy themselves at the slightest whim of the emperor as punishment over the most minor infraction."

I swallowed the strong, bitter stout again and set it down on the homely wooden table.

"I feel you are about to say: 'And, yet . . .'"

"I was. And yet . . . they are most often a gentle people. They love gardening, revere flower arranging and painting on screens. They write the most beautiful poetry. They are glorious in battle, but will cry before or afterward. They are an emotional people, while making a great show of stoicism in front of you. They are endlessly fascinating."

Grant put down his empty pint glass next to his empty plate.

"Let us repair to my flat, Mr. Llewelyn," he said. "I've got a few things to show you."

He stood, threw a couple of sovereigns on the table, enough to pay for both meals twice over. Then he took his stout umbrella, a product of James Smith & Sons nearby, just a street over, and led me outside into the rain.

The Alpha Inn is opposite the left end of the British Museum. Grant's flat was opposite the right end. In just a couple of minutes we crossed the pavement and came to his door. I held the brolly while he turned the key in the lock. Then we went up a flight of stairs to his flat on the first floor.

I'd never been there before. His rooms were densely packed with bookcases. Not merely did they line the walls, but they stood out perpendicularly into the room like their more professional brethren at the British Museum. Every shelf was full of books, quite old ones, bound in leather. Every space above was crammed with still more books, even down to the teetering stacks on top, which looked like they might fall on our heads. In front of the books, in the scant few inches between the spine and the lip of the shelves, were curios from foreign lands: Egyptian figures carved of stone, small Arab daggers, shrunken heads from some unknown tribe of cannibals, a small Chinese village carved of cork and pressed between glass.

I started when I saw an owl staring at me from atop a bookcase, but it was stuffed and dusty.

"The man fancies himself an alchemist," I told myself.

I leaned forward to read titles on one shelf, as any bibliophile is wont, then wished I hadn't. *The Magic of Moses. The Apocrypha. The Gospel According to Thomas.* Not this Thomas, mind you. I'm just a plain old Methodist.

Meanwhile, Grant was changing his shoes for a pair of carpet slippers and his jacket for a tattered jumper, out at the elbows.

I had before me an example of what might be termed *confirmdus bachelorum*. It was as if everything in the entire flat had been designed to win the disapproval of women.

"Where is it? Where is it?" he was asking himself, searching among some dusty maps rolled and crammed into an elephant's-foot umbrella stand. He had quite a menagerie going. "Here it is!"

He showed me a map of the islands of Japan. They did somewhat resemble England in size, shape, and relative placement. There were cities whose names I recognized. Yokohama. Edo.

"This is an old map," he said. "Edo is called Tokyo now. The capital city. Take it with you and memorize it. You can return it when the case is over."

He started taking down books that might be helpful: a history of Japan, a book of Japanese fables, another on Shintoism. He took down a sword from the wall and unsheathed it, discussing the process required to smelt it and beat it down over and over again. I was beginning to be overwhelmed.

"They are very clever," Grant was saying. "Show them any piece of equipment—a pistol, for example—and they'll figure out how to manufacture it, then how to save money using lesser materials, then how to add improvements to either the pistol or the manufacturing process. They are canny businessmen and expert hagglers. They won't be taken in a swindle."

"You sound as if you admire them."

"I do, in a way, I suppose. And yet I wish the Americans had never arrived. I preferred when the Japanese thought themselves invincible and the center of the universe. Now it's as if while showing themselves outwardly to be calm, inside they are panicking.

They are liable to do anything. One would have to live among them for some time to figure what they might do next."

"Barker has," I said. "Lived among them, I mean."

"Has he, by Jove? I'm not surprised. Very interesting chap, your Mr. Barker. He knows more than I what they will do, I suppose. Trust his lead. And study those books. You never know what will help you. Just remember this: the Japanese will never tell you what they are really thinking. They are always on their guard, so you should be, as well, especially if one of them is carrying a sword. You cannot imagine how sharp their swords are. You can drop a hair on an open blade and it will be cut in twain by the mere force of gravity."

"I really shouldn't borrow your books," I told him. "These are your own personal copies."

"Nonsense!" he cried. "All knowledge must be disseminated. Return them when you can, or don't. I'll always buy more to fill the shelves. I've ingested most of the subjects in these books, anyway."

"I shall return them just the same," I promised.

"Of course you will, Thomas. I'm not concerned. But use them! That's what they were written and published for."

"I will," I said. "Tell me about the Boshin War."

"As I recall, the war occurred in 1868. It was a civil war, or if you prefer, a revolution, between the Imperial Army and the shogunate, allied with the old samurai. It was swords against artillery. The samurai class was effectively exterminated and swords outlawed. The traditional methods gave way to modern technology, as it always does. As I said, it would have been so nice if the Americans had left Japan alone, but one cannot put the genie back in the bottle, eh?"

"I suppose not. Anything else?"

"Not off the top of my head."

"What about Shintoism?"

"Shintoism! Such a wonderful subject. It's an ethnic religion.

Only the Japanese practice it. One performs certain rituals in order to establish a connection between modern times and the ancient past. There are shrines where one can pray to a host of ancestral gods and many annual festivals."

"Wait, wait!" I said, holding out my hand. "Am I getting this right? Shintoism is a bridge between the present and the past, but meanwhile, modern weapons and 'self-improvement' have eliminated the aristocracy and everything must be in the most modern style possible."

"Well put."

"A Shinto leader, then, no matter how well embraced by the people, would be considered a danger to modernists. And a pacifist would be a danger to the military status quo."

"Certainly," Grant said. "I assume you are speaking about Toda Ichigo. To these English, an ambassador was shot. To the Japanese, a beloved leader of peace, a living saint, if you will, was assassinated. This could be the failure of the visit. In their mind, to kill such a hero would be unthinkable. Therefore, an Englishman must have done it. Are there any English involved in this?"

"Possibly," I admitted. "A Foreign Office man, and Lord Diosy, head of the Japanese Society."

"Neither sounds a likely candidate."

"True," I answered.

"I'm glad you came. You must come round more often."

"Thank you for the information. I'll do that."

"Can I offer you some tea?"

I had a mental image of him blowing dust out of the bottom of a cup, and pouring water into an old and hoary cauldron.

"No, thank you. Really, I must be going."

"Nonsense!"

I did, in fact, have the tea, which was green gunpowder tea in Barker's honor, and was less revolting than I had feared. He talked about Japan for another half hour. I did my best to retain what he was telling me, but my brain was soon waterlogged with facts. I was finally able to escape into the night a little past ten. By then, the rain had stopped, but the ground was actually steaming.

Lugging the stack of books and the fragile map, I was able to flag down a cab outside of James Smith & Sons, which was just as well. The shop was closed.

CHAPTER FOURTEEN

Each night, Cyrus Barker falls asleep in this manner: he lays his head on the pillow, he closes his eyes, he relaxes his body, and within sixty seconds, he begins to snore. It's that simple and that quick. It's another gift that God or nature has bestowed upon him, as opposed to lesser mortals.

I, on the other hand, stare at the ceiling for hours, while all my insecurities and inadequacies parade above me, like the Lord Mayor's show. I change positions, fluff my pillow, and when worse comes to worst, go downstairs and try reading something in the library. I would not wish insomnia upon my worst enemy, but over the years we have established a kind of truce. Someone informed me once that it is a malady of particularly intelligent people. I assume the person who told me that was a fellow sufferer.

That night I went to bed and followed my usual routine. When last I looked at the clock by the feeble light of the moon it was a quarter past twelve.

There was a tinkle and a loud thump reverberated through the house, seeming to come from nowhere. I had finally fallen asleep and it woke me immediately. I opened my eyes and ran the back of my hand across my forehead.

"Lad!" Barker bellowed from his chamber above me, and then pandemonium ensued. There were heavy footsteps and the sound of metal clanging against metal as a pitched battle broke out overhead.

I seized my thick fighting stick and ran into the hall. After climbing the narrow and steep stairs to Barker's garret room, I found my employer fighting with a large man. The intruder wore gray clothing and his head was wound in dark cloth, so that his eyes alone were visible. It was unsettling. I stepped forward into the room and my bare toe encountered something sharp. There was glass all over the floor. Looking up, I saw that the entire skylight had been shattered.

The room looked as if it had been shaken like a pair of dice in a cup. Chairs were upended, tables broken, books tossed all over the floor, and under all, a layer of broken glass. The only thing untouched was the fireplace.

Barker drew a hatchet from his wall, which is covered in all sorts of weapons from various countries. He threw it, but the man ducked out of the way. He pulled down a bronze sword and suddenly there was a loud clanging as he defended himself again from the intruder's attack. I caught the gleam of one of those long Japanese swords as it beat down upon the Guv's defenses.

I tried to pick my way among the shards of glass, aware that the stick in my hand was no match against a sharp blade. As I watched, the assailant wrenched the sword out of Barker's hands and tossed it behind him. In response, Barker pulled another weapon from his wall, a long stick of whitish driftwood. It seemed an unlikely choice.

The man attacked, but unaccountably I heard the sound of metal on metal once more. The clanging reverberated across the wide, low chamber. I made my way over to a desk where I knew my employer kept a pistol in a drawer. I was in the act of retrieving it when the drawer was struck with the sword. Having no luck with the Guv, the assailant had decided to come after me.

I raised the pistol to fire it, but had trouble finding room to extend my arm. I stepped back, but the man closed in on me. He must have realized if I got my arm free I would shoot, so he would not give me the opportunity.

The intruder was massive, or at least it seemed that way to me. He drove me back, crushing me between the wall and his heavy body, knocking the air from my lungs. I was still trying to breathe when he swung me by my nightshirt down the stair. I plunged head over heel down the hard mahogany steps. Striking the wall of my bedroom, I fell to the carpet. A moment later I heard, or rather felt, the assailant step over me. I groped after him, seizing an ankle, and received a hard kick in the face for my troubles.

There was a bright flash and a loud bang downstairs. I recognized the sound. It was Mac's sawn-down shotgun. He'd given our visitor a parting shot, literally. Then I heard Harm in the backyard, baying. Poor blighter, I thought. This assassin had no idea what he was doing when he decided to drop in on Cyrus Barker.

"Thomas?" Barker asked, surveying the damage. "Is anything broken?"

"I don't think so, sir, but ask me in the morning."

I looked up. Barker's left cheek had been laid open and was bleeding to his chin. The rest of him seemed sound enough.

"Sorry I couldn't stop him," I said, as he helped me to my feet. I was banged and bruised, but the worst was the piece of glass I'd stepped on as soon as I'd entered the chamber.

Mac came up the staircase with his shotgun broken over his arm, removing the shell. A moment later Harm entered from the stair, a scrap of dark gray fabric between his hideous teeth. He seemed very pleased with himself, growling as if to say, "Look what I did!"

My employer took the cloth from Harm, who gave up his trophy most reluctantly. He examined the simple dark cloth a moment before returning it to the dog, who carried it off to his bed as if it were treasure.

"It was an assassin," Barker explained. "A Japanese assassin. His sword was different, not a samurai sword. Still, he was very definitely Japanese."

"And large," I said. "He was very large."

"Ohara."

"The ambassador's bodyguard? Why attack us?"

"I shot his master, or so the Foreign Office will have informed the embassy. It was revenge. Without a master, he is a lone wolf, fending for himself."

Mac had gone downstairs and returned with a shaving bowl full of water and some gauze.

"Let's get that glass out of your foot."

"Ouch!" I said as he touched it to see how deeply it was wedged in my foot.

"It's only a sliver of glass," he said.

"That's easy for you to say. Be careful."

He pulled the glass, dyed my toe with iodine, and wrapped my foot. He put another sticking plaster on Barker's cheek. Then he went upstairs to look over the state of the skylight and all the glass on the floor.

"See you in the morning, lad," the Guv said.

"That's it?" I replied. "He could come back in the middle of the night."

"Surely not."

"Shouldn't we talk about it? I mean, we both nearly got killed ten minutes ago!"

" 'Nearly' being the optimum word. We both survived, relatively unscathed."

"I feel very scathed, thank you very much. He squashed me flat against the wall there. Then he threw me down the bloody stairs."

"The fact that you are protesting is proof that you still have air to protest with."

I could not argue with that logic, I supposed. I listened as he went out of my room and up the stairs again. I heard Mac sweeping up glass on the floor above me. By the time he was finished and had turned out the light, I could hear the steady rumble of Barker snoring again.

"Barmy," I said, to no one in particular. "Absolutely bloody barmy."

I was still sore the next morning. Dummolard was in the kitchen, cooking breakfast. He took down one of his copper saucepans and handed it to me for a mirror.

"You are keeping ze pet mouse these days, Thomas."

I regarded my reflection. There was a purple lump under my right eye, where the hilt of the assassin's sword had caught me. My face was drained of all color otherwise as far as I could tell.

"Where is he?" I asked, referring to the Guv.

"Out there," Dummolard said, gesturing with the fag end of his French cigarette. He was a bear of a fellow, unshaven and ill-tempered, but he was part of the household, so he was one of us, for good or ill.

I looked outside. Barker was in the yard, not gardening or performing one of his martial forms, but sitting in the pagodalike gazebo by the back gate. He was not alone, though it was not yet half past six.

"Who is he sitting with?"

"Ze general. They are playing Go."

I was curious. Very curious. However, every atom of my being was in pain and in need of coffee. Go, a game from China that Barker had tried to teach me before quitting in frustration, involved black-and-white stones on a wooden board. A game can last all day. I had time for a cup of coffee or two, and probably a bite of breakfast. Or lunch, perhaps.

"I understand you had some amusement here last night," Dummolard continued.

"How did you know?"

"The skylight, she is out. I saw it from the street."

"Ah, yes."

"Eggs, in truffle butter, perhaps?"

"I have no objection."

"Bon!"

There are positive reasons for having a graduate of the Cordon Bleu in one's home, even if he is an ill-tempered Frenchman who smokes continually and complains about everything. Barker doesn't actually pay him. He used our kitchen to experiment on new recipes for his award-winning restaurant and, I suspect, to avoid his wife.

A few minutes later a plate was set before me. My body might have been ailing, but my mouth was serenely happy. Truffle butter will do that to a fellow.

"This is perfect, Etienne."

"Mais oui," he said, and mashed another cigarette into the flagstone floor.

One omelette and two cups of coffee later, I pushed myself up from the table and stepped outside.

The morning was warm, the smell in the air loamy. Harm lay on the bridge which straddled our narrow stream, his head up but his eyes closed in the warmth of the sun, a king in his kingdom.

My mind went back for the hundredth time to when Barker encountered the Japanese delegation and had stiffened. One doesn't do that when someone one likes arrives unexpectedly, only when someone one dislikes arrives. But if it was Mononobe, why invite someone you dislike to play a game with you in your own home? Perhaps it was someone else in the entourage.

Cyrus Barker is not one to play games, unless there is a very good reason for it. As a Baptist, he does not play cards. However, he once told me that Go is not a game of chance, but of strategy. All Japanese generals play it in order to discover each other's weaknesses. Who would be the first to show fear or to make an unconscious mistake?

It's a deceptively simple game, far easier to learn than chess.

One player has white stones, the other black. Each puts down one stone on the gridded board. If one encircles the other player's pieces completely, they are removed from the board. That's it, really. And yet, people play this game for hours every day. There are masters at the game who are revered. It is taught in military academies, and not merely in the East.

We were playing a game of Go here in London, using real lives. It wasn't a mere delegation or an official visit. A slice of Japan had been carefully cut and set down in a mansion in Bermondsey. They disdained our British rules of decorum. They were playing by their own.

I came near to the gazebo. Both men were concentrating on the board. General Mononobe looked up from the board and glared at me. My movement had distracted him. Anyway, our eyes met, possibly for the first time. Perhaps it was my mood at the moment, after the difficult night and all it had entailed, but it seemed to me I was staring into the face of the very devil himself.

CHAPTER FIFTEEN

We invited Tatsuya Akiba, the minister of arts, to the Northumberland Arms Hotel, which is just round the corner from our chambers. It has a square of tables and chairs outside with umbrellas shading them in hot weather. It was the closest thing to a Parisian café in Whitehall. One could eat slowly and drink coffee, while watching the world go by.

When Tatsuya arrived, I was amazed at his appearance. He was of average height, and his black hair was cut in a perfect bowl on top of his head. Every hair came down to his ears and was cut off severely, with no hair whatsoever at the back of his neck or in front of his ears. He wore round spectacles with black frames, very thick, and he had long, thin hands. His clothing was impeccable, worlds better than the ones the bodyguards wore, but his waistcoat was canary yellow and his tie a fish-scale green.

"Mr. Barker," he said. "It is very nice to meet you. How fares your lovely garden?"

"It thrives, sir."

Tatsuya offered a boneless hand to the Guv, who accepted it gingerly.

"Ah!" he said, sliding down into his seat.

"How are you finding London, sir?" I asked.

"It's amazing, gentlemen. I have stereopticon slides back in Tokyo, but they don't do your fair city justice!"

Tatsuya was trying so hard to fit in, he only succeeded in standing out. His language and his clothing were mere approximations of our true speech and manner, but Barker did not care what one wore or how one spoke, as long as one answered his questions. As for me, well, I found him rather entertaining.

We had not intended to eat there, but Tatsuya ordered a tray of various cakes and tea all around. He lifted his teaspoon by the very tip of the handle, like a plumb line, and let it dangle carefully into his tea before stirring it. Then he availed himself of the sweetmeats.

"Now, what can I do for you, Mr. Barker?" he asked, wiping icing from his mouth.

"I have some general questions, if I may," my employer said, avoiding the sweets, which he almost never consumed, save at the insistence of our chef.

"Don't be shy, Mr. Barker. Ask me anything!"

I glanced over and noticed that every other table was watching us. The waiter looked as if he were debating whether to throw a certain foreigner out into the street. Most people in London had never seen a Japanese person before.

"How were you chosen as the subambassador to the arts, if I may ask?"

"Of course. I am a professor at the University of Tokyo on the subject of Western culture. I've given lectures all over Japan discussing art and literature. I have memorized all of your major streets and your Underground system. Having received a letter of introduction from Lord Diosy, I've been visiting all of your museums, as well as Liberty's of London, and taken a tour of some of your art galleries. I'm having such a wonderful time, but really, every minute is accounted for. I wouldn't have been able to come now if one of my appointments had not canceled."

"Have you made many purchases?" Barker asked him.

I knew the Guv. He had no interest in someone's purchases.

"Enough to fill a ship, sir! Bolts of Orkney tweed, tartan wool, china, paintings, sculptures. Everything down to penny postcards to mail to my acquaintances while I am here."

"Have you purchased works of art?"

"Yes, I did buy a Turner at auction just yesterday."

Barker turned to me. "Turner?"

"A landscapist, sir, around the middle of the century," I said.

"Have you been given an adequate budget?" Barker asked Tatsuya.

"Oh, scads of yen. Pounds, if you prefer. Not only has the government contracted me to make purchases, but several prominent families have paid me to find something for their homes. I can't say why a traditional paper-walled home would need a painting of Venus coming out of the water, but I'll do my best to secure it."

"What about your compatriots? Have they the same budget as you?"

Tatsuya chuckled.

"'Compatriots.' I love English. I've never heard the word pronounced before. To be honest, none of us have discussed our budgets with one another. You'd call it bad form. I suspect, however, that my budget is the smallest of all. Our trade minister will be purchasing all sorts of goods, while the general and admiral will be looking at ships and modern military equipment. I overheard the three of them the other evening discussing the feasibility of contracting a drawbridge to be built, similar to London Bridge, in Tokyo. Oh, yes, we have been sent here to purchase, and purchase, we shall."

Barker poured himself a cup of tea from a samovar by the front door and I took a gooseberry tart while he wasn't looking. I like a sweet myself from time to time. He returned, inspected me visually as if I were a child about to get into trouble, and sipped his tea.

"May I assume you are shown about these museums and companies on some kind of private tour?" he asked our guest.

"Oh, yes. They whisk me in and out and point out everything. To be truthful, sir, I'm but a humble professor without much money, but a great fondness for your country. They almost treat me like royalty here."

"Have you been interviewed by reporters?"

"Yes, and photographed wherever I go. I am to appear in the *Woman's World*. They asked my opinions about everything. It has been bloody marvelous, as you would say."

I tried to keep from laughing. Barker wouldn't have said it in a thousand years. I marveled at the minister, babbling what I would imagine were state secrets, while Barker was taking it all in.

"What is Lord Diosy's place in all this?"

"He's the one who makes all the appointments and tours for us. He knows simply everyone and has exquisite taste. His collection is first-rate for a Westerner. There are a few pieces I, as a Japanese, wish were in museums in Tokyo."

"Do you have a bodyguard who travels with you?" the Guv asked, finishing the last sip of his tea.

"Yes, though he's a bit of a dullard, I'm afraid. He's in the cab there. Spends all his time at swordplay. Very serious. Bushido, and all that. I say, that was the past and this is the present. One must change when it is necessary, as Japan has learned to adapt."

"I'm sure the general would agree with you. Have you had much chance to talk to him?"

"We don't get along, I'm afraid. He believes all men should be soldiers. I don't care about his opinions. I have a wife and four sons."

"What is your opinion of the bodyguards?" my employer asked.

"A mixed lot. Some of them are young. Kito is a guard in the Imperial Palace, and is vain about it. Ohara was near mad over the loss of Toda Ichigo. He vowed to avenge his death and ran off. Poor chap. The man took his disgrace very hard."

"Isn't he rather heavy for a guard?" I asked.

"You'd think that, wouldn't you? With my own eyes, I have seen him turn a cartwheel, and land as gently as a rabbit. I suspect he is the most dangerous of all the bodyguards. Some of the young rakes use a sword, I'll give them that, but Ohara Kogoro, he's far more than a fat man."

"I understand. Was he not with the rest of the guards hired by the general?"

"No. The general desired another man for the role, but Toda insisted. Ohara was his own personal bodyguard, I believe."

"Was the general always interested in *bodigado*?"

"You clever fellow! You speak Japanese, but you haven't told us. I must tread carefully around you, Mr. Barker!"

"Pray answer the question," the Guv rumbled.

"Oh, rather," the minister exclaimed. "He picked them as if they were thoroughbreds. He fussed over them, and when he chose his men, he drilled them unmercifully. I swear Ohara was two stone heavier when he was chosen. His sumo weight."

"Sumo?" I asked.

"Japanese wrestling among the heaviest of men," Barker explained.

"You mean there are more like him?"

"Oh, aye. It is the national sport of Japan."

"Imagine that."

I was hoping that this was a country in which I might possibly be considered tall. Kito, for example, was no taller than I. The thought that there was also a race of giants there rather dampened my enthusiasm.

"You said the admiral told you about the general's past. Are the two of you confidants?"

"He'll listen to me, unlike the general or the minister of trade. He's not much of a talker, however."

"Do the general and the admiral get along?"

"Just barely. There's no love lost between them, but they were shipmates once and are now living in the same house. One must learn to be civil."

"What of the minister of trade?"

"Akita? He's all right. He's younger than the rest of us, and understands he must perform his duties well. I don't think he has looked up from his orders, save to visit a factory or two. He hasn't seen Big Ben or Westminster Abbey. Hasn't passed Buckingham Palace. I imagine he has not read about them or taken any interest whatsoever. He might just as well be in Yokohama. He's everything I fight against, in a way. Traditionally, the samurai class was required to learn other things besides the use of a sword. They wrote poetry or painted. They arranged flowers. They appreciated the beauty of nature around them. The general, the admiral, Mr. Akita, they concentrate so much on what they must do that they never notice the beauty that is all around them."

"I see," my employer said.

"I came for another reason today, Mr. Barker: to apologize to you. Your garden is sublime, the ambassador told me. He was most impressed, and when I returned from an appointment he chided me for not coming to see it. I am sorry, sir, that I did not come. The number of hours you must work to create such beauty, it is a great sacrifice. Bravo, I say!"

"Thank you, sir."

Barker turned to me.

"Have you any questions for Mr. Tatsuya?"

I cudgeled my brain for a question that would not embarrass Barker in front of a guest.

"What is your impression of the general himself?" I asked.

Barker nodded. It was a fair question.

"I could write a book. He keeps to himself when he doesn't need something. He's a nationalist. Japan first. He wants to restore our 'self-respect,' whatever that means. I love Japan, I really do, but it isn't everything. If he could rewind the course of history, he would return to 1853, when the Americans arrived, and fight them to the death. Even if he died, it would have been a noble cause. I feel a nobler cause would be feeding starving children and tending to the elderly. However, there is no glory in that, is there?"

"There is," Barker said. "But few see it. Thank you, Mr. Tatsuya, for speaking so openly with me."

"I liked the ambassador. He gave you the feeling that when he talked to you, whatever you had to say was both important and worthwhile. None of these other chaps will give me the time of day. An arts minister is completely unnecessary to them."

He rose in a fit of pique.

"I have come thousands of miles from my wife and four sons. I am taking art back to Tokyo which will revolutionize textiles, painting, ceramics, fashion, architecture, and design. What are they doing? They are playing at war."

He bowed formally, his bowl-cut hair hanging from his head. Then he left, heading back toward Whitehall Street.

"Unusual fellow," Barker said, once he was gone. "I suspect he feels outnumbered."

"Yes. I suppose even Japan can have its Anglophiles. He must be having the time of his life, at the government's expense."

"You think him harmless?"

"Of course."

"Don't!" Barker chided. "Just because a fellow seems a certain way, don't assume he is. Tatsuya didn't merely come to chat and have tea. He was warning us. Every message has a message within it."

"But sir, if he's come to warn us, why suspect him?"

"Because we don't know why he is warning us. It may be to cloak his own activities."

"Or it might be that he is warning us because we need warning."

Barker shook his head. "Why should a Japanese, who only just met us, choose to warn a pair of complete strangers against his own countrymen?"

"I can think of two reasons," I said.

"Two? Very well, what are they?"

"Number one, he is an Anglophile. He cares about our country as much as his."

"I don't like it," the Guv said, frowning. "There is a difference between liking a country's culture and giving government secrets away. And the other reason?"

"Because Ambassador Toda is dead, and he fears he shall be next. He is the odd man out."

Barker pointed a finger at me. "Now that is possible. Until new knowledge comes to light, let us consider that. Do you suppose he is naturally guileless, or he deliberately wishes us to know what Mononobe and the admiral are doing?"

I considered the question, weighing my answer. Barker would not want a platitude or an off-the-cuff opinion. When he asked me what I thought, he actually expected me to think.

"Tatsuya certainly threw some opinions about. Mononobe is taking the embassy in an entirely different direction. Toda would have helped the poor and visited schools. He would have toured Whitechapel as well. Instead, Mononobe will only be touring Sandhurst or the Royal Armory in Leeds."

"I agree. There was no reason for the minister of arts to come here and talk openly to a pair of enquiry agents. Our opinions would not be of interest to him, unless we can pass the information on to someone, or watch closely what is going on. Tatsuya would not have spoken to us unless he was concerned."

"You think not? He wasn't merely being loquacious?"

"You must understand, lad, that Japan is a very subtle country."

"To them, then, we must be rather gauche."

"They do not have a high opinion of the rest of the world, save in terms of technology."

"They want what we have, but not to be like we are."

"Well put, Thomas."

"Thank you. But you were around them for a time. I hardly know anything about them that you don't tell me or that I can glean from Mr. Grant's books."

"How do we know anything without asking?"

"Seek, and ye shall find; knock and the door will be opened unto you."

Barker smiled.

"Well, well," he said. "So he can quote scripture."

"As Shakespeare said, 'The devil can cite Scripture for his purpose.' "

CHAPTER SIXTEEN

London is full of grocers, public house owners, and restauranteurs quite willing, for a small remuneration, to deliver food to one's door. In fact, one could say there is an entire reticulum expressly set up to deliver a product to the consumer. Messages and telegrams are dispatched; stores deliver goods to the homes of customers who are too important to be seen carrying parcels; and fresh, hot food is taken to hardworking clerks and members of Parliament in Whitehall. It is not necessary in this advanced year of 1891 to have to go on foot and fetch meals from a pub the way one did in 1501. But just try explaining that to Cyrus Barker, Esq., and see how far it will take you.

Perhaps he thinks he is doing a favor by keeping me active, or perhaps he prefers his pork pie to be as hot as possible. In either case, I was expelled the next day near lunchtime, to bring back sustenance. Not pâté de foie gras, mind you, but a humble pork pie, working man's food. I ask you, is that any way for a wealthy man to eat?

There are dozens of public houses and restaurants within walking distance and I knew them all well. That was the problem, you see. One served the best fish, another the best chips, a third the best meat on a bun, and therefore I had to go far and wide if one of us had a craving, such as the Arms in Charing Cross, which served an incomparable pork pie. One might wonder why I waste time discussing what we had for lunch, rather than something pertinent to the case. Because in this instance, it was pertinent to the case.

I was coming back from the Arms, with a greasy paper sack containing three pies, including one for Jeremy Jenkins, and I was passing through Trafalgar Square. I didn't bother to look up to where Lord Nelson was standing, one hundred and fifty feet above the pavement, because I was not a tourist and had seen Nelson's Column practically every day since I arrived in London.

No, I was walking for a purpose, which was to get the pies back to Craig's Court as quickly as possible while they were still hot. I had folded the paper over twice to retain the heat and was holding the sack close to my body the way a forward holds a rugby ball under his arm. Nothing was going to dissuade me from my mission. That is, practically nothing. Ahead of me, I saw a Japanese fellow standing among the pigeons, as unmoving as old Nelson himself. I was not so simpleminded as to think his presence was merely a coincidence.

I hadn't noticed this fellow at the embassy. He wore a bowler hat like the rest of them, along with a long, European-made coat though it was hot. As I approached, he reached into his coat and drew a sword.

I looked about. It was a little after noon and a samurai was standing in the middle of Trafalgar Square about to attack, yet nobody seemed to be paying any attention. The square was nearly empty at that time of day.

Fair enough, I thought; if he wants to fight me, I'm ready. I was no beginner any longer, and was the best pupil of Mr. Vigny, who sometimes taught at our Barjutsu studio in Soho. I'm not good with a pistol, but a piece of hickory, such as the fighting stick I held in my hand made for me especially, was my forte. Of course, it would be useless against a samurai sword. However, as I drew near, I saw that it was not a sword in his hand at all. It was a bokken, a wooden practice sword. It could cause a bruise or break a bone, but it could not kill me. The chances were good that we would be evenly matched.

I set down my parcel of pork pies and circled him, raising my stick in my right hand while my left came out wide, balancing my right. It was exactly how my ancestors fought with sword and buckler. My adversary glared at me and raised his blade so that the unsharpened side rested on his right shoulder, ready to strike. I am normally cautious on the street, but this somehow felt as if we were in our training school and I am aggressive there. I attacked.

I swiped the ball of my stick at his head, but he ducked just barely in time and deflected it with his curved stick. In turn, he tried to rake me across the ribs. He might have succeeded in breaking one had I not circled my stick around in time to block his attack. Thrust, parry, and riposte. Tit for tat, if you prefer.

He gave one of those bellows Japanese fighters give and struck down at me with an overhead attack. It set the pigeons about us flying up into the sky, so for a moment we were encircled with them. I raised my stick and caught the strike squarely. He brought it back and, as if as an afterthought, he flicked it out again. It smacked across the knuckles of my free left hand. Pain bloomed. Had he carried a real sword my fingers would be littering the pavement. I frowned and shook off the pain. A look of smug satisfaction crossed his features.

What are you up to? I wondered. Why attack me with just a stick? Did you think I could not fight? Are you trying to humiliate me or injure me so that I cannot help Barker anymore? Did you come here on your own or were you sent, and if so, by whom? Whoever it was, I suspected it was the man who killed the ambassador.

He attacked again. I jumped back, sucking in my stomach as the sword swung horizontally, batting one of the buttons off my waistcoat. He swung again and as he did, I twirled my stick and avoided the move. I came down and caught him on the shoulder with the ball of my cane, two inches in diameter of solid silver just where it would do the most damage. He winced and growled what might have been an oath. There was muscle and nerves and bones in that spot and I knew it was suddenly feeling nerveless and weak just then. He stepped back, stomped a foot in anger more at himself than me, angry at his own carelessness. Perhaps he assumed this was going to be easy. I was, after all, just an Englishman. Well, a Welshman, anyway. To him, it must have been like swatting a mosquito; a slow one, at that.

Suddenly, my progress was impeded. I was aware of a large field of blue on either side. Looking back, as the wooden blade came rushing toward me, I saw a sleeved arm come down and club my opponent across the back of his cockatoolike head. We were encircled by a squad of constables.

"Was this person bothering you, sir?" a sergeant asked.

"He was rather," I said.

"You must come with us to 'A' Division."

"I have some pies for lunch."

I looked back. The parcel was open, and the pigeons on the pavement a hundred yards distant were enjoying a meal. Our lunch, to be precise.

"Never mind."

"Friend of yours, sir?" a sergeant with thick side whiskers asked. Poole said side whiskers were out of fashion that year but now was probably not the time to inform him.

"Never saw him before in my life."

"Come along, then," he said, fixing darbies to my wrists. "You must answer a few questions and sign a warrant if you wish."

We arrived at and passed by Craig's Court. I looked helplessly at the windows of number 7, hoping Barker might randomly glance out the window. Meanwhile, I was being peppered with questions by the sergeant while my assailant was being silently dragged or carried by another pair of constables behind us.

"How did you come to be chased by this foreign person, sir?"

"I was coming back with lunch for my employer. He seemed to be waiting for me."

"Did this person seem intent upon you personally, or do you suppose the attack was random?"

"Oh, he very definitely singled me out."

"Can you think of any reason why such a person would choose you over anyone else in the square?"

"Well, I work for Cyrus Barker, and—"

The sergeant came to a stop, rather quickly.

"Would that be Mr. Barker of Craig's Court?"

"The same. Anyway, I was defending myself. He attacked me."

"Have you any reason to be attacked by a foreign person?"

"Yes, in fact. We are investigating the death of the Japanese ambassador."

"So, we might assume this young Japanese lad had reasons for trying to stop you."

"I'm not certain why. We're only trying to find out who killed his ambassador. Perhaps he had something to hide."

"If he does, we'll get it out of him. Here we are! Home sweet home, as the antimacassar on my mum's easy chair says."

I was shoved through the gate and eventually through the doors of Scotland Yard.

"May I please get word to my employer?" I asked. "He'll wonder where I have gone to."

"In due course, Mr. . . . ."

"Llewelyn. Thomas Llewelyn."

"After you've answered questions for us."

Inside the facility, the hustle and bustle of "A" Division went on just as it had, though now it was at different quarters. However, I missed the homely oldness and wear of the previous building, and its more formal manner. This was the modern way now. Methods had changed since the days when Jack the Ripper stalked White-chapel, the sergeant's side whiskers notwithstanding.

I was taken into an interrogation room and left for half an hour. Until one has had one's hands locked behind one's back for such a time, one cannot imagine the discomfort. Eventually, I heard a key being placed in the lock outside and the door swung open. Inspector Dunn, whom I had seen in the Japanese embassy, entered.

"Mr. Llewelyn, you do tend to get yourself in trouble," he said.

"Put it on my gravestone."

"I will. At this rate, I shall be doing it before September. What happened in Trafalgar Square?"

I related an abbreviated version of what had occurred. He looked slightly skeptical.

"If you don't believe me, ask him," I said. "Provided he speaks English."

"He does, after a fashion. He has said exactly six words, but he keeps saying them over and over."

I tried to imagine what they might be. Most of my guesses were facetious in the extreme. Scotland Yard brings out the worst in me. The inspector was waiting to tell me.

"Very well, Inspector. What words did he speak?"

"He said, 'I confess. I killed Ambassador Toda.' I'm going to tell the commissioner now." Dunn leaned forward and slapped me on the back. "Congratulations, Mr. Llewelyn. You've cracked the case."

CHAPTER SEVENTEEN

The samurai and I were still shooting daggers at one another, so we were put in separate cells. They were adjoining, but with a wall between them. I've cut up in the past, knowing I had an excellent solicitor in Bram Cusp, but it was safer to keep quiet until I knew who was interrogating me. If it were Chief Inspector Poole, I was safe. If it were a few others I knew, I'd be collecting teeth from the ground.

"Might I be permitted to send for counsel, please?" I asked politely. I asked just once. More than that, and one becomes a burden.

After about thirty minutes, I was moved to an interrogation room, where I waited another twenty minutes. Finally, the door opened and a harried-looking detective with a pencil behind his ear entered. I'd never seen him before.

"Name, please," he said in a bored voice.

"Thomas Llewelyn."

He removed the pencil and misspelled my name in a notebook. "Occupation?"

"Private enquiry agent."

Most Scotland Yarders take umbrage to my profession, and this is usually when they start chaffing me, but this one was content to take notes.

"Private. Enquiry. Agent. Age?"

"Twenty-six."

"All right, Mr. . . . Llewelyn, how came you to enter into an affray with the chap in the next cell?"

"I was coming back from the Arms with some pork pies for my employer's lunch. That chappie was waiting for me in the square."

"You mean, you personally?"

"Yes, Officer. It must be because my employer, Mr. Barker, has been retained by the Japanese embassy to investigate the death of the ambassador last week."

"Barker?" he asked. "Is he the one with offices in the next street?"

"Yes, sir."

"So why did he attack you, if you were working for the embassy?"

"I wish I knew. I suspect he is one of the bodyguards, but I had never met him before."

"Why did you raise your stick?"

"Because he'd raised his."

"Why didn't you just walk away or call a constable?"

"Two reasons," I said. "The first is that I help teach a class in antagonistics, and I wasn't going to be seen running through the square being chased by some stand-in but by a character from a Kabuki play."

He'd been writing with his pencil the entire time. "Spell Kabuki."

I did.

"And the other reason?"

"He seemed to know how to use it. I preferred not to be hit."

"Not to be hit." He looked up. "He attacked you with a stick. Then what?"

"I defended myself. He was as good as I imagined, but I got

lucky once or twice. He definitely had murder in his eyes. Luckily, your man stopped the fight there and then."

"So, Mr. Llewelyn, you admit it was a fight."

"Of course we had a fight! We weren't having a quadrille. I participated, but I did not instigate it. Would you prefer I stand there while he batted me around, and me with a fine stick in my hand?"

"Were you injured?"

"No, not really. A bruise or two."

"As you recall, did you hurt the foreign gentleman?"

"No. As skirmishes go, it was unsuccessful on both sides. I was concerned at the time, but looking back, I've had worse fights in the schoolyard."

"Do you intend to press charges?"

"No, I don't think so. As I said, I wasn't injured."

"I'm going to take you back to your cell and then bring your opponent in to compare your stories."

"May I contact my solicitor?"

"No one's charged you with anything yet."

"I'd like to telephone my employer."

"From what I hear, your Mr. Barker is a smart bloke. He'll figure out you were waylaid."

"Can I at least get a cup of tea?"

"I'll have one brought to your cell. Dunno how good it is but it's hot."

"I've made tea here."

He snapped his fingers. "That's where I've seen you. You was a special constable during the Ripper investigation, weren't you?"

"Yes, I was," I said with some relief.

"How the mighty have fallen, eh? Constable! Take this fella back and bring me t'other one."

I went back to my cell. Eventually, tea was brought in a tin cup. Cocoa tastes better in a tin cup, but tea requires china. Still, I see the reasoning in not serving tea to prisoners in Aunt Primrose's best Cantonware. I drank it. It hadn't improved since I left. In fact, it might have been from the same pot, warmed on a hob.

I saw the bodyguard led down the hall, his hands braceleted. He looked at me with no expression. Here he was in a strange country in a prison cell and it was of no concern to him, or so it seemed.

I heard the door slam and continued to ponder the situation. Why had the fellow attacked me? Did he know I was working for the general? Well, Barker was, anyway, and that amounted to the same thing.

Nothing happened for an hour. No more tea, no telephone call, just silence. I listened to the sounds of the building, the muffled voices all around me. We were in New Scotland Yard now, a different kettle of fish. No one had carved initials in anything or kicked the plaster off a doorway entrance while drunk and disorderly. Everything was sterile.

Finally, the prisoner was brought back and I was taken out again. The inspector met me in front of the interrogation room.

"I'm letting you go."

"Thank you."

"He confessed."

"To attacking me?"

"No. Well, yes, he did. As well as killing the ambassador."

"But he was shot. This fellow had a stick."

"That doesn't mean he can't pull a trigger. You just point and squeeze."

"I suppose you're right, Inspector. Sorry. I didn't get your name."

"McNaughton."

"Thank you. Your cell was very nice."

"Get out."

I'd actually meant it, but there was no convincing him. "So, what happens next?"

"I have no idea, but the commissioner will have plenty to sort out. This chap's a foreign national. It will be tricky."

"He'll do the right thing," I said, though I didn't believe it for a minute. "How is the prisoner?"

"Agitated. He barely speaks English. Do you know what he

asked for? He wanted a haircut. Like he was strolling down Piccadilly and wanted to spruce himself up a little."

"Are you going to give him one?"

"We will, but we'll watch him closely, and he'll be in irons. I'm going to have his belt removed. Maybe even his suit. He might try to top himself."

He looked about at the floor.

"What are you looking for?"

"My pencil. I've lost it."

"Am I free to go?"

"Said you were, didn't I?"

One of the best experiences of life is being released from jail. The air is sweeter, birds sing; the very clouds look like candy floss. I hopped around the corner into Craig's Court.

All was as it had been. There was Jenkins with his perennial copy of the *Police Gazette*. There was Barker digging for the dottle in his pipe with a small tool. He looked up at me and stared.

"No pork pies?"

"No pork pies."

"Explain."

I did, from the fight in Trafalgar Square to our arrest and my questioning.

"I'm not familiar with Inspector McNaughton. He must be new," Barker said.

Then I explained that the prisoner had confessed to killing the ambassador. I expected him to jump up and run out the door, but all he did was press the tips of his thick fingers together and sit back further in his leather chair.

"Interesting."

Finally, I described things as I left them, how McNaughton had let me go. Then, he jumped out of his chair.

"He asked for a haircut!" he rumbled.

"Yes."

"They generally shave their heads before killing themselves. It is a form of self-humiliation."

"It's all right. They were going to remove his belt and even his clothes so he couldn't hang himself."

"Even so. Come! We may be in time to stop him!"

We bolted out of there and only stopped when we came to the gate at Scotland Yard. They tend to stop anyone who appears boisterous or excitable. Finally, we slipped through and entered the building.

"Mr. Barker," the desk sergeant, Kirkwood, said at our arrival. "Good to see you again."

"Thank you, Sergeant. We must speak to Inspector McNaughton immediately. I suspect a prisoner brought in recently will do himself a mischief."

"Got it. I'll send for the inspector. Have a seat."

"Cannot I go through?"

"Sorry, sir. Not the way we work now. You can't just go wandering the halls anymore. Commissioner Munro's orders."

I wondered if the rule was made especially for us. There was no love lost between him and the Guv. They'd been adversaries since Munro had been in charge of Special Branch.

After about five minutes of Barker pacing, McNaughton appeared. He was a self-contained fellow, very calm and patient. I liked him better than most of the Yardmen already. He came forward and shook my employer's hand.

"I've heard of you, Mr. Barker."

"Inspector, did the Japanese prisoner ask to have his head shaved?"

"He did. He had it all cut off."

Barker explained that a Japanese, after admitting to a crime such as murder, will shave his head prior to killing himself.

"But he had no weapons. And we took away all his clothes but his loincloth. We considered this might happen and acted accordingly."

"I admire the precautions you have taken, Inspector, but I suggest you look in on the prisoner immediately. A man determined to kill himself will surely find a way."

"Very well, Mr. Barker. If you gentlemen will follow me, we'll check on our foreign friend."

I wanted to run, but the new Scotland Yard building was not a "running" sort of building. At best, we strode as briskly as we could, considering someone whisked from one hall doorway across to another in front of us every fifteen seconds. I could feel the passage of time.

"Keys!" Inspector McNaughton bellowed to the turnkey, who jumped at our arrival.

McNaughton took the keys and strode down the hall. It was not a long distance, but I felt as if we were standing in water up to our waists, trying to push through in time.

But we weren't in time. Our unnamed bodyguard was dead. He lay crumpled naked on the floor. He had strangled himself with his *fundoshi,* the thong of material he wore around his groin. And what do you think he used to twist the tourniquet so tightly about his throat that it had asphyxiated him? It was Inspector McNaughton's pencil.

CHAPTER EIGHTEEN

That evening I decided to stay in. London was feeling decidedly unsafe, and as it happened, both my best friend and the woman I loved lived in the City, not far from Limehouse. I had been attacked once and there were still two more bodyguards out there who might be looking for me.

I did not want to think about Japan. I'd barely thought about it before this case and I hoped never to think about it again as soon as it was over. Since then, I had thought of nothing else and was certain there would be more to come before it was resolved. I had a nice glass of cold milk from the icebox in the larder, a rare treat, and was reading the part in *Far from the Madding Crowd* where the fellow dropped the bacon in the road.

Just then the doorbell rang. I sighed but continued to read. One of the characters was saying the bacon was gritty, but if one just made sure one's teeth didn't meet in the middle . . .

"There is an Asian gentleman at the door wishing to speak with you, sir," Mac said, standing in front of me. I don't know how he moves about so silently.

"Me?" I asked.

"He said either you or the Guv, and I'm not climbing two flights to inform him when you are here in the library."

I put down the book, took a swallow of the milk, and got up from my chair, a comfortable gentleman's club chair in faded brown leather, with a matching tufted ottoman, that had become perfectly comfortable over the years. I gave Mac my best put-upon look. One cannot let a butler have his way or he'll be running the household.

"Asian gentleman?" I repeated as I walked toward the door.

"Yes, sir. A large one."

I reached for the pistol that Mac kept hanging from a hook by the stick stand, then opened the door while aiming it. Granted, it's not the most welcoming way to treat a guest, but we all know what desperate times engender. I'd been attacked already.

Ohara stood outside, his bowler in his flipperlike hands. He bowed. He was very obviously the fellow who had not only crashed through our skylight and fought Barker, but kicked me down the stairs. It still hurt.

"What do you want?" I asked. I was not prepared to be friendly.

"I wish to speak to you and Mr. Barker, sir," he said and bowed again.

"Why should I? You kicked me down a stairwell."

"I apologize. It was most regrettable."

"It is regrettable when someone treads on one's foot. This is another matter entirely."

Just then Barker came along behind me, having come leisurely from upstairs. His face, as usual, was without expression. He was wearing an Asian dressing gown over his waistcoat.

"Mr. Ohara," he said.

Ohara bowed.

"What does he want?" he asked.

"To speak to us."

"Does he have a weapon?"

"He is a weapon."

Barker turned his head. Mac was in the doorway of his butler's pantry, holding his sawn-down shotgun. Ohara probably still carried buckshot from it.

"Let the fellow in," my employer announced. "Put him in the library."

I waved him in with the pistol and led him down the hall. Meanwhile, Barker stepped out the front door and looked about, in case there were more men in the bushes. Outside the back door, Harm was barking and scratching, informing us that there was an intruder in the house, as if we could not work that out for ourselves. I ushered Ohara into the library and offered him a seat. But not in my chair.

"Is that milk?" he asked.

"Yes. Do you want a glass?"

"No, thank you. Goat milk?"

"Cow milk."

He shook his head. "You English eat the strangest things."

Barker came in and looked at each of us as if we were conspiring. He gave a nod toward my hand and I set the pistol down on the table by my glass.

"What can we do for you, Mr. Ohara?" Barker asked.

He reached into his bowler and removed a thin needle perhaps four inches long, attached to a red puffball, either fur or feathers. Barker reached for it.

"Careful! It is poisoned!"

"I am familiar with darts," the Guv rumbled. "Whom do you believe wishes you harm?"

"The other bodyguards. They were each chosen by the general, personally."

Cyrus Barker stood and went to the fireplace, resting an elbow on the mantel. The grate had been cleaned out for the summer and a spray of dried flowers set inside it.

"But Ambassador Toda asked for you personally?"

"He did."

"Did you know him before you were asked?"

The big man hesitated, debating with himself. He finally decided, slumping his shoulders. Harm was still barking on the other side of the door. For once, I agreed with him. He is a good judge of character.

Ohara reached up and removed his tie pin. He unscrewed the shaft and brought it up to his mouth. Blowing into one end he then retrieved a slip of paper from the other, no more than an inch and a half square. He uncurled it and gave it to Barker. I could see Asian lettering in red and black and some sort of symbol.

"The Kempeitai," Barker growled, as if he had expected it.

"What's that?" I asked.

"Secret police, military police. May I assume you are here to watch the delegations' movements?"

"I am."

"Then you failed. The ambassador is dead."

"*Hai,*" he replied. His head sagged, and he turned the brim of his hat in his hands.

"Tell me about that."

"There was a meeting that night. I guarded the door. The ambassador was upstairs with his foot up. He had gout. I heard a popping sound and ran upstairs. He was dead. I assume one of the bodyguards must have killed him."

"Which one?" Barker asked.

"Kito, I would think. He loves pistols. The others have their own specialties. However, any one of them could have pulled the trigger. It is not difficult and requires no skill. It is a coward's weapon."

"Then I suppose you heard I was outside and thought that I had done it," the Guv said.

"Yes, sir. In my ignorance I came here and attacked you both. I apologize. I was mad with grief."

"You cared for Mr. Toda?"

"No, not particularly. He was a great man, but I did not really know him. I was ordered to protect the ambassador. No, I had failed in my duties. I had—I have disgraced the Kempeitai."

"And now you fear you will be assassinated."

Ohara frowned. "I fear nothing, sir, save the dereliction of my duty. But my life is in danger."

Barker twirled the dart in his thick fingers.

"Are any of the guards trained as assassins?"

"None that I know of, Mr. Barker. But then, they each required some skill to be chosen by the general over the others. Not just anyone can become an imperial guard."

"Nor a member of the Kempeitai. Your methods are greatly feared in Japan, even by the military."

"We are ruthless, sir," he admitted. "It is necessary."

"You were charged by your superiors to watch someone. Who was it?"

"The general."

"For what crime?"

"Treason, sir. I believe he hopes to become prime minister and then overthrow the Meiji government, to start a new shogunate. He is supported by some powerful manufacturers that, a generation ago, were samurai families."

"Have you collected much evidence so far?"

"No, sir. General Mononobe is shrewd and does not commit his plan to paper."

Barker handed the scrap of paper back to Ohara and sat down.

"Why are you here?"

"I—I need a place to stay."

"Get a hotel room," I said.

"Why would you trust me?" Barker asked.

"Because you concern the general, sir. Very much. You are not a member of the government. You are a private citizen. A detective."

"Private enquiry agent," I corrected. "But we're currently working for the general."

"He's trying to keep you occupied."

"I know that," Barker said. "Are you working alone?"

"I am."

"Why? There should be at least three of you."

"The general suspects my identity. He only allowed me to come because Ambassador Toda insisted. Had there been three of us, he would have known he was being watched."

Barker moved forward and stood over Ohara. "Why should I trust you? How do I know you don't work for Mononobe, and are another distraction?"

"The paper—"

"Could be a forgery."

"My attack upon you—"

"Could have succeeded. What then?"

"I—I don't know why you should trust me," he said, ducking his head.

"Mac!"

I crossed my arms and tried to look resolute in case Ohara tried to cut up rough. Mac glided in a moment later.

"Sir?"

"Put this gentleman in the guest room. Oh, and double locks on the doors tonight. You and Thomas can guard in shifts. Work it out as you wish."

"Very good, sir." He looked at our guest. "If you will come this way, please."

Mac led him out into the hall. The man's bulk barely cleared the doorway.

"Thomas," the Guv said, "do you have something to say?"

"Oh, no, sir. It's not for me to say. Obviously, you trust him, since he has proven you have no reason to trust him."

"Precisely. Had he been dishonest he'd have invented a reason. And remember, he came to us first. He trusted us first."

"Do you expect an attack tonight?"

"Perhaps. Ohara is the sort of fellow whom people notice. Let us hope he arrived by hansom. I would suggest you sleep on the sofa in the front room. Put Harm out all night. He's an excellent watch dog. I doubt they will come tonight, since the general is coming here tomorrow morning to play Go. More likely, he'll find some way to search the rooms then. However, if we are caught unawares, Ohara's life could be forfeited. And ours with it."

"I blame the Americans," I said.

Barker's mustache curled just a fraction. "I'm sure there is enough blame for everyone, but why precisely the Americans?"

"If Perry hadn't steamed into Edo harbor forty years ago and frightened the hell out of them, they wouldn't be here now, trying to become a world power. It would have been better for everyone if they had been left in peaceful isolation."

"You've been studying, I see."

"Mr. Grant from the British Library lent me a book or two."

"I'm glad you are using your time wisely."

"You really think Ohara can be trusted?"

"One thing to admire about the Japanese is their self-sufficiency. He'd have choked on his own tongue rather than ask for help from a stranger. An Englishman, especially."

"Scotsman," I corrected.

"Even worse," he said. "You must work out your shifts with Mac and get to bed. The sooner you start, the more sleep you'll get."

"And what will you do?"

"I'll make some plans for the morning. Oh, and one more thing."

"What's that, sir?"

"You cannot light a lamp overnight."

"Not even enough to read by?"

"If they see you awake, they'll know you are guarding the house."

I sighed. Not even a book to keep me company.

" 'Night, sir."

"Have a good evening, Thomas."

He turned and left the room. Harm was still barking in the yard.

"Marvelous," I said, to no one in particular.

CHAPTER NINETEEN

My relationship with Bok Fu Ying was complicated. When I had first met her five years before, I had been intrigued with her, but Barker told me in no uncertain terms that he did not want me to be her suitor, even before the idea had actually occurred to me. Also, I was not yet certain that I was willing to consider a bride who would forever be outside of society, beautiful though she was. The unanswered question was whether she had foreseen my interest, as women tend to do, and how she felt about it.

It is not my intent herein to discuss my relationships. It would be jarring to introduce them in the middle of an account of the first embassy of Japan and I would not do so, save that two unrelated elements suddenly became related in a way I could not have foreseen. The first element was Bok Fu Ying herself. The second was Rebecca Cowan, to whom I was affianced. I had not foreseen that these two would meet. It was never my wish, but Fate does not always take what I prefer into consideration.

It was Saturday and Barker had told me he had nothing particular for me to do, knowing this was the time I visited Rebecca every week whenever possible. At one time we had discussed the difficulties of being both a husband and a private enquiry agent, but he hadn't discussed it lately, probably because it would sound hypocritical. He was very near an understanding with Mrs. Philippa Ashleigh, the woman whom he had followed here from China years before.

I was done with work, and out the door as soon as possible, walking toward Trafalgar Square to find a hansom cab willing to take me to the City. As I was walking I noticed a young woman coming from the other direction in a maroon dress and heavy veil. To be truthful, I didn't give her a second thought until her elbow snagged mine and we were both arrested in our movement.

Lifting my top hat, I said, "Excuse me, miss."

She laughed. "You know perfectly well I am no miss now, Thomas."

"Fu Ying?"

She pulled back her veil. "Some enquiry agent you are."

"Are you looking for Mr. Barker?" I asked.

"No, I'm not," she said.

"I'm on my way to an appointment."

"I know, Thomas. I'm going with you. As your elder sister. I declare the right to examine anyone interested in joining the family."

Were we in our antagonistics school, she would have the right to call herself my elder sister. The problem was she saw that relationship as no different from the rest of the world.

"I'm perfectly capable of choosing my own bride."

"Mrs. Ashleigh sent me. I've been deputized. Something must be wrong with her if you won't bring her to meet us."

"There is nothing wrong with her. She's perfect."

"I'll decide that for myself, thank you."

"You're not coming with me."

"Then you're not going. If I start a fight I promise it will be you who is arrested. You're well acquainted with jail cells."

"Mrs. Ashleigh is a fine and noble woman, but she has no right—"

"Oh, she's not the only one. Mac sent me. And Etienne, and Jeremy Jenkins, and Ho."

"Don't tell me Ho gives a damn if I live or die."

"If you are preoccupied you might not be there when Sir needs you."

"It's not you we are hiding from. It is Mrs. Cowan's relations. Some of them don't approve of me."

"What? Someone does not approve of you? Then they do not approve of me. What are their addresses? I will answer for you."

"I'm not trying to see them beaten, I merely wish them to approve of me. Rebecca—Mrs. Cowan's late husband was a Jewish politician famed throughout the East End. Beside him, I don't amount to much."

"You are young, Thomas. We all expect great things from you."

"Anyway, you aren't expected."

"Fine. I'll wait in the drawing room until you leave. I would rather speak to her alone, anyway."

"Really, you can't do that!"

"I can. Do I have to summon a policeman?"

"No, don't bother."

"What's the matter?"

"You look stunning. It would be better if you had chin whiskers or baggy eyes."

She smiled. Every girl likes to hear a genuine compliment, even if it is not intended.

"I'm sorry to disappoint you. Now, will you summon a cab, or do you intend for us to walk?"

Soon we were in a cab heading from Whitehall on the way to the City. My fiancée lived in Chamomile Street, hard by the synagogue.

"I don't think this is a good idea," I said.

"So, tell me," Fu Ying went on, ignoring the remark. "Does your family know? Have you informed your mother?"

"Not yet. We're estranged. I was going to tell her."

"When? Afterward?"

"I don't know yet."

"Thomas, you cannot keep your life divided into so many compartments, like an express train."

"I prefer it that way. It's simpler."

We arrived in Chamomile Street and were shown into Rebecca's house by the maid, who was slightly disturbed that there were two guests when one was expected. There was a small flutter of activity before Rebecca came downstairs to see what the fuss was all about. She raised a brow slightly when she saw that I was not alone, but her manners are impeccable.

"Mrs. Cowan," I said, "allow me to present Mrs. K'ing. She is the former ward of my employer. Mrs. K'ing, Mrs. Cowan."

Fu Ying then lifted her veil before accepting the hand Rebecca offered. I'll say this for Rebecca: she did not hesitate or flinch or do what other hostesses in London might have done when finding an Oriental woman in their home unexpectedly. She merely smiled.

"Welcome! I'm so pleased to meet you," she said. "Tea? I'm afraid it's probably not up to your standards."

I should have known better than to worry. Rebecca is a master at putting people at their ease. She led us into the drawing room and offered us a seat.

"I'm afraid I have not had the pleasure to meet Mr. Barker yet," she said. "I've only seen him at a distance. He seemed very forceful."

"He can seem that way at times," Fu Ying replied. "But inside, he is very gentle. He purchased a house for me in Limehouse, in Three Colt Lane, and would not stop until it was full of the most beautiful furnishings. Most men would not care about such things."

"Thomas called you Mrs. K'ing. Have you married?"

"I have. My husband is a powerful political force in the East End. He also runs an establishment called the Inn of Double Happiness."

"Yes, I know the name well. My brother visits there often. So do many of his friends."

I wondered if Rebecca knew that on Friday nights, the establishment rivaled the synagogue for the number of Jews in it.

"How did you meet Thomas?" Fu Ying asked.

"He came to our house as a *Shabbos goy*, a Gentile who lights the fires in the house during the Sabbath. We are not permitted to work then, you see. I didn't know until later that Mr. Barker had sent him to investigate my father. I just knew within about two minutes I wanted to marry him."

Fu Ying looked up from the dainty cup in her hand. "Yet you married someone else."

"Yes."

Both were too formal to ask why, but it was implied. I was watching some sort of subtle jousting.

"My parents did not approve of Thomas, you see, and anyway, he did not ask."

Both pairs of eyes turned to me. I was suddenly under the microscope.

"I understood that her mother refused to allow me to see her and forbade the marriage," I said in my own defense. "Also, Barker told me that enquiry agents do not necessarily make good husbands, our work being what it is."

"Did you not care for her that you didn't pursue her?" Fu Ying asked with a tone of disapproval.

"I did!" I said. "Very much. But I didn't know how she felt."

The two women smiled at each other.

"Mrs. Cowan, I apologize for the thickheadedness of my brother."

"Call me Rebecca, please."

"Fu Ying."

They had finally come to an understanding. They were united against me.

"Why do you think," Fu Ying asked, "that men cannot see the subtleties of life when they happen right in front of them?"

"I've wondered that, myself," Rebecca answered. "My late husband was no better than most in that regard. I believe my father had to speak to him before he asked for my hand."

"I live in Limehouse, in a most respectable residence, not far from here. Perhaps you might consider visiting sometime."

"Dear girl, I should love that."

The maid arrived with a cart. I noticed in deference to Fu Ying, we both took our tea black.

"So, how came you to be Mr. Barker's ward?"

"I was a present to Sir from the Empress Dowager of China. He solved a mystery for her and in return she gave him an imperial dog. Every palace dog must have someone assigned to look after him, so I was chosen out of one of the orphanages in Peking."

"Did you lose your parents?" Rebecca asked.

"They abandoned me on a mountaintop. I was a girl, you see, and they could not afford to feed me."

"So you were some kind of servant."

"A slave, madame. I am owned by Mr. Barker's dog, according to my papers."

For once, Rebecca lost her composure. "Surely Mr. Barker has given you your freedom."

"Alas, Xixi still rules, and her word is law. But as Sir says, she is half a world away. How is she to know? I visit the dog, Bodhiddharma, every other day or so. The rest of my time I spend helping my husband."

"He's very prominent among the merchants of Poplar," I said, still trying to dig myself out of a hole.

Fu Ying picked up a morsel of shortbread and ate it daintily. Then she changed tactics.

"Actually, madame, I am here on the behalf of several friends of Thomas. He has been keeping you to himself and we wanted to be certain he is making a wise choice."

"Oh, ho," Rebecca said, not batting an eye. "Is that how it is?"

"In particular, I am an emissary for Mrs. Ashleigh, a close friend of Mr. Barker's. She hopes to meet you soon, either here or at her estate in Sussex. I have stayed with her often and it is a lovely home, not far from the ocean."

"I would love to meet her," Rebecca said. "Please tell her to forgive Thomas for not introducing me sooner, and I hope to become better acquainted with her."

I was looking down at the carpet, trying to work out how to get myself out of this social blunder, when something caught my eye.

"I say—" I began.

"She understands," Fu Ying said. "What can one do?"

"I think . . . I believe that your bag just moved," I said.

Fu Ying was carrying a brown leather bag with her, like a small Gladstone. She now picked it up and opened it. There was a small puffball in it, pure white with bright black eyes like marbles.

"This is Butterfly. She is a descendent of Harm. She goes with me wherever I go."

"What a beauty!" Rebecca exclaimed. "May I hold her?"

She lifted the little dog to her face, and when their eyes were at a level, the dog licked her nose with the smallest tongue I've ever seen. She hugged the dog and set her in her lap.

"I'm sorry. I couldn't resist," she said. "You may continue the cross-examination. I am being examined, am I not?"

"You like Thomas. You like dogs. What else is there?"

"I do like Thomas. He is important to me."

"You realize he is necessary to Sir's work. If you were to convince Thomas to find different work, it might mean death to Mr. Barker."

"Is that it?" Rebecca asked. "You fear I might make Thomas quit? I met him because Mr. Barker sent him to our home. One might almost say he introduced us. I would support Thomas in whatever he does."

I turned to Rebecca.

"I suspect Mrs. Ashleigh is concerned about the safety of Mr. Barker. She would like to get him to the altar someday."

"One certainly cannot blame a girl for that."

Butterfly yipped. She had not been adored in nearly a minute. Both women converged upon her and cooed. I made a face, the result of which was the dog being placed in my lap.

"Hello," I said.

The dog looked up at me. She was a white ball, more head than body, with two black eyes separated by a black nose. She yipped at me again. I picked her up, and she nuzzled against my neck. For some reason the women found this satisfactory. I could barely believe that this puffball had come from the loins of a seasoned warrior like Harm. He was small, but he was mighty.

Rebecca poured some more tea for us all.

"Mrs. Ashleigh said if he has any bad habits which trouble you, you are to let her know."

"Here now!" I said, as the pup's fur tickled my neck.

"You needn't worry on that score," Rebecca said. "I have experience getting husbands to heel. Tell her if he starts pinching constables' helmets she will be the first to know."

"Husbands can be difficult," Fu Ying said. She had been teasing, but had gone serious for a moment.

"They can be," Rebecca said. "But you mustn't knuckle under to them. You must be fearless."

"And you know," I said, "that we are your friends here. If you are ever in need of anything."

Bok Fu Ying suddenly looked down, struggling to keep her composure. I think it surprised her most of all. Butterfly was watching her mistress.

Rebecca stood and turned to me. Then she gave me the first command of our lives.

"Thomas," she said. "Take the dog for a walk."

I obeyed her at once. There was a tiny leash of pink leather in the purse. Apparently there was a collar underneath all that fur. I found the ring and clasp and took the ridiculous little toy outside.

One could take a dog, a real dog, around an entire park. To this one a single street was like a mile. When I reached the second corner I stopped. Somehow I had picked up two dozen children along the way. They began cooing over Butterfly and taking turns playing with her.

After half an hour, I scooped up Butterfly amid the children's protests, and carried her back on my shoulder. She was asleep and snuffling within half a minute. Perhaps she wasn't so bad, I thought. She was from Harm's brood after all.

I stepped back inside. Fu Ying was actually laughing, though her face was a trifle red.

"Thomas, you must see Fu Ying home."

They both stood and Rebecca took her hands. Both wore the most delicate of gloves. Rebecca's were a sort of black lace, while Fu Ying's were gray kid leather. She could break boards with those little hands.

"I'm so glad you came," Rebecca said. "Have you a telephone set?"

"I do. Sir might need me."

"I'll give you my exchange number, then. We must have lunch soon."

"I would like that. But I must look a fright. May I powder my nose?"

"My room is at the top of the stairs on the right."

Bok Fu Ying bowed and climbed the stair. Meanwhile, Rebecca turned and looked at me. There was an adorable dimple by one side of her mouth. Back then, I hadn't worked out that two dimples are safe, but one is dangerous.

"Very pretty, Miss Bok Fu Ying," she said. "It's a wonder you didn't marry her yourself."

"Think, Thomas, think," I said to myself. I was skating on thin ice.

"Don't be silly," I said. "She's my elder sister."

"Of course," she said. Her dimple broadened into two. "You haven't worked it out, have you?"

"Worked what out?"

"Mrs. Ashleigh didn't send Fu Ying here. Mr. Barker did."

CHAPTER TWENTY

The Japanese delegation are eating lunch here regularly," Ho said to us from a cushion in front of his legless desk. Barker had sent word to me and I had met him here.

Barker bit into a leprous-looking thousand-year-old egg. The white was tea stained and the yolk a bilious green. They aren't actually a thousand years old but they are buried in the ground for a hundred days, and I have a hard-and-fast rule about consuming anything which has been, in fact, embalmed. The Guv likes them, but then, he also likes snail dumplings, so his tastes are rather suspect.

"Have you been preparing food for them especially?" he asked.

Ho was drinking plum wine from a bottle, using a cup the size of a thimble. He tossed back another one.

"A little sukiyaki, some *yanagi*, and tempura."

"You have enticed them here!" Barker said. "Very good."

"All travelers are the same," Ho said. "In a strange country they will try the food for two days, then they want the old, familiar things."

"Do all your waiters speak Japanese?"

"A few of them do, but the Japanese are suspicious. They stop speaking whenever we get near."

"Does General Mononobe come?"

"He does. He has a preference for soba noodles."

"You've got a plan?" Barker said.

"Let the sake flow and prepare fugu."

"Fugu?" Barker asked. "Do you know how to prepare it?"

"It cannot be difficult if a *xiao riben* can do it."

Barker smiled. Whatever Ho had called the Japanese, I'm sure it was derogatory.

"What is fugu?" I asked.

"Puffer fish," my employer explained. "They throw it away here. No Englishman will eat it."

"Well, no wonder," I said. "It sounds dreadful."

"A pig is ugly, but pork is delicious."

"Agreed," I said. "Is fugu delicious?"

"No, it is nearly tasteless," Barker answered. "But it has other attractions for the Japanese. It is poisonous."

"Poisonous!" I cried.

"Only if served incorrectly," Ho said, holding up a finger. "The liver is poisonous. If the meat has not touched the liver, it is fine to eat. If it has, you are dead almost instantly."

"Dozens die every year," Barker added.

"But it's tasteless," I argued.

"Yes," Ho said, "and cut so thin one could read through the flesh."

"Death and beauty," Barker murmured. "They are a unique people."

"They are *xiao riben*," Ho grumbled. He spat on the floor.

I looked at Barker.

"Ghost devils," he supplied.

"K'ing is up to something," Ho went on. "He flatters them too much. That man does not do anything that is not for his own benefit."

"Perhaps you misconstrue," I said. "Some would call serving food to the Japanese a form of patronage."

Ho looked ready to strike me. I was merely Barker's satellite and had no right to an opinion. Barker seemed not to notice the exchange. Or perhaps he was deflecting a response.

"You plan to get them drunk in hopes that someone will blurt out their strategy?" he asked.

"I don't see you proposing a better plan," Ho snapped.

"I was not criticizing, merely trying to understand your plan. If there is one weakness, it is that one of the people you hope to catch is Asian and will assume your waiters understand what he is saying. You cannot rely on the anonymity of your waiters."

"My men walk softly and they hear very well. I trust them to do the work I ask."

"Have you gathered anything so far?" the Guv asked.

"Of course. There are five bodyguards, are there not? One of them, the one with the big mustache—"

"Kito," Barker supplied.

"He has a liking for low women, and tries to convince the others to go with him. One of them is a fop, interested only in purchasing Western suits. The big one has a prodigious appetite, and does not like English food. The one who died trained all day and they suspect he preferred young men to women. The fifth is completely taciturn, and does nothing but scowl. He doesn't like being here."

"They all come in as a group?" I asked.

"No, never. Only ones and twos. Once, three of them came in together. They are beginning to relax here. I believe one of them will say something worth listening to sooner or later."

"What of Mononobe?"

"He has been here three times. He likes my dim sum, especially rice balls in tea leaves. Once he came in with K'ing, but they conversed very quietly. Another time he came with the Foreign Office man, the one with the yellow hair and pale mustache."

"Campbell-Ffinch."

"He picks at my food as if I were serving rat."

"What can you do about something like that?" I asked.

"I serve them rat."

I shuddered. "Did you ever hear anything of worth from their conversation?"

"K'ing spent his time trying to humor the general. Anything the delegation needed, he would be glad to oblige."

"Did you hear anything clandestine at all?"

"K'ing mentioned the Blue Funnel Line."

I had heard K'ing mention it before, myself.

"That's the line running between here and China, is it not?" I asked. "The officers are European, but the sailors are Asian. Most of the sailors belong to the Blue Dragon."

The final phrase I had whispered. The Blue Dragon Triad was a secret organization to which many Chinese sailors belonged. The triad, run by K'ing himself, looked after aging sailors and the Chinese population as a whole, a benevolent society. It also existed on another level, gathering weapons and passing information to overthrow the Qing government. They were revolutionaries, part of the Heaven and Earth Society. On a third level they ran criminal enterprises, helping their members to flee one country or another, changing money and counterfeiting. K'ing's gambling house and opium den were part of that concern. So which was the mask, and which the true face? Somehow, they were all true. Criminal and benevolent. Rebellious, and money-seeking. He was everything at once.

"Interesting," Barker remarked. We had finished eating and were drinking tea, except for Ho, who was still taking wine tiny cup by tiny cup.

"Interesting?" Ho repeated acidly. "This is the man you married your ward to."

"It was whom she chose," Barker replied, with an air of patience.

"She shouldn't have been given a choice! She was too young. It was your duty to find a proper husband for her," he chided.

Barker finished his tea and poured another cup. He wasn't about to be drawn into the argument Ho was spoiling for. The decision was already made. Ho just could not accept it.

"Blue Funnel," he mumbled to himself.

"There was money to be made. Anything brought from Japan— tea, silk, jade—would have to be carried on Blue Funnel ships if K'ing could force a contract. That's hundreds if not thousands of pounds," I said. "And it would provide work for sailors right here in Limehouse. Then there are docking fees, and storage in nearby warehouses. Oh, yes, that could be worth a lot of money."

"Enough to make K'ing work with the Japanese?" I asked.

"As far as I can tell, he is a pragmatist. A businessman. He has lived here most of his life and has left prejudices behind in the Old Country."

"Or he's a traitor," Ho said. "Trying to impress the general. A merchant. A lickspittle!"

"You're a merchant. You've opened your doors to them."

"You know opening my doors to those cursed ghost devils was to gain information about their plans!"

Barker got out his pipe, filled it with tobacco from his sealskin pouch, and lit it with a Bryant May match, made nearby in Poplar. He had that thoughtful look on his face, if I was reading it correctly.

"You should invite K'ing to your little party here."

"Never!" Ho bellowed.

"You are trying to get information, are you not? In order to do so you must bring all of the conspirators together."

That set both of us thinking. That is, if Ho was not too drunk to think.

"Conspirators," I repeated.

"Aye."

"Implying that there is, in fact, a conspiracy."

"Correct."

"What kind of conspiracy? Conspiracy to do what, exactly?"

"I don't believe it is to corner the market in silk."

"They're opening an embassy," I said. "It sounds perfectly reasonable."

"What is the purpose of an embassy?"

I shrugged my shoulders and took a sip of tea. My little cup had gone cold, but I was tired of tea.

"To form a bond between two countries, and establish commerce."

"Idiot," Ho said to me.

"I liked it better when we weren't speaking."

"Ha!" Ho threw back his head and laughed, then smote me on the back.

"The purpose of an embassy is to say, 'You have to deal with us now. You cannot afford to ignore us anymore. We are equals. Make peace with us, or make war. We are ready for either.'"

"Is he right?" I asked Barker.

"He's not wrong."

"They didn't merely happen to send an admiral and a general along," Ho added.

"But Ambassador Toda was a pacifist."

"Correct. He wasn't here a full day before he was shot."

"Something is very definitely occurring," Barker said. "And I don't like it one bit, Thomas."

"What do you mean?"

"I mean the Foreign Office, in the person of Trelawney Campbell-Ffinch, has been too friendly. It is something else, other than a war."

"What, then?"

"I don't know," the Guv admitted. "Perhaps the Japanese want to buy Hong Kong."

Ho's eyes grew big. The wine appeared to not be affecting him at all.

"That would leave your beloved Canton unprotected," he said.

"But if the British were forewarned, they could get out in time."

"Suppose," Ho continued, "that they signed an alliance with England, in order to fight someone else."

"Such as?"

"The Japanese want Formosa very much. I suppose they would not mind owning Korea, either."

"Would the English help them?" I asked.

"If they could find a reason," Barker answered.

"Find!" Ho barked. "They could make a reason. Remember the Arrow incident about fifty years ago? One English ship stuffed with opium went down on the Pearl River and England nearly went to war with China. And England retaliated by supplying plenty of cheap opium to China from poppy fields in India. It ruined a generation of men."

"The English, in matter of diplomacy, are not the gentlemen they appear," I said.

"Ah," Ho said. "Light dawns. He can be taught."

"Thank you. And the Japanese?"

"Ghost devils!" Ho cried, lifting his bottle. Perhaps the liquor was finally starting to affect him.

"Perhaps not as bad as that," Barker said, trying to pacify his friend. "They are a small, isolated nation which was thrust into the limelight when the Americans arrived with their black ships. To some degree, I suppose they are frightened it shall happen again. But they have weapons and they are not afraid to fight. I believe plans are afoot in Tokyo, but we know not yet what kind of plans. If the ambassador's death is any indication, the time for peace and flower arranging is over."

"So how do we know what plans are afoot?"

"The best way, I think, is to make certain everyone is at the party. Especially Campbell-Ffinch."

"Why?"

"Because he is lazy and has never bothered to learn Japanese, which means everything has to be translated for him."

Ho chuckled. "This is going to be an interesting party."

CHAPTER TWENTY-ONE

S ometimes one must state the obvious in order to receive an answer. People tend to be loquacious, but not all of us, I'm afraid. Some of us consider silence a virtue. I happened to work for one of them. Explain things to me when I could eventually work it out for myself? Perish the thought.

"We're heading toward the inn," I said that evening.

"Aye."

"You intend to speak to K'ing himself?"

"I do."

"About what, exactly?"

"Whatever occurs to me."

Barker was walking in that way he has, his head down, his hands behind his back.

"He's not liable to tell you his plans, sir."

"I don't expect him to. But he might say something of use to us."

"I just don't want to see you waste your time."

Barker sat back in the cab. We were in Limehouse again.

"There's always enough time for a patient man."

That's it. Give me an axiom instead of an answer. The Analects of Barker.

The room was full. Most of those assembled were Asian. The population was not large, but it seemed as if all of it was here. As we entered a wide, open room with Persian carpets, a Chinese man detached himself from a position near the wall and came forward. He was very large. Not in the way Ohara was. He had big muscles and a trim waist.

"Who are you?" he asked.

"Shi Shi Ji," Barker replied. "I wish to speak to my son-in-law." The guard crossed his arms, blocking our way.

"He is occupied."

"Five minutes," Barker said.

I followed the Guv down a hall and then up a set of stairs. K'ing's lair, if one wishes to call it that, backs onto a disused sewer line where his staff and patrons could escape during a raid. The Guv seemed to know exactly where he was going. At the end of an ornate hall, he opened a door and stepped in.

K'ing was reclining on a couch, holding a two-foot-long pipe with an outsized bowl. I have that kind of occupation which allows one to be able to identify opium where he smells it. The atmosphere in the room was charged with it.

K'ing's attention was focused on some point beyond us, possibly at some point beyond the wall. The smoke he was exhaling curled upward from his mouth.

"Cyrus Barker," he said, about a minute later.

"At your service."

"Hmmm. What can I do for you?"

"I wanted to ask you a question regarding my former ward, Bok Fu Ying."

"Too many words. Far too many."

"What did you send her to find?"

"An offer from the government."

"An offer to ship items to and from Japan?"

The casino owner nodded and took another pull on the pipe.

"The government was working against the Blue Funnel Line?"

"I don't know. No time to see, with Toda dead."

"But you suspect it did?" Barker asked.

"Why hand over a moneymaking contract to us? Best to keep it with the English lines."

"But that endangered the plan, didn't it?"

"Oh, it did," K'ing murmured, shifting on his leather chaise longue.

"The plan," Barker continued. "What was it again?"

K'ing sat up and cleared his throat. "You won't catch me out so easily, Cyrus."

The Guv shrugged his thick shoulders and gave a cold smile.

"I believe," Barker said, "that you have been building a relationship with the general in order to foster trade between here and China. So far as I know, you are the only Chinaman who doesn't despise the Japanese. I presume it is a business opportunity."

"Believe or presume whatever you wish. I'll neither confirm nor deny your story."

"However, I don't think you would take such matters seriously if it were but one big voyage. There must be a steady flow of goods from the English government. Not merely food or timber or simple goods."

K'ing rested his head against the back of the chaise. He took another puff of his pipe, then let it leak back out of his mouth. As it rose, he sucked the smoke back into his lungs at the last minute. "Chasing the dragon" meant opium smoking, but originally it was this method of smoking it.

"You're getting boring," he said, and closed his eyes.

He slumped a little in his chair, and I wondered if he had succumbed to the fumes and would be of no use to us. He rallied, however, and raised his head.

"Bless my soul, if it isn't Thomas Llewelyn. Still following in Barker's shadow?"

"As you see."

"I'm making money hand over fist. Come join my organization."

"Thank you for the offer, but no," I said.

"Don't be . . . Don't be . . . What's the word? Precious? Don't be precious. Take the money."

He laid his head back again.

"Don't fall asleep, K'ing. We have another matter to discuss."

"What is it?" he demanded irritably.

"My ward."

He spoke with his eyes closed. "She is your ward no longer. She is my wife. I own her now."

"You cannot own her, like she is a milk cow or a piece of furniture," I said.

"I can and do. Shi Shi Ji, you relinquished what few rights you had to her when we wed. By English law, she is mine."

"You're ruining her life. And yours, by the way."

"That's touching, but it's none of your concern."

"When was the last time you even saw her?"

"What day is it?"

"Tuesday."

"I saw her last week. No, the week before. It doesn't matter."

"I gave her to you with the expectation that you would care for her and see to her comfort."

"She's in a fine house. She lacks for nothing. I've given her baubles and fresh flowers. I'm a businessman. I have work to do."

"When you're not sucking on that blasted pipe."

"It was Sebastian Nightwine's fault. He kidnapped me and forced this habit on me. May he rot in hell!"

He actually leaned forward toward us and spat out the words. It was the only true emotion he showed in our entire conversation.

"K'ing, there are ways to conquer your addiction. The Mile End mission has made great strides in the treatment of opium abuse."

"You'll take my pipe over my dead body!" he shouted.

I thought then that his words seemed prophetic.

Cyrus Barker looked at his son-in-law with something approaching disgust. Fu Ying was not his actual daughter, of course, but it amounted to the same thing. What a disappointment her suitor had become. My employer believed in self-strengthening. Indulging in the pipe without even an attempt to throw off its tentacles was a sign of weakness in his book. It was indulgence when there were things to attend to, such as Bok Fu Ying being neglected in Three Colt Lane.

"What are you here for again?" K'ing asked.

"We were seeing how you were."

"I'm in excellent health, as you can see. The casino is doing well. Gambling is even more successful than running an opium den. Half the East End is Chinese and the other half is Jewish. Both have a weakness for the gambling table."

"It had to be done," Barker said, leading him along. "One wouldn't want to spoil the plan."

K'ing shook his head, but it was wobbling as if it were too heavy for his neck.

"It had to be done," he repeated.

"Now you can join with Mononobe and set up a trade alliance. You'll make a lot of money that way."

"I will," he said. His eyes closed.

"All those goods going to Japan, and others coming back here. Cloth and timber, silk and art work. And eventually a warship, all delivered by your crews."

"Of course," K'ing said.

"You'll need more ships and merchant sailors."

"Lots more."

"A big plan."

"Big plan."

His hand tilted forward and dropped the long pipe onto the table in front of him. In a minute we could hear his steady breathing. He would answer no more questions.

"Come along, Thomas."

I followed him out. His bodyguard brushed past us, past Barker, anyway, and walked in to look on his employer. His charge now, I thought. The man had probably become his caretaker.

"I feel sorry for him in a way," I stated. "He had such promise. He looked after all the Chinese here, he set up funds for them to secure their money, he did good works. K'ing always had a reputation as a criminal, but in fact, he really cares about this little colony."

"Don't waste your sympathy," Barker growled. "I was a fool to marry Fu Ying to him. He is a grave disappointment."

"That was a fine trick, leading him along when he was half unconscious. It was a confession of sorts."

"A confession of what, exactly?" the Guv asked. "His plan is not illegal. His casino and his opium den are not illegal, either, by law. To the Chinese community he is a veritable saint, thanks to his benevolent society."

"Except to Ho," I said.

Barker chuckled. "Aye. Except to him. Perhaps I did my old friend a disservice. I should have encouraged Fu Ying to marry him. He's old, but he would not have mistreated her."

"Water under the bridge," I said.

"We could kidnap her," he mused. "Help her divorce him."

"It wouldn't work," I said. "He has solicitors. Actually, he is one, blast him."

We stepped out into the street. It was raining in Limehouse. Misting, rather. I watched it fall through the nimbus of a gas lamp. It made the sordidness and misery of the district look temporarily quaint. That's the thing about England, you see. We can do our best to savage it, and somehow it always grows back or reveals its natural beauty. The landscape will outlast us all. Eventually, when we are gone, it will all become a forest again, after all we've done to it.

"What do we do now?" I asked, tugging my bowler down a bit more and putting my hands in my pockets.

The Guv pulled up his collar.

"Home, I suppose."

"Don't you want to see Bok Fu Ying?"

"She is self-sufficient. I would not intrude upon her."

My employer is rough sometimes, but I think he treats me better than he does his ward. For all his Scottishness he is a Chinese father. There is no coddling. Children are trained to be prepared for a difficult world. He was right, I suppose. Fu Ying would not appreciate his help. But she needed it, which was more important. Barker wouldn't listen to my advice, any more than K'ing would listen to ours. There are a good deal of stubborn men in London.

CHAPTER TWENTY-TWO

The next morning, I had plenty of coffee and for once the old Llewelyn noggin was working.

"Forgive me, sir, but if the general were the actual killer, why hire you to find him? Is he undervaluing your skills?"

We were back in Whitehall in our chambers. Meanwhile, Ohara was back in Newington with Mac. After seeing the destruction he had wreaked in Barker's rooms, I didn't trust him. There were still three floors left to demolish.

Barker had his boots up on the corner of his desk, scratching absently under his chin, deep in thought. It was his standard method of cogitating. He'll sit there all day if I let him.

"I don't believe so," my employer said. "It's the easiest way to see what I am about, and how I'm progressing. For that same reason, I have him come to the garden for Go every morning. We are engaged in a battle of wits over a game of strategy."

"You think he committed the murder, then?"

"I have no evidence, but I consider it likely," the Guv said.

"But at the time of the murder, the general was downstairs giving a dinner speech. How could he kill Toda?"

"He could have moved the bodyguards around like a game of thimblerig. They all wore identical suits and Ohara was at the front door, separated from the ambassador."

"Perhaps the murderer is under our own roof," I said. "You told me the Kempeitai were ruthless, like the Special Branch. He could have had orders."

"For what purpose?" Barker asked.

"I have no idea. I'm not an expert in Japanese politics. One party is against another for whatever reason. Somehow the ambassador became an impediment or merely expendable. He was a peaceful man in a dangerous game. It might not even be Mononobe. The admiral has as much to lose as he."

"Two new suspects in as many minutes. You scintillate this morning, lad."

"The law of averages said it would happen sooner or later."

"Does it not seem that the admiral has been avoiding us?"

"It does," I admitted. "You left word for him to contact you."

"He did not speak when he came to view the garden. Perhaps he does not speak English, which doesn't matter, since you speak Japanese."

Barker lifted the telephone receiver in his hand and spoke into it. "Good morning. Shall Admiral Edami be in the embassy today? Excellent. Thank you very much."

He dropped the receiver into its cradle.

"The admiral shall be there within the hour. Come, Thomas, let us waylay him when he comes by."

We took a hansom to Lord Diosy's house and a man detached himself from the bushes, a shaggy-looking fellow with a white beard. I recognized him.

"Henry Cathcart!"

"Hello, young-fella-me-lad."

Cathcart was a reliable watcher. He kept an eye on things. He had such an ability to memorize conversations that his moniker was "The Sponge."

"Henry, has the admiral arrived yet?" Barker asked.

Cathcart tugged on a disreputable top hat. "Not so far, sir, no. Left about an hour and a half ago."

"Thank you, Henry. I'll send you back to your post. Have you been taken care of?"

"Not yet, sir."

"Mr. Llewelyn, give Henry two shillings. I want him reasonably sober for a day or two. He's got work to do."

"Thankee, sir. A true gentleman, as always."

We waited nearly half an hour before a brougham entered the gate. I could not mistake that erect posture or the peaked cap with gold braid. My employer let him enter and waited five minutes before we followed him inside. We were at the door, speaking to one of the guards, when the admiral came out again. I hazarded he was leaving because he heard we had called. He blanched momentarily when he saw us, but recovered well.

"Mr. Barker, it is good to see you again. How is your investigation into the death of Ambassador Toda?"

His English was slow and laborious, but we understood him. Now that I saw him again, he was not as tall as I had imagined.

"We are making progress, sir," Barker said. "We would like to ask you a few question about the ambassador's death."

"Regretfully, I have an appointment," he replied.

"Truly regrettable. I would hate to inform Lord Diosy that you were hindering an enquiry. It would be highly suspicious if a murder occurred in this residence while you were in it, yet you said nothing."

"I am an extraterritorial diplomat and am not subject to your laws."

The man was trying to sound authoritative, but there was a tinge of panic in his voice.

"Perhaps, but I am sure the Kempeitai would be interested in your refusal to answer questions about the death of such a well-known and much beloved ambassador."

The admiral deflated again. "Very well. Come along to my office."

We followed him up the stairs to the first floor. His heels echoed as he ascended. He led us to the left, to his so-called office. It was actually the anteroom to a suite. His desk, if one may consider it one, was a secretary stacked with papers. The general had the only actual office in the building.

"Have a seat, gentlemen."

We sat. The room was built in the French style, with interior wardrobes that rose to the ceilings. It was an ostentatious symbol of wealth. Three quarters of each closet was useless, and there was no ladder to reach them.

"Ask your questions."

"Where were you, sir, when Toda Ichigo was killed?"

"I was downstairs in the meeting room. The general was speaking to us about how best to plan our schedules so that we knew when we were coming and going."

"What was the decision?"

"He said we should each have a sheet of paper at the entrance, where we write the time and where we are going, and when we anticipate returning."

"When did you become aware of Toda's death?"

"We heard the shot. We could not tell where it came from. Then a minute later his bodyguard called out from the top of the stairs. We followed all the guards up the stairs to the room. Toda was sprawled out on the rug. There was blood and I could smell cordite in the air. It was a tragic loss to our country. I'm not sure how we shall ever recover."

"Where was the bodyguard when the ambassador was shot?" Barker asked.

"I do not notice bodyguards, Mr. Barker. He was not down in the meeting room. I understand he has left the embassy. He ran away. The other bodyguards are looking for him."

I doubted they were tracking him to buy him a pint. The thought came to me that Ohara was resourceful. No one would think of looking for him in Lion Street. They were probably combing Limehouse for him.

"We are hunting him as well, sir. If your men find him, I hope someone will inform me."

"Of course."

"Forgive me. You have no men. I understand your bodyguard has died."

"Yes. He confessed to killing the ambassador, then he killed himself in the proper manner. I don't see why the investigation has not ended."

Barker nodded, as if he understood it was a trial to Edami to answer questions, but bureaucracy required it.

"What was your guard's name, sir?"

"Mitsuo. He was the youngest of the guards. I would have preferred a sailor, but Mononobe chose the best of the Imperial Guards."

"Very unfortunate, sir, to have two deaths and one missing guard at the opening of your embassy."

"Mitsuo has confessed."

"Fortunate, indeed. Do you have any idea why he should kill the ambassador?"

"None."

"Did you happen to notice him in the meeting hall?"

"I saw him once when he brought me tea. I do not recall the time. Of course, it is difficult to keep them apart in one's mind. I could not tell you, for example, which guard belongs to Akita-san."

"Excellent, Admiral! We are making progress. You are an excellent witness."

The admiral smiled and bowed his head. The Guv was acting bumptious, a typical bureaucrat sent to cover over a scandal. Edami was susceptible to flattery and visibly relaxed.

"The general has informed me that your government has

ordered a destroyer," my employer said. "That is wonderful news. Now you need not rely upon the Americans to patrol your coasts."

That was a kind of test, I thought. The fact should not have been known to Barker. Would Admiral Edami confirm it?

"Yes, sir. No longer will we have to submit to the barbaric and overbearing Americans that plunder our country. Your people are much more civilized. I hope we shall agree to trade in the future. I am very impressed with your navy. They are truly a marvel."

"That is so. We very much look forward to a treaty with your country. Two countries so very much alike! But, sir, we have taken up too much of your time. You have been very patient. Come, Mr. Llewelyn. Let us leave the admiral to his important work."

We stood and bowed. I still hadn't worked out the bowing yet. It was more complicated than it looked. We were certain to bow lower than the admiral out of respect.

We stepped in to see General Mononobe, but he was out. Likewise, Minister Akita. We did not look for Tatsuya. He would keep us from our duties as we kept Edami from his.

In the street again, Barker turned and began to walk without searching for a cab. The sun was shining through the trees, breaking up its rays, creating dappled shadows at our feet.

"'An honest witness doth not deceive, but a false witness pours out lies.' Proverbs 14:5."

"In his defense, sir, he's probably not a Christian. What lies did he tell, precisely?"

"He said he heard the shot, but it was muffled by Toda's robes."

"That's right, and Toda had powder marks. The general said he heard nothing in the same room."

"Then there was the cordite. The murder weapon was a revolver. There would be very little odor, especially with an open window nearby. Cordite was invented a few years ago. The pistol is probably older than that."

I was thinking to myself how fortunate I was to have a situation that allowed me to walk freely under an avenue of trees in an afternoon when everyone else was working in a hot, stuffy office. It was very warm. Every window one saw was open. Other than that, I was thinking random thoughts. In the back of my mind, I was trying to remember an impression I had received and immediately buried.

"Sir."

"Aye, lad?"

"When I got a close look at Admiral Edami, I had the feeling that I'd seen him before, which of course is impossible, since he only arrived last week. But I still recognized his features, and not because I'd seen him in the garden."

"Continue," Barker said, his hands behind his back, flipping the tails of his coat.

"I had seen his face before in the face of Mitsuo, the bodyguard. There is a family resemblance. They may have been father and son."

"I must take your word for it, Thomas. I never saw the bodyguard's face. Are you sure?"

"The resemblance is such that I'm sure I'm not mistaken. Are you sure he didn't kill the ambassador?"

"Of course not, lad."

"But he confessed and then he killed himself! How and why would he do that?"

"Traditionally among the samurai, a young man, often the youngest and least proven among his comrades, will volunteer to accept the blame for a crime or even a decision, then kill himself immediately afterward. The police are satisfied, tranquility is restored to society, and a father is proud of his son for his sacrifice."

"What would the mother say? A young man just ended his life, years before a normal death, and why?"

"He earns the respect of his peers, the gratefulness of those he reveres, and he will be remembered for years for his sacrifice."

I couldn't help but think I'd rather die in my eighties and be well remembered by my own family instead.

CHAPTER TWENTY-THREE

The party was that evening. The embassy, Campbell-Ffinch, and Mr. K'ing had been invited. We had debated asking Fu Ying, but Barker reasoned she would distract everyone. The tearoom had been closed to its usual customers, although one or two had worked their way into the far corners of the room and would not be moved. There were crates of bottles with Chinese lettering, containing what I assumed was plum wine. All the staff was in the steaming kitchen, preparing course by course: noodles with prawns, sea snail dumplings, beef with peppers, stuffed fish courtesy of Billingsgate Fish Market, and even more exotic dishes such as shark's fin soup, and an actual bear's paw. However, by far the one that drew everyone's attention was the fugu, the poisonous puffer fish.

Ho was in the kitchen with a small slab of translucent fillet and an assortment of knives, all on a metal-covered counter, since the regular wooden cutting boards might be poisoned by the slightest touch of the flesh. Between the heat in the kitchen and the duty he was performing, Ho's forehead was covered in sweat and a member of the kitchen staff was wiping it constantly with a cloth. The puffer fish was sliced paper thin. He set aside the knife, picked up a second one, and excised the flesh around it. He set that knife aside, picked up a third, and sliced the meat on either side. A fourth knife was brought out and the rest of the fillet sliced into thin strips. The knives were thrown into a bucket full of brine. Ho would not risk contaminating another fillet. Finally, he ran water over the entire fish.

"I trust you know what you are doing," I said.

"As do I. Everyone, clear the kitchen, except for the chefs!"

We were herded out. As we were, I noticed a case of bottles smaller than the plum wine.

"What are these?" I asked.

"Sake," Barker replied. "Japanese rice wine. It's rather potent. Lord Diosy was able to provide it for us. Take no more than a cupful. I want your head clear tonight."

"Yes, sir."

The tables had actually been polished and the floor mopped. I doubted such a thing had ever happened since the tearoom opened. Serviettes were set out, as well as chopsticks. There were little ceramic dishes at each place setting, since it was considered ill manners to allow the tips of the chopsticks to touch the table.

Paper lanterns covered in gold kanji were hung from the ceiling, and a few posters placed on the wall. This was an attempt by Ho to liven the dark room. Closer to the time of the arrival of the embassy, a small oil lamp was lit on each table.

Barker leaned in and spoke. "The menu will be a mixture of Chinese and Japanese. There is a dish which contains pork and chicken called sukiyaki, and rice and raw fish wrapped in seaweed. Ho has done his best. The embassy may criticize the menu, but I'm sure they will be too well-mannered to voice it in front of us."

A quarter hour later, the embassy delegation arrived. There was a great deal of bowing and niceties given in three languages. Cyrus

Barker stood and welcomed the guests in their own tongue. Then Ho spoke, translated by Barker.

Afterward, the Guv came over to where I stood, and murmured to me, just loudly enough for me to hear, "K'ing has not arrived."

"He was the worse for wear when we saw him last," I said. "Perhaps he is still somewhere in a stupor."

"It's not like him to miss a business opportunity."

The general rose and bowed, and the crowd grew quiet, waiting for his speech, which he gave in English.

"The embassy appreciates your generosity," he began. "We understand to what trouble you have gone in order to make us comfortable. I fear some of us have found the food in London to be unpalatable. We shall adapt to the cookery here eventually, I am sure, but this meal is a fine treat to us. The embassy thanks you."

The door from the tunnel squeaked open and Trelawney Campbell-Ffinch sauntered in, the last to arrive. He made a face at the odor of the food in the room. No doubt he would have preferred boiled mutton and roasted potatoes.

The rest of the speech concerned the need for countries to come together for the support of both civilizations. Rather tactlessly, China was not mentioned. It was a rousing speech, but did not elicit a good level of enthusiasm from the audience. However, the general was satisfied, and as he returned to his seat, he was encouraged by his countrymen.

Campbell-Ffinch rose without permission from the host, and gave a short speech himself. The British government was honored to have the embassy here, and they looked forward to a long and profitable relationship. The Foreign Office was pleased. It was as if Campbell-Ffinch had set up the event himself, as a representative of the English government, and Her Majesty. For all the embassy knew, Campbell-Ffinch had gone into the kitchen and prepared the meal himself, after setting up the tables. He sat down with a smug expression, and I waited to see what would happen next.

The dishes were brought in from the kitchen. Two tables had

been put together for the embassy guests, the ministers seated on one side and the bodyguards on the other. All of them looked restless. The ministers had been dragged to a social event for several hours, which they had rather spent meeting with contractors, arms dealers, and ship makers. The bodyguards, now reduced to three, were looking nervously about at the Chinese waiters, as though expecting an attack. There were half a dozen poisoned knives in the kitchen. All a waiter had to do was to stab someone and all political and diplomatic hell would break loose.

Barker sat, as usual, self-contained. He glanced about the room, taking everything in: the expression on Mononobe's face, the unease of the guards, Campbell-Ffinch's self-satisfied expression, and Ho glowering in the kitchen entrance.

The waiters moved about, replacing empty bottles of sake. They wore white gloves and immaculate matching jackets. To a man they presented an expressionless mask, as if they had no feelings or concerns about anything. One would not know that they were working in concert, and straining to hear every word said on one side of the room.

Things were going well, and then suddenly, they weren't. One of the waiters served new plates to the Japanese delegation and returned. His face was pale. Barker put a hand out to stop him, but he passed by, as if he hadn't seen it.

A minute later, Ho came to the doorway. His face was red, almost volcanic. Barker stood quickly and put an arm across the doorway, barring him from coming in.

"What has happened?" he asked.

"They have insulted my cooking. They said the beef and peppers were too dry."

I rose and stood beside Barker, hoping to defuse the situation before it could escalate.

"Who said it?" the Guv asked.

"One of the bodyguards!"

Barker smote him on the chest, more in bonhomie than anything else.

"Why should you care what a bodyguard thinks? They are uneducated oafs. They have no knowledge of cuisine and very little else except fighting. None of the ministers have said anything. I'm sure they found nothing to complain about."

"I shall give them something to complain of. I shall remove the poisoned fugu from the dustbin and wipe the fish with it!"

Barker still had his arm across the doorway. Ho was doing his best to move beyond it, muttering a string of Chinese oaths under his breath.

"You know, if you put the poison in the fugu, you'll cause an international incident."

"I don't care," Ho said. "My skills have been impugned. I believe I shall stop him and demand a duel."

"Come now," I said. "You don't need to fight over something as unimportant as the remark of a hireling. Why don't you bring out the fugu tray?"

Ho turned his anger my way. "As you said, why should I pay attention to something as unimportant as the remark of a hireling?" he asked.

I wasn't going to fall for that one. "Because I know your beef and peppers is sublime, the closest thing to perfection on the planet."

Ho's brow was set, but he wheeled about and went back into the kitchen.

Barker nodded. "Very good, Thomas."

"Thank you, sir."

Everything was fine again. A few minutes later Ho brought out the fugu, on a large silver salver. The flesh had been layered to look like an imperial dragon, the slivers forming scales. Salmon and a few other fish were added to give the beast color. What a beautiful engine of death it was.

"You must try some when it comes to our table, lad."

"What? You've got to be joking. I don't know their culture. I don't want to know. I'm not important to anything happening here. Why should I risk poisoning myself?"

I wasn't going to add that I was affianced, having already played that card several times.

Barker sighed, much as a headmaster over a slow student. "The embassy would be quite suspicious if you refused the dish, and Ho would be insulted again."

"Fine, sir," I said. "I apologize."

It seemed like only seconds until the tray was presented to us. Barker helped himself to a large helping. I took two slices. Then Barker put half of his on my plate. No one ever said he wasn't cunning.

I put the first piece in my mouth. The fact that I had already made a will was a small comfort. Twenty-six was not a bad age at which to die. I would look better in the coffin than most, like I had just fallen into a quiet sleep, once the look of horror had been expunged from my face.

The fugu was moist and completely tasteless. No one would eat it for its flavor. Its only allure was that one might die from it. Apparently, several did every year. Even famous people in that far-off land died, officials and Kabuki actors. In fact, the meal was only for the wealthy. The poor never saw it. It was a game of edible roulette for the pampered rich.

My death would have served the Guv right. I had been shot at, stabbed, beaten, and nearly hung. It would be ironic if I died from a sliver of fish.

Needless to say, I lived. All of us did. Nobody fell to the floor, writhing in agony. I suspected that some of us were disappointed. Nothing makes one feel as totally alive as one's neighbor keeling over dead.

That was enough excitement for one night, I told myself. Unfortunately, the evening had only begun. The waiters had been milling about in the back of the room, growing increasingly angry about the slight to Ho, his restaurant, and by association, to themselves.

Finally, one of them came to the table with another salver containing a pot of tea and some cups. He bowed several times and attempted to place the teapot on the table. Of course, the Japanese were drinking sake. They had no need for tea. In fact, bringing the tea to the table inferred that they were being drunken bores. They did not appreciate the offer.

Then the waiter attempted to insist, placing a cup by one of the bodyguards' elbows. He tried to pour the tea, but it went down the guest's arm. Of course, it was steaming hot. The fellow jumped up and tried to swing his fist at the waiter, which only brought the compatriots from the back of the silent room. For a moment, I thought the entire restaurant was about to break out in a brawl.

"Silence!" Barker growled in a booming voice.

Everyone stopped what they were doing and stared at him. He made his way to the delegates' table, then put his hand on the waiter's shoulder.

"Sir," he said gravely. "You are sacked."

The young man slunk off into the kitchen with his head down.

Barker bowed to the people at the table.

"Good sirs, I hope you won't hold this man's clumsiness against us or this restaurant. You are our honored guests and there are still courses to come. You have not had the bear paw yet, which was brought here at great expense."

Mononobe rose and bowed as well. "You must forgive our behavior, sir. These men are young and hotheaded. It was merely an unfortunate accident."

He sat. Beside him, Campbell-Ffinch looked ready to have an apoplexy. He might have a patch of gray in his hair by the morning.

Barker went into the kitchen, as composed as if he had been taking a walk in Hyde Park. I followed behind. We met a seething Ho.

"You have no right to sack one of my staff!" he shouted.

"That is correct. I am a guest here, like the embassy, and have nothing to do with the running of this establishment. I would suggest you give the young and brave fellow the rest of the night off, and possibly a bonus. I shall pay it, if you wish."

"I will pay it! As if I could not pay my own staff!"

"We shall get back to our table. I should point out that your waiters congregating in the back of the room means they aren't listening in on the conversations, which is the real purpose of this party."

Ho slapped his forehead and raked his hand down his face. Then he marched out of the kitchen.

"Come, lad," my employer said. "I hope there is still some fugu left."

CHAPTER TWENTY-FOUR

Ho kept them for as long as he could, but there is just so much food a human body can digest. Mononobe and his guards rose and bowed and made to leave. Barker offered more sake, more plum wine, and every type of sweetmeat he could conceive. It was all to no avail. They bowed and walked to the door, and then they were gone.

The waiters gathered around Ho then, and a hurried conversation took place. The restauranteur burst out into the foulest Chinese he could think of, and for once I was very glad to only know a few words of Cantonese.

"Nothing!" he bawled, falling into a chair. He was glossy with perspiration and his shirt was wringing wet. "My waiters discovered nothing. Anytime we neared the general or his men, they shut their lips tight. Even your Foreign Office friend said nothing."

Barker was not as temperamental as Ho. He looked as if he were taking the loss philosophically.

"Do you realize," Ho went on, "how much money I put into this dinner? It cost a fortune! I'm going to have to sell this restaurant and move back to China!"

I looked over at the waiters, in their black trousers and white jackets. They were completely dispirited. Most had removed their brimless cloth caps, the picture of abject failure.

"You are being melodramatic, Ho," Barker said. "You're richer than any man in Limehouse, Mr. K'ing included. Send the bill to me. I'll pay it."

Abruptly, Ho did an about-face. It was the second remark about Ho's fortune. "I can pay it. Don't think I can't. I just cannot believe I humbled myself in front of those Japanese demons for not a single fact."

"Henry!" Barker called out.

I looked across the room. In a far corner, an old man lay with his head on the table. The disreputable hat he wore did not conceal his shaggy white hair or his identity. It was Henry Cathcart. He raised his head a little at hearing his name.

"Yes, Push?" he asked.

"How was your meal?"

"Excellent, sir. I like a bit of Chinese now and again, washed down with plum wine."

"Did you hear anything of interest?"

"'Course I did, sir. I always give good service, don't I?"

"What did you hear, then?"

"The English cove with the yellow mustache was trying to convince the Japanese general not to trust Mr. K'ing," Cathcart said.

"'He'll pat you on the chest today and stab you in the back tomorrow,' he says. 'We've got the steamships to move or escort them.'

"The general, he shushed him up, 'cause the waiter was coming round behind him. They ate the food that was served. English said the food is all cabbage and catgut, but the general says it's the best he's had since he left Tokyo."

I looked at Barker. "English" had to mean Campbell-Ffinch.

Ho gave no response, having received an insult and a compliment at the same time. He merely sat and glowered.

"Continue, Mr. Cathcart," Barker prompted.

"The waiter went away with a sour look on his face. English said: 'You shouldn't trust the Chinese. Their motives are counter to yours.'

"'Agreed,' the general said. 'But then, we never planned to pay K'ing, anyway. A report to the Qing government that he is allied with the triads, at just the right moment, should settle the matter.'

"'We could get goods to you much faster,' English says.

"'Best for you if England's name never comes up,' the general says."

The Sponge stopped to pour himself a glass from a nearly empty bottle of plum wine and drank it down.

"Is that all?" Barker asked.

Cathcart belched, then shook his head. "They didn't talk for about five minutes. The waiters were bringing more food and trying hard to listen for anything said. When they gave up, the English cove spoke again.

"'We want assurances that Hong Kong and Australia are safe.'

"'Of course they are safe. We would not turn on our allies.'

"'This is all speculation, of course,' the Foreign Office toff says. 'Since you haven't convinced the emperor yet.'

"'We have the military,' the other says. 'We'll convince him one way or the other.'

"There was a toast then, which interrupted their talking for a while. When it started again, English had been thinking.

"'Why don't you go east? Give them bloody Americans a taste of their own medicine.'

"'We have considered it. Certainly, we will need the Sandwich Islands for provisions.'

"'With a steam warship you could inflict a good deal of damage upon San Francisco.'

"'With ten we could burn the entire coast. Ah, but these are dreams. Let us deal with the matter at hand.'

" 'The matter,' English says, 'is that K'ing was supposed to be here and where is he? Sucking on a pipe, I'll be bound. We English are more reliable.'

" 'But more cunning,' the general said. 'You toy with us. Where are the promised ships?'

" 'They are being built and will be ready when the shipment is ready and the deal signed,' English said. 'I'll have the maps for you within the week.'

"The general was displeased. 'Very well,' he said.

"That was all, Your Lordship."

Barker said nothing. Ho said nothing. Henry Cathcart was wrung dry, but he had come through where Ho's waiters had failed.

"Maps," Barker growled. "That's it, the final piece of the puzzle. The Japanese have very poor coastal maps. The English are famous for them, but they are not very generous in lending them to foreign governments. That is why they have not signed a deal with K'ing, at a lower price. They need the maps."

Suddenly, he smote the table, nearly reducing it to kindling. "I should have seen that! Living among the English has made me muddleheaded."

"You're English yourself," Ho said.

"I am Scottish," the Guv insisted.

"English, Scottish, you're all of a piece."

"As the Chinese and Japanese are all of a piece."

Ho crossed his burly arms and looked away. Barker was not that obvious, but he turned away, as well. Henry Cathcart cleared his throat.

"I'm sorry, Henry. Thomas, give the gentleman a tenner."

"If it's all the same to you, sir, I'll take five now and five in a week or two. Ten slips straight through the fingers."

"Good work, by the way. There is no better informer in all London."

The Sponge tipped his hat. "Always glad to oblige you honorable gentlemen. I hope to be of use to you again. Mr. Ho, good victuals, as always. What was that stuff I was eating?"

"Sukiyaki."

"Marvelous. Well, gents, mustn't leave the publicans waiting."

We watched him stagger off. Some claim Henry's abilities are God given, but I know better. With few skills to offer the workaday world, he had developed one which some would envy. No one needs an informant that cannot recall the exact words of the people he is following. The ability to do so while appearing drunk or even unconscious was worth its weight in gold.

"What sort of maps is Mononobe negotiating for? What country do you suppose he will attack first?"

"Japan," Ho stated. "He cannot do anything without the consent of his countrymen."

"What would he do? Overthrow the emperor and establish a . . . What's the word? A shogunate?"

"He's already got the backing of the important families in Japan," Barker said. "More likely he will convince the emperor to accept him as prime minister. The Meiji dynasty has lost power over the last few decades."

"What about the people?" I asked.

"They have little say, and would probably fall for speeches that claim Japan will become a world power."

"What if he succeeds? Will he threaten Britain?"

"Not yet. They would sign some kind of cordial treaty. England and Japan would divide the world between them. That is why Campbell-Ffinch was so concerned with Hong Kong and Australia, English colonies in that part of the world."

"But Japan is such a small country. How can they hope to take over China or Korea?" I asked.

"They are roughly the size of England, and they will be armed with the latest munitions."

"I hate politics," I admitted. "Why can't countries leave each other alone?"

"Envy. Jealousy," Ho stated. "Somebody wants what you have and plans to take it."

"I don't think—"

One of the Chinese waiters, the one whom Barker had sacked, burst into the room and breathlessly spoke to Ho. Immediately Ho jumped and ran toward the stairs.

"What is it?" I cried.

"The Inn of Double Happiness is on fire!"

We followed Ho up the steep staircase to the roof and ran to the edge. Off to the south against a jet-black sky, an orange glow lit up the night. Until that sight, I had not realized that Ho's tearoom and the inn were on the same side of the river, a few warrenlike streets away.

I was mesmerized by the fire. It is a common weakness to be stopped stock-still by a conflagration. We all stared in wonder, but Barker was the first to speak.

"Let us see if we can help."

To a man we followed after him, not down the stair to the tunnel, but down a metal ladder affixed to the river side of the building. There were over a dozen of us: guests, waiters, and cooks. Some, perhaps, had homes in the area. One building could kindle the whole of Limehouse.

We did not wait to collect the group on the ground. As each man reached the street, he began running toward the inn. Barker, the first on the ladder, was long gone by the time I touched the ground. I ran through an alleyway, and turned south toward Limehouse Docks, toward the blaze ahead of me.

I could see flames rising from the windows, the latter having been already blown out. However, the exterior was not yet affected. As I ran, a fire pumper pulled by a pair of big Friesians raced past, carrying a battery of volunteer firemen, all of them English. I suspected the Chinese were barred from rescuing their own district.

As the way was already made for me among the crowd, thanks to the engine, I ran into the midst of them. The firemen had jumped from their vessel, and were already gathering hoses and pumping to add pressure. Soot covered everyone who was being pulled from the casino, coughing and retching. A secondary hose was used to draw water from the Thames. It wasn't potable, but for dousing a fire, it was ideal.

Unfortunately, there was little we could do. Bucket brigades were unnecessary. But watching the blaze was not enough. We must help. I pushed my way through the crowd, but not as easily as my employer. I reached the door and we stepped inside.

The heat was searing. The large roulette table was on fire, and the curtains and wallpaper, up to the ceiling, were licked by flames. As we watched, a giant crystal chandelier crashed to the floor.

I began to gag on the heavy smoke that filled the room. It was as if I had walked into Dante's Inferno. Barker led me to a man trapped under a charred beam, but it was too late for him, poor blighter. There was a woman lying on the floor in a dress which was already smoldering. Her sightless eyes gazed at the ceiling. Her addiction to gambling had proved her undoing.

Barker waved me back. I was in danger of collapsing. His coat was suddenly caught on fire at the shoulder and I literally ripped it from his frame. There was no time or need to stamp it out. We backed out of the room, and as we stepped into the cool, delicious night air, I noticed that my employer's face was both red from the fire and blackened by smoke. I reached up and ran a finger along my cheek. It came away black.

We had suffered burns in the one minute we had stepped into the building. I dragged the Guv along to the water lapping in Limehouse Reach to a small sandbar, where we both bathed our faces in the filthy water. As far as I was concerned, we had done our duty.

The casino was past saving. Unfortunately, all of Limehouse was still a tinderbox. So was Poplar and Bethnal Green and White-chapel. An uncontrolled fire could destroy the entire East End. The first in line would be Ho's restaurant, where we had just been having a party. Fire doesn't take anything into consideration.

Cinders and soot were raining down upon our heads. The heat and fire were growing to the levels we had found inside the building. Worse, in fact, for the oxygen was aiding the flames, and there was no limit to how high they could go. The glow I had seen from the top of the tearoom was now a ball of flame thirty feet tall.

"You don't think Fu Ying is inside, do you?"

"No, she has always done her best to avoid the place."

A final second-story window shattered then and a figure clad in black leaped out of the frame, toward the river. He was aflame from his long queue to his trousers. The building sucked in air and flames, and the sound seemed to intensify. Meanwhile, the flaming man's body hit the water with a hiss and was swept along by the river. Disaster may come and go, but it could not stop the steady flow of Lady Thames.

"Mr. K'ing," Barker said.

"That was K'ing?"

"Aye."

"Is he dead, do you think?"

"Probably not. But he'll wish he were."

He suddenly raised his head.

"What is it?"

He pushed himself up off the sandbar we rested on.

"Come with me," he said.

Reluctantly, I followed. He moved through the crowd to the south and stepped into the next street. Reaching a sewer cover, he pulled it to the side and immediately began to descend.

In the sewer, we could hear the roar of the fire, but there was little or no heat. As I stepped forward I realized this was the entrance to K'ing's underground passage. As we walked, the trickle of water ended, and a few feet later one came upon carpet. The old leaden walls gave way to wallpaper, and eventually to works of art. Chinese landscapes, and works under glass, carved from cork. Finally, we came to a door.

"As expected," Barker said.

A thick metal pipe was wedged under the handle of the door. I reached for it and he quickly pulled my hand away.

"Don't touch it!" the Guv ordered. "Open that door and the flames will shoot out into the street behind us. We'd be cremated instantly."

"The fire was set deliberately," I said. "K'ing's way of egress was blocked."

"Someone endangered the lives of all the gamblers to try to kill one man."

"Who would do such a thing?" I asked.

"Oh, I could think of a name or two."

CHAPTER TWENTY-FIVE

I never thought I would say this, but I did not fully trust my employer. He kept secrets from me and I did not like it one bit. I knew he was a private man, and I also knew that he preferred not to speak about a case until he had solved it, but this was a combination of the two. For all I knew, he had already solved the case but was dragging it out for reasons of his own. I had seen him face an adversary from his past before, Sebastian Nightwine. Apparently, he was not alone. A man like the Guv attracts enemies. I don't mind that. It is part of my work. However, I would like to know who is a friend, and who an enemy.

It wasn't that I was curious. I needed to know, if only for my self-protection. Very deliberately, without anesthetic, I needed to probe the wound with a scalpel and he was not going to like it one bit.

"Sir," I said. "You were in Japan for a time, were you not?"

We were in the dining room at dinner the next evening. We had spent the entire day helping Limehouse with the tragedy. I was fortifying my courage with a glass of red wine. We were not wine bibbers in the Barker household, but it went with the braised duck confit Etienne had made. After the chef had prepared it, Mac had gone to the lumber room in the basement and unearthed a cobwebby bottle.

Barker gave me a stony look and said nothing, but I was undaunted.

"That must have been in the sixties. Were you in Honshu or Hokkaido?"

"Hokkaido. Since when did you know the name?"

"Liam Grant lent me a map. Let's see. That was the northernmost island and the hardest to get to. Why did you go there?"

Mac came in and gave me a warning look that said, "Don't do it! Don't talk about this!"

I ignored him.

"There was a war going on," Barker finally said. "The imperial forces were determined to destroy the samurai class. They were in need of supplies. I brought the *Osprey* there, and delivered supplies to the exiled samurai."

"Guns?" I asked.

"No, not guns. If anything, the war was an ideological battle between traditional samurai warfare and modern Western weapons. My cargo was tea and rice. Hokkaido is little more than a black rock, you see. There are few fields for growing much there."

"So, what happened?" I asked, helping myself to another glass of claret.

"A woman. I married her."

The wine went down the wrong pipe. I choked and then coughed a dozen times, while Barker and Mac glared at me with disapproval. I was beginning to regret having asked. However, this was the most interesting news I'd heard in ages.

"You married her?" I squeaked. "Did you reveal to everyone that you were a Scotsman?"

"No, I still wore my spectacles and maintained that I was

Chinese. Only Miyoko knew. That was my wife, Miyoko. She cut off my hair after the Japanese fashion, and taught me the language. The local samurai tolerated a Chinaman in their midst because I had not cheated them on the rice and was willing to take up arms if necessary against the imperial government and because a typhoon had decimated their numbers. I supported their cause. The emperor was trying to usher in a new age on the dead bodies of the old one."

"And did you fight?"

"Eventually. For eight months I was a simple farmer, cultivating a crop of radishes and catching fish with my young wife. I count it one of the best times of my life."

"But they came."

"Aye, they came, with their bayonet rifles and their cannons. We were a simple village of peasants and displaced samurai, still loyal to the old shogunate. The port town nearby was Goryokaku. Our village was called Nanaehama. There was a castle there that the samurais hoped to defend."

Barker stopped and took a small mouthful of wine. He had no taste for it. He appeared to be looking off, far away, perhaps as far away as a remote village in Japan. I was losing him.

"What happened then?" I asked.

He was staring at a corner of the tablecloth, but there was no telling what he was actually seeing. I was about to repeat the question when he spoke.

"They came by sea. The Imperial Army had purchased an American ironclad and had brought French advisers to show them what needed to be done in order to storm the castle. I will not call it a massacre, but the castle was shelled to pieces and whoever was left inside was shot before they could even draw a sword. Let us call it a rout. Those left alive escaped into the countryside. They were pursued by imperial soldiers in their blue modern uniforms, armed with their rifles and bayonets. The first village they came to—"

"Was Nanaehama."

"*Hai.*"

I don't think he realized he had answered in Japanese.

"We had heard the shelling of the castle nearby, of course, and tried to prepare the best we could. I had brought two rifles and a box of shells, which probably made us the best prepared family on the entire island. I had trained Miyoko to shoot. We knew the end was coming. There would be a skirmish until we ran out of ammunition, and then we would both die in a hail of bullets. They had an unlimited supply of them. We would die as all the other rebels had died. My wife would die as the daughter of a samurai. I would die as an anonymous Chinaman who had arrived at the wrong place in the midst of a war and been stubborn enough to stay in order to defend a stupid little radish patch. But I loved that woman and that stupid little radish patch." He paused for a moment. "I cannot talk about this anymore."

Abruptly, he stood and left the room, his wine nearly full and his meal half eaten. He had been too agitated to even finish his meal. I felt sad that I had caused him pain, but it was necessary that I know, and perhaps necessary that he say it. Secrets can fester if not shared.

The next I knew, I was struck on the arm. Mac stood at my elbow.

"I say—"

"Idiot! Can you not allow a man his privacy?"

"No!" I snapped. "I'm in a dangerous position, being beaten and followed and I don't even know whom I'm fighting or why. It's not merely myself I'm worried about. Mrs. Ashleigh has tasked me with the promise to look after him. I can't do that if I don't even know what's going on!"

"The Guv knows what he's about," Mac insisted.

"Does he? I've never seen him so emotional before. Normally, he prays and ponders before he acts. Now I feel as if he makes his decisions off the cuff. If he's not going to take me into his confidence, or listen to my advice, what in hell am I here for? I'm not a bloody mushroom that thrives on being kept in the dark."

It felt good to say it, even to Mac. If I didn't vent my steam, the boiler was going to explode. Mac was about to defend our employer again, but I was having none of it. I threw down my serviette and marched upstairs, the duck confit left to grow cold on the table. It was one of my favorite dishes and Etienne had slaved over the meal.

This argument had been brewing for a long time. Keep your plans secret from your enemies. Keep them even from Scotland Yard. There is no obligation there. But don't keep them secret from me. The slightest scrap of information could mean the difference between safety and having a bullet ricochet around my brainpan. I wasn't going to let that happen now. There was a woman who cared very much whether I lived or died. I had searched for her all my life, had gone through hell, and I wasn't going to give that away merely because my employer was recalcitrant.

I was inclined to pack my bags and leave him to his stewing. Take myself to a hotel and consider my next step. I was thinking for two now. Perhaps I should follow her advice and find a good, safe situation somewhere else. Her father, a rabbi, had connections in the City. I could become a banker or something. Work on the stock exchange. A nice, steady, boring position, which brought me home to dinner and her sweet face, like clockwork.

I brooded on my bed, arms and legs crossed, and considered resigning. Harm came in, slightly wagging his feather of a tail, and jumped up on the bed and settled in with a sigh. He knew we were fighting. We had tipped the balance of order and tranquility in his home and it worried him.

An hour later, I began to feel differently. Harm had long before decamped for a safer spot, and I realized that Barker needed me, even if he didn't see it. He's intelligent and a dangerous man to cross, but he is not invincible. His opinion might be different, but he cannot take on the world by himself.

Had my friend and confidant Israel Zangwill been there he would have told me I was talking out of both sides of my mouth.

I couldn't wish to remain safe for Rebecca's sake and want to take more of the brunt from Barker's shoulders.

The apology would have to come from me, I realized. Not that I was wrong, but Barker wouldn't apologize. He would brood. He'd stare into the grate for days, watching the flames flicker. He wouldn't investigate, he wouldn't talk; sometimes he wouldn't even eat.

Mac was right. I had instigated an emotional fugue. I needed to make the first move, even if it meant swallowing a good gagging lump of pride. I had started this. I had to be the one who finished it.

With a sigh that rivaled Harm's, I stood and assembled myself, pulled on my boots, straightened my tie, and ran a comb through my hair. I tugged on my waistcoat and cuffs. One must look one's best when facing the guillotine. Perhaps he would sack me. Then I wouldn't feel guilty and my problems would be solved.

Going downstairs, I encountered Mac in the hall. He was where he was supposed to be, but right then I didn't want to see his face, or I might put a fist into it and rearrange his perfect features. He crossed his arms and glared at me. No amount of disapproval on his part was going to move me. I passed through the back door.

The garden was perfect then. I wished the embassy could have seen it at that moment. Frogs croaked on the lily pads and I heard a dove in the willow tree at the far end. Barker was in the gazebo, leaning a hand against one of the posts, his head down in thought. I climbed the shallow steps and seated myself on a bench inside.

"I apologize for intruding on your story," I said.

He said nothing, not a blessed word. I had apologized, but I wasn't going to grovel. We were at an impasse. Five whole minutes went by until he finally spoke.

"Eventually they came. Miyoko filled each rifle while I shot the other. I was a better shot than she, and we didn't want to waste a single round. I had barricaded our little hut with logs, and had shot close to a score of imperials before we finally ran out of ammunition. Miyoko and I stared at the other for what we imagined was the last time.

"Then the commander of the squadron called us out. He told us to give ourselves up, that we were his prisoners.

" 'Don't trust him,' Miyoko told me.

" 'Let us get this over with,' I said.

"I stepped out the front door, facing a clearing full of men in blue uniforms with rifles pointed at me. They had trod all over that patch of radishes I'd slaved over. I was prepared to be slaughtered. I held the sword of one of my comrades in my hand. I could use it about as well as Miyoko could use one of my rifles. The colonel in charge saw the sword in my hand and drew the sword from his scabbard. He approached me, and when he was little more than ten feet away, he ground his boots into a particular spot and waited for me to attack, which I was foolish enough to do."

Barker took off his spectacles and tossed them on the bench. I had seen his eye before, but it was still hideous. A cut ran across the cornea and the skin below it was notched in a *V.*

"The colonel slashed down once. He nearly cut out my eye. I slashed with my sword, but met only air. It felt like a hot poker to the face. I screamed and walked in circles as the soldiers laughed and poked at me with their bayonet rifles. I felt rather than saw the colonel walk past me toward the house. My house, my patch, my land. My wife. I tried to follow him, but fell in a flurry of bayonets.

"Later, I woke alone. It seemed I was the last man on earth. I heard no soldiers, no shelling. Nothing. My kimono was covered in blood from a dozen wounds, but few of them were deep. I dragged myself into the house, calling my wife's name. I found her body against a wall. She had been beheaded."

I was dumbstruck. There was nothing one could say after that. I merely stared at him in the darkness, unable to speak.

"The man who killed my wife was Colonel Mononobe."

It was too much, like when a wire shorts in one of those new electric generators and one is plunged into darkness. I raised my hands to my face and rested a palm against each eye.

Barker had seen and done, had experienced things no one should ever have to endure. His bones had been broken and healed imperfectly, his tissues and tendons torn, his psyche assaulted, his sanity pushed to the brink. I was being trained to follow after him and groomed to replace him.

"What happened to you?" I asked. "How did you survive?"

"Ho arrived. He had left the harbor ahead of the gunboats and came back when they were gone. He buried Miyoko and helped me to the ship. I understand I had a fever that lasted a week, but he stitched my wounds as best he could."

"And you never returned to Japan?"

"No, never. Never, ever shall I set foot on those cursed shores."

Jacob Maccabee was right. I stood and left him to his memories and his demons.

CHAPTER TWENTY-SIX

Tower Bridge is both the newest bridge to span the Thames and the farthest east, crossing from Southwark to a spot hard by the Tower of London. It is two hundred and thirteen feet tall with two open-air walkways that span it high above the bridge itself. It's a good spot for looking over the city in the day, and for more clandestine activities at night. Pickpockets and women of ill fame ply their trade there and effectively bilk every penny from those who come to the bridge at night. No one comes there to get their pockets picked, but as for the other, that's a different story.

The next afternoon, Barker had asked me to look in my notebook for where Kito had gone to find the exotic Englishwomen. As it happened, they were at Tower Bridge.

I suspected there were too many men in London who did not take their marriage vows seriously. They go out for a pint at the corner pub and keep going east. The price for a prostitute here was more than that of nearby Whitechapel, but it was still under a shilling. Women of the Chapel, then, came here because the money was better, but they had to deal with others before them, ready to protect their patch.

"No less than five quid," a woman told us, her burly arms crossed, when Barker told her his plan. She was in her forties and life had been hard. Her hair was brassy and she was gap-toothed. She had no man to support her. Perhaps she was supporting him.

"That's steep," Barker noticed.

"They'll see," she said, nodding at the hawkish faces of other unfortunates. "And will think I work for the peelers. I'll have to pay a few sisters to show them I ain't."

"Give her a fiver, lad."

I had liberated it already and stuffed his wallet deep into my pocket, safe and sound. I handed it over and avoided her gaze as she pushed it down her cleavage.

"My beat is from this side of the bridge to that stairwell," she said. "There's a nook where the deed is done. Watch out for coppers. Their beat is down below, so they only come up here once an hour or two. It's a long walk up these stairs. So, I just go about my business, right?"

"As you say," Barker told her, as she turned and stepped aside.

"It stinks up here," I remarked. "And the wind is strong."

The wind moaned among the wires that held up the structure we stood on. For so large an edifice the walkway seemed flimsy, buffeted by the wind. Every man and woman here looked hungry. To them we were nothing but prey.

"What's this bloke I'm supposed to entice look like?" she asked.

"He wears a black suit, a bowler with the brim rolled up all around, and a very thick waxed mustache."

"And he's a Japanese?"

"Aye, he is. He is rather difficult to miss. He has already visited this area since he arrived. I'm hoping he'll pass the time here."

"Where shall you gents be?"

"At the other end of the bridge. When he comes, solicit him, get him to follow you into the darkened corner. Then come out a few moments later claiming he assaulted you. We'll raise a hue and cry and that should be enough to get him arrested. You may choose to back out if you wish. There is no shame in it."

"I said I'd go through with it, didn't I? I'll give you your money's worth. I don't go back on a deal."

"Very well. The choice is yours. Is there anything else you require?"

"No. All right, then. Wish me luck, gents."

We left her and walked to the other end of the bridge. Once there, we rested our elbows on the railing and looked over the side. The Thames lay like an enormous black dragon asleep on top of the city. The breeze whistled through the railing while clouds scudded low over our heads. I felt a bit light-headed. A hundred and forty feet is still fourteen stories high. I gripped the railing rather tightly.

"We don't know for certain he will appear."

"We don't," Barker agreed. He stepped into the alcove nearby and somehow managed to light his pipe. The wind shredded the plume of smoke about his head and carried if off. Indifferently, the meerschaum merely produced more.

"You think he'll come?"

"He seems to be guided by his baser instincts. As I recall, Japan is not a country where unsavory women are tolerated. Another point in Tokyo's favor, I think. I believe Mr. Kito's world is very circumspect, consisting of the embassy, wherever the general sends him, possibly the Inn of Double Happiness, and this place. I assume a cabman upon enquiry sent him here."

"Not the kind of enquiry work we do," I said.

"Most certainly not."

"Yet here we are."

He puffed. "We are after a murderer. Did you expect to find him in chapel?"

"Good point."

"Are things moving forward with Mrs. Cowan?" Barker asked suddenly.

"Glacially, but intractably," I said. "Her mother is dead set against me, and Rabbi Mocatta merely wants peace in the family, but Rebecca feels we can wear them down."

"Mmmm," he said.

I'd never considered my employer's opinion of my marrying. It would be a nuisance to him, I suspected. I might not live nearby, I would not be on call twenty-four hours a day, and Barker's opinion would always be the second one I considered. If he tossed me out, there went all my plans. A family could indeed interfere if a daughter was about to marry a young man with no occupation or prospects.

"There he is."

I stopped contemplating my future or lack thereof, and watched as the Japanese figure of Mr. Kito strolled by. It was as if he were a strip of steel and the woman a magnet. He was drawn straight to her. He raised his hat and spoke to her, though of course we could not hear him. He even bowed once. She simpered. He took her arm and led her to one of the alcoves where they could have privacy.

Someone should stop them, I told myself. She'll go too far.

Barker's hand came down on my shoulder. "Wait for it," he said.

We waited. Ten seconds, twenty. Thirty. My nerves were raw. Suddenly, she screamed. We began to run toward the alcove. The woman came running out of the darkness into the light provided by a few gaslights. Her dress had been rent, and as she ran, she tried to hold the tattered remnants of it over her bare flesh.

Then Kito came out of the pool of darkness with a face like thunder, pursuing what he supposed he had purchased with a shilling. The man was fast, I'll give him that, lithe and athletic. He was much faster than a woman hobbled by a long skirt, attempting to cover herself, and crying for help.

We wouldn't reach her before he caught up with her, I realized. We were too far away, and as I said, he was devilishly fast. Then suddenly, he stopped and backed off. For a moment, I wondered what had stopped him, until I heard a police whistle behind me.

"What's going on here?" a loud voice demanded.

I turned my head and saw a welcome sight: a good, solid police constable with side whiskers and a mustache, the very image of one of the Met's finest. I felt reassured. This was in hand once again. We would explain our role in this and Kito would be detained, possibly in connection with the death of the ambassador.

Then a bright red blotch appeared dead center in the constable's forehead. He gave a startled look, just as the sound of the report reached my ears. The man fell back. He toppled, not like a man collapsing, but like a bureau tipping over full length. Kito had shot him, had shot a police constable in the pursuit of his duties. I'd never imagined that such a thing was possible.

By then the unfortunate had reached us, practically bowling into us. Barker had removed his long coat, and threw it around her shoulders. Then he stood between her and Mr. Kito, who still held a pistol in his hand. The woman seized my arm, and I could feel that she was trembling.

The Guv stood and regarded Kito, and Kito regarded him back. Obviously he recognized us. Perhaps he had already worked out that we had set a trap for him. He was debating whether shooting Barker, or indeed, all of us, would enable him to escape. He hesitated, which was all the time Barker required to pull a pistol from his pocket.

Everything seemed to slow down for a moment. Kito was holding out his pistol in our general direction. My employer was raising his arm in response. The streetwalker had her arms around me now, clearly frightened. Then from nowhere and everywhere came a second report.

Cyrus Barker had not had time to raise his British-made Colt revolver to the proper height, and anyway, the shot did not sound as if it had come from a pistol. It spun Kito around and threw him against the rail of the bridge. For a moment I feared he would fall, but he steadied himself, and fell to his knees. His shirt was slick with claret-colored blood.

Confidently, Barker walked toward him, presuming that who-ever shot Kito must be an ally, and would not shoot him. He was nearing the spot where Kito crouched, and I thought it was over. But at what cost? One of London's finest had paid the ultimate price for his service. The Met had lost what I assumed was an ex-emplary officer.

In fact, it was not over at all. When Barker was no more than five feet away, Kito sprang up and tried to dive over the side of the bridge.

A bystander reached over the side and caught him by the boot. His arm was already straining, but he was a burly fellow. He swung Kito out a foot or two and brought him back again, so that the bodyguard's head thumped against the side of the bridge.

"Some help here would be appreciated!" Inspector Dunn called.

Barker was the first to reach him, and they pulled the limp form back over the railing.

"You cut it rather fine," the Guv said to him.

"Oi!" the woman beside me cried and clutched the fragments of her clothing. "I didn't ask for this! Nobody said he'd be like this!"

"Give her another fiver, lad."

"I think a trip to Scotland Yard is in order," Dunn said.

"Not another one!" I complained.

"Perhaps a change of venue is in order," Barker said. "I sug-gest The Grapes for a pint of stout, at my expense. If you agree, I shall tell you everything I know, as I promised Detective Chief Inspector Poole I would."

Dunn looked at him as if wondering whether he could trust us. It was a consideration.

"Done," he said.

True to his word, Barker told him everything. Well, within reason.

CHAPTER TWENTY-SEVEN

I didn't want to go to work the next day. I hadn't had enough sleep since the Japanese embassy case had begun. I vaguely remember dreaming an assassin was chasing me about the house, lopping off parts of me as I ran. That morning I felt deflated and irritable. However, I was not actually ill, so I had no excuse for staying home, and anyway, he would say the only cure for whatever ailed me was going to work. One couldn't argue with that.

Despite a bout of nausea, I drank two stout cups of coffee, which was enough to wake up a bull elephant. Our chef, Dummolard, likes his coffee strong. He was peevish that I refused his eggs. Chances were even that he would sulk for a week.

Going out into the garden, I found it drowsy with the summer heat. Dragonflies hummed over our pond, avoiding the frogs on the lily pads. The small windmill, which looked out of place in the garden, pumped water up from an underground stream.

Cyrus Barker was seated on the floor in the center of his gazebo. His limbs were crossed, his shoes beside him, and his hands rested in his lap. I couldn't tell if he was meditating or merely thinking. Harm lay beside him, drowsing in the sunlight that came through the low slats. I didn't want to disturb him, but my mere presence was enough. He gave a sigh and stood, pushing down on the sides of his feet until he was upright.

"Good morning, Thomas."

"Sir."

"Are you ready for work?"

"As you see."

"Come then," he said.

Between the Metropolitan Tabernacle and the Elephant and Castle public house, we found a hansom cab and climbed aboard. The ride did not settle my stomach.

"Did you sleep well, sir?"

"Why do you ask?"

"You look deep in thought this morning," I said.

"There is much to think about."

He leaned back in our cab and crossed his arms, which always halves the space inside the cab, pinning me to the side window. It was a sacrifice I was willing to make if he was able to work out who had killed the ambassador soon.

"I certainly would not call this mission a success, from their point of view," he said.

"Could the killer possibly be Lord Diosy? It is his house, after all."

"What possible motive could he have, lad?"

"I don't know. Perhaps the bodyguards were pinching the soap from the water closets."

His mustache curled, almost into a smile. "You do talk rot, sometimes."

We reached Whitehall and were soon ensconced in our offices. Barker put his feet up on the corner of his desk facing the bow window and stared for half an hour without moving. As for me,

I began taking notes on everything that had transpired, along with a timeline of events.

This all reflected badly on Her Majesty's government, which in a way reflected poorly on all of us as British citizens. These were guests in our country and they were dropping like skittle pins. The gentle ambassador, a treasure to his country, lay cold and dead, packed in ice, ready to be sent back home. Diplomatic bodyguards were dying one by one. From whom were they protecting the delegation? What secret was worth dying for? The Guv and I were both deep in thought when Trelawney Campbell-Ffinch entered our chambers.

There were circles under his eyes, and he looked even worse than I felt. He came in without a word and fell into one of our visitor's chairs. He lit a cigarette with a shaky hand. As he puffed, he raised his right hand and pressed his palm against one eye. None of us moved a muscle for at least a minute.

"It's quiet in here," he noted.

Barker nodded.

"This entire embassy business is unraveling."

"Then find one end, and follow the thread to the other."

"That's easier said than done. Simla."

"I beg your pardon?"

"I have been threatened by my superior, that if I don't stop these murders, I am to be stationed in Simla. It's burning hot in Simla in the summer."

Barker shook his head. "Simla is up in the Himalayan foothills. It's where the English go to escape the heat."

"Well, anyway, I don't want to go. I like it here in London. I've worked hard to stay here, developing contacts and informants."

"Forgive us for not sympathizing," I said. "I suppose being socked in the eye will do that for you."

"You've run face-first into a brick wall, and now you want to compare notes," Barker rumbled.

Campbell-Ffinch tapped his cigarette ash into the ashtray at his elbow. "Something like that."

Barker turned his head toward me, while still perching his feet on the coaster.

"What were you doing for the past half hour, Thomas?"

"Setting down the events of the day and night in question, in order. A timeline."

"Read it to us," he said.

"The times are approximate, of course.

>*"August 17th. Eight o'clock A.M.: The delegation arrives at our house.*
>*"Nine o'clock A.M.: They return to the temporary agency.*
>*"Seven forty-five P.M.: A meeting occurs at the embassy.*
>*"Eight P.M.: The ambassador is shot.*
>*"Eight-thirty P.M.: Mr. Barker is arrested outside the embassy and taken away.*
>*"Eleven P.M.: I visit the embassy and am also arrested.*
>*"Midnight: I'm escorted to see DCI Poole in Scotland Yard.*
>*"Following day: Go to Penge, a crime in itself."*

"I was born in Penge," Campbell-Ffinch said.

"You have my sympathies."

>*"Next, our solicitor and I help to release Mr. Barker."*

"Allowed him to escape, you mean."

"That's it, Ffinchy old boy. Jolly us up and see where it takes you."

>*"Ten A.M.: General Mononobe comes to our offices and asks us to find the ambassador's killer.*
>*"We are given access to the mansion. The occupants are as follows:*
>*"Lord Diosy, owner of the house and liaison to the government.*
>*"General Mononobe, the military ambassador.*
>*"Admiral Edami, the naval ambassador.*

"Mr. Akita, the trade minister.

"And finally, *Mr. Tatsuya, the arts minister."*

"That ponce!" Campbell-Ffinch spat out with a puff of smoke. "He should study less art and more warfare."

"And be more like you," I said.

"Exactly."

I decided not to waste any more sarcasm on him. He wasn't worth the effort.

"What about the servants?" he asked. "And the bodyguards, Ohara, Kito, Mitsuo, and two others, whatever their names are."

Leave it to the Foreign Office to arrest some poor footman just to show they were doing something and let the courts decide if he is innocent. Of course, any footman who has been in a trial would never be rehired, nor would he be employed elsewhere. For the rest of his life, the cloud of suspicion would encircle his head.

"I assume you questioned them," my employer said.

"Apparently, all the servants had been with His Lordship for years and, of course, had no connection to any Japanese person."

"How fares your investigation?" Barker asked.

"Were still searching for that bodyguard, Ohara. Oh, and I should mention Inspector Dunn and his constables. They were in possession of the premises when I arrived. They're not on your list."

"You're suspecting Scotland Yard now?" I asked.

Barker turned to Campbell-Ffinch, which required that he put his boots on the floor again.

"What is your opinion of Dunn?"

"Not the brightest candle in the box. A good follower, but some were surprised when he achieved inspector. He's dogged, I'll give him that. What did you do next?"

"We questioned everybody," the Guv said.

"So did we. What do you think of Mononobe?"

"Military. Tough old bird. But he was downstairs in a meeting when the shots were fired. All of them were."

"No, one of them complained about the food and went upstairs early," Campbell-Ffinch said.

"We were told all were there. Which one left early?"

"The trade fellow. What's his name?"

"Akita. I put in. Did you question him?"

"I did," Campbell-Ffinch said. "He's been purchasing a great deal of supplies. Cotton, wood, coal, tar, rope. Enough to fill several ships, I should think."

"Interesting. And the admiral?"

"He's having a ship built. Steamship. Well, battleship, actually. And the general has been ordering artillery and munitions."

"What about the minister of arts?" Barker asked.

"We suspect he is only there to make the mission seem innocuous. He may not even know what is going on."

"I know what is going on: conquest and colonization, of course. The Japanese have been a downtrodden country for too long. Now, either the imperial government itself or a contingent of it is preparing for war. The people want a show of strength. And the English government, by which I mean you yourself, are in it up to your ears."

Campbell-Ffinch rose and put his hands on his hips.

"I've tricked you, Barker. I've got you to admit you're suspicious of our actions."

"You haven't tricked me at all, Trelawney. I know you do the Foreign Office's unsavory work. As soon as I saw you in my garden, I suspected something dangerous was going to occur. But, really. Allowing a national treasure to be slain over a treaty!"

"The treaty will be extremely lucrative to Her Majesty's government."

"No doubt. And thousands will die. Perhaps millions."

"We'll be there as advisers. We shall try to avoid bloodshed whenever possible."

"Oh, that's good," I put in. "There will be less rape and murder. You can't know how relieved I am."

"Spare me the sanctimonious attitude, Llewelyn, you gutter rat.

First of all, I freely admit that your suspicions are coming to pass, but there's nothing you can do to stop it. Barker, now that it is confirmed and not mere suspicion, I'm afraid you are sworn to silence. It is a government secret. You are bound to respect that. Is that clear? Breathe one word and you'll go to prison as a traitor. I don't mean jail. I mean prison. That is, until they strain your neck. We don't like traitors in this country."

Barker frowned. I wondered if he had really been manipulated by a man like Campbell-Ffinch. It was insupportable.

"Do I have your word as a gentleman, Mr. Barker? I know you consider yourself such, though I cannot imagine why. Do I have your word that you will not breathe a word to another soul? This is your government speaking."

The Guv put his hands on the desk, thinking furiously. Finally he gave out a bushel of air in a long sigh.

"You have it, sir. I promise not to breathe a word."

"Thank you," Campbell-Ffinch said. "I actually didn't want to arrest you, but I could not have you revealing state secrets. I respect you, sir, at least in the ring."

Barker did not answer. If the Foreign Office man was expecting a similar confession, he was in for a wait.

"And you, Mr. Llewelyn. Do you swear as a . . . Wait! You're not a gentleman, are you? Nothing like, in fact. You'd best button your lip if you know what's good for you."

"Oh, yes, sir. Thankee, sir. You are too kind."

Campbell-Ffinch came over to my chair and leaned over me. "Your cheekiness is going to get you hanged one of these days. And I'm going to have a front row seat to it."

I let him crow. He was having his day and I was sick of it. Muzzled. That's what we were. Sworn to secrecy by Her Majesty's government.

"Oh, don't take it so hard," Campbell-Ffinch said, crossing to the bay window and looking out into our narrow court. "Your hands are tied. I let you in on what is happening. We'd have left you out of it if it weren't for your blasted garden. You would have the one Asian garden that Kew approved of. I knew you'd kick up a fuss."

"We were hired. By the general, no less."

"Yes, it was his idea. It seemed a good way to keep you occupied for a few days."

"And what about the bodyguards?" Barker asked.

"They all worked for the general. Except for the fat one. He was loyal to the old man, and took his death very seriously. He seems to have left, possibly on a boat to Japan to unburden himself about what's going on here. Of course, he'll be too late by then."

He turned around and faced us, hands on his hips.

"You were surprisingly easy to manipulate, Barker. I thought you were supposed to be so clever, both in the boxing ring and out. I'd still like to take you on in the ring someday. I hope for your sake you're more clever there than—"

The glass of the bow window on either side of him shattered. It stained his collar and he fell into a heap on the carpet. We both stared at him, nonplussed.

Carefully, Barker crouched and moved over to the window. He put a hand to Campbell-Ffinch's throat. As he did so, I glanced at the window and saw that a bullet had shattered the first pane and exited on the other side.

"He'll live," my employer pronounced. "It creased the back of his head. Chipped his skull, I'll be bound. He'll have a headache for a while."

Barker peered over the window frame for perhaps a minute. Then he stood up as if daring the killer to shoot him. Finally, he went to the telephone, and gave the operator a number on the same exchange as ours.

"Hello, Terry. I think you had better come over here. Campbell-Ffinch has been shot."

CHAPTER TWENTY-EIGHT

Poole appeared, we were questioned, and Campbell-Ffinch, good riddance, was taken away to Charing Cross Hospital in an ambulance vehicle supplied by St. John's Priory. I noticed Barker was not forthcoming to Poole the way he was to Dunn the night before. Then it came to me. He'd made a blasted vow to Campbell-Ffinch not to talk and he would honor it.

When Poole left, dissatisfied, and the glazier was repairing the window, I turned to Barker.

"You didn't tell him."

"No. I told Dunn. That should be enough."

"Whoever shot Campbell-Ffinch must have shot Kito as well. That must make him K'ing's man."

"Yes. I suspect that burly fellow at the inn who barred our way. Jeremy!" he called to our clerk. "You are on call tonight."

"Yes, sir, Mr. B.," Jenkins said to him, trying not to look crestfallen. He was much revered at the Rising Sun public house down the street and he looked forward to his ale all day.

"No more than two pints, then home."

Our clerk's mood improved. He seized his hat and stepped out before our employer changed his mind.

"Anything for me, sir?" I asked.

"Quite a lot, actually. How would you like to exercise your literary talents?"

"I'd like that very much."

"I'm going to gather together a series of facts and I'd like you to turn them into an article such as might appear in a newspaper."

"I can do that."

"We've got about half an hour."

"Half an hour! How long is this article supposed to be?"

"No more than two columns."

"Two columns!"

"Are you going to continue to repeat yourself?"

"Two columns," I said. "Half an hour. Go to it, sir. The topic?"

"How the Japanese are purchasing British warships and munitions to foment war in the East, and how the British government is colluding with them."

"Ah! And who is going to publish this little story?"

"Someone who owes me a favor."

It took me a moment to add two and two.

"Stead," I said.

William T. Stead was editor of the *Pall Mall Gazette*. We had once stopped a mob from burning his offices after he purchased a child and delivered her to the coast, merely to prove how easily it could be done. The *Gazette* and its editor were innovators, using photographs in its pages, for example. They also had a reputation for daring journalism.

"Do we have enough facts to glue it all together?" I asked.

"Just enough. I pray just enough. No more questions. We have work to do."

We worked, but it took more than half an hour. Without speaking, we both were concerned that Stead might be done for the day, or out to dinner. It was near six when we finished and closer to half past when we arrived in Fleet Street, due to traffic. We could almost have arrived faster on a run.

We were in luck. Stead was still there, his omnipresent cigar between his teeth. I've always wondered if there were any editors who didn't smoke, or didn't have a bottle of Scotch secreted in their desks.

"Mr. Barker," the grizzled veteran said to him as we entered his office. "To what do I owe this honor?"

"I have some information which may be of interest to you and your readers."

"I'm always glad to help the British public. Come in and have a seat."

This was better treatment than I expected. Possibly better than we deserved. My story was a tissue of facts, inferences, and innuendos. It was also damning, not only to Mononobe, in particular, but also to the Foreign Office.

"I have stated the facts such as they are, and Mr. Llewelyn has cast them in the form of what might appear in a newspaper. Of course, I am not implying that you should use it as is or give him a byline. We were merely attempting to give the facts some cohesion."

"Understood," Stead said. "Let me read."

Stead was fiftyish, his beard shot with gray, and his stomach showing a habit of too many cutlets and not enough exercise. He was a liberal Democrat, bordering upon socialism, and always looking for a downtrodden group or government scandal to feature in the pages of his *Gazette*. His politics were exactly the opposite of Barker's. I prefer not to discuss my own, which tended toward the former.

He began to read aloud.

"*Sources within the British government have confirmed that the ministers of the newly arrived Japanese delegation have been purchasing goods at an alarming rate. Those include not only base materials such as wood and food, but battleships and artillery for the country's military. General Mononobe, current head of the delegation after the recent death of the original ambassador, Toda Ichigo, has assured the government that any munitions purchased are strictly for defense of the small string of islands, and yet an original order for a single battleship has been augmented to several, which sources have suggested is too many for merely defensive purposes.*

"'General Mononobe and Admiral Edami have proven war records and a desire to see Japan join their neighbors to the west in colonization, but where and how much is in question. Equally uncertain is why the delegation is here in England at this critical time, and what arrangements might be agreed upon by the two countries. Foreign Office liaison Trelawney Campbell-Ffinch has not been available for comment.

"'Should Japan wish to join the nations which are considered world powers, it would cause concern among Her Majesty's allies in Europe, who have not been included in the negotiations. Whispers of a secret treaty have affected the stock exchange and raise questions in both Houses of Parliament. Whether the sources are correct has not been fully verified, but the possibility of an Asian armada armed with so many English weapons has caused concern in all quarters of government. Hong Kong, Canton, and Macao, with so many English residents, might be at risk from Japanese saber rattling, but so far no firm confirmation of precisely which countries or colonies the imperial government might consider necessary to acquire in the name of Japanese safety have been revealed.'"

"Did you write this?" he asked me.

"I did."

"It's good." He turned and looked at my employer. "How much of this is substantiated?"

"Most of it," Barker said. "Well, some of it."

"Would the army or navy admit to arms sales?"

"Probably not, but the admiral and general were both seen attending demonstrations of this country's latest weaponry. What purpose would it serve if not to promote sales of those very products?"

"Is there any proof that the Japanese government would use

these weapons against local countries with whom they are in contention?"

"Not the government," Barker corrected. "A coalition of powerful families who hope to force the government toward militarism."

"How do I know this information is reliable? On whose testimony have you built this theory?"

"On that of the late ambassador's bodyguard, who is a member of the Kempeitai, the Japanese secret service."

"I would need proof that he exists."

Barker reached into his pocket and retrieved a folded letter. He opened it and passed it to Stead. I saw a Japanese signature at the bottom, though the letter was written in English.

"Damning enough," Stead admitted. "But I would need to speak with him directly. What's his name?"

"Ohara," I said.

"And when would this article need to appear?"

"Tomorrow morning."

Stead tossed the letter with finality.

"Impossible," he said. "We're going to press within an hour. We're just finishing setting type. This article needs to be substantiated."

"You've gone to press with less."

"Indeed I have," Stead said. "Many times. But not with an indictment against the government."

"Ah," Barker said. "But I have not stated that the government is culpable. The army or navy can sell battleships to an ambassador with impunity. Rather, it is the ambassador, knowing they are meant for a third party and not the Meiji government, who bears the blame."

"You're trying to stop him."

"Desperately."

"You can't. Not with this, by tomorrow morning. The information must be vetted if I am going to face scrutiny by Her Majesty's government. A bee can sting, but he can also be stepped on."

"Very well," Barker said, folding the letter and putting it back in his pocket. "I would like to call in a favor."

"I knew it would come eventually. What is it?"

"I'd like to make use of your press tonight for about half an hour."

"That's hard. What do you need it for?"

"To make a false newspaper front page with a limited run."

"How limited?" Stead asked, lighting a fresh cigar, and tossing the spent vesta in an ashtray full of them.

"No more than thirty or so. Enough to catch the embassy and the Foreign Office unawares."

Stead shook his hand in the air, fanning himself. "That's hot. I could get into a lot of trouble."

"Why? Suppose your hardworking staff stepped out at eleven P.M., before the pubs closed, leaving the equipment unattended, for half a pint of bitters."

Stead whistled.

"That's an awfully big favor. But then from you I would expect nothing less. Won't you need typesetters and inkers?"

"I've got a crew of my own."

"I just bet you do," the newspaper editor said. "The Swell Mob."

"So what is your answer?"

Stead closed his eyes and considered long and hard. If there was any way for him to get out of it.

"Very well, but I want this done right. My boys will leave at eleven, shut and lock the door, and come back one hour later. You can print what you like within that hour, as long as it's not about the royal family. Am I clear?"

"As crystal."

"I may need an alienist. Or a solicitor. Or a one-way ticket to France by tomorrow morning. We're square after this, Barker. No more favors."

"Done."

"It might have been better to let this place burn to the ground."

We let him have the last word on the subject.

Outside in the street, we walked until we came to The Old Bell tavern and finally had dinner. However, that was not the only reason for our being there. After our meal, Barker got up and walked to the bar to speak to the publican.

"Sir," he said. "I should like to have this room for a private party."

"I believe we can accommodate you, sir. When would you like to borrow our rooms?"

"Eleven o'clock will do."

"Eleven . . . You mean tonight?"

"There is no time like the present. I believe that is the phrase."

"Will there be alcohol consumed?"

"Well, I should say, or I would have rented a temperance society hall or a family hotel."

"That is after hours, sir. Drinking hours are until eleven, not a moment later."

"That is why I requested a private party, my good man."

"What am I to do with my customers?"

Barker paused and nodded. "I suppose you could tell them to leave. After all, they are no longer bringing in custom."

The meaty-faced publican scowled at my employer. "And for what should I tell my best and most loyal customers to leave?"

"For twenty-five pounds, I should imagine."

The man's busy eyebrows came within an inch of his hairline. He was calculating. A glass of bitters was sixpence. Even illegally, he'd probably make no more than a pound that hour. This was twenty-five times that.

"I'll tell you what," Barker added. "Any one of your regulars wishing to stay after eleven can have drinks on me, provided they only leave through the back way. I would make certain you have plenty of beverages on hand. My guests will be printers and newspapermen, a thirsty lot."

The publican's demeanor changed as I set down the twenty-five pounds on his well-worn bar. He lifted the flap, came around the bar and shook Barker's hand. He promised to have some nuts and sweetmeats on hand, and to go round everything with a rag. New sawdust would be lain down, and a piano player brought in. Would the gentleman have any other stipulations?

"No. I shall not be attending. Expect the men to be here shortly after eleven."

We left the pub. The Guv rubbed his hands together in satisfaction.

"What next?" I asked.

"I'll go to the offices and call Mac. He'll meet us there at ten-thirty. You go to the Rising Sun and tell Jeremy the same. Wait, on second thought, tell the barmaid. She'll keep better time than he."

"I fear this will be a long night," I said.

"Aye," he growled. "And a long morning shall follow it."

CHAPTER TWENTY-NINE

We arrived at the Rising Sun that evening shortly after eleven o'clock. We had hired a brougham, which would seat the four of us, Mac included. We used the back entrance to the courtyard in Great Scotland Yard Street, and pulled up to the old public house.

Barker and I looked at each other, thinking the same thought: what if Jeremy Jenkins had not kept to his promise and was now unconscious on one of the tables? He loved his pint, not to mention four or five of its brethren. We tended to speak in low tones the first hour of the day, due to the fact that he was often the worse for the night before. It would have been wiser to have warned him off the Sun entirely for the night, but Barker did not have the heart. I opened the brougham door and stepped down while Barker and Mac waited. If I needed them I would return.

Our clerk is a tall, thin fellow, with a hawkish nose and pomaded hair with a widow's peak. He has a thick Cockney accent. He used to live with his father, but the senior Jenkins had passed away a couple of years before. The old man had been an infamous engraver and forger, who had passed on his skills to his son. I presumed Jenkins still lived in the same house on the Lambeth side, but we didn't trade confidences. Our clerk is very self-contained.

I walked in and looked about. Jenkins was nowhere to be found. Circling the tables, I finally found him in a corner with his jacket off and his sleeves rolled up. A mostly empty pint glass was on the well-worn table in front of him.

"What number is that?" I asked, indicating the glass.

"My second. And it wasn't easy. I promise you, Mr. L. I had to order Liddy the barmaid not to give me a third, no matter how much I pleaded."

"Are you ready?" I asked.

"Willing and anxious. I need to see what sort of equipment they have at the *Gazette*."

"I'll help you set the type, if you like, Jeremy."

"Set type? This isn't the Middle Ages. They must have a linotype machine, if they expect to stay current with the other London newspapers. Set type, indeed."

"Sorry," I said, shrugging. "I had no idea."

"It will take all four of us to work the rotary press, however. You'll have to keep your wits about you, since you have to climb up onto the machine. There are very sharp blades to cut the paper."

"That's good to know. I can hardly wait."

We climbed into the brougham and passed down Whitehall Street, headed north. Fleet Street was at the north end of Charing Cross, which begins almost exactly at Craig's Court.

"How are you, Jeremy?"

"Never better, sir. Eager to get to work." He paused and nodded at Mac, who had been sitting silently in the cab. "Mr. Maccabee."

"Mr. Jenkins."

Jenkins and Mac parsed Barker's day between them. Jeremy had him for roughly eleven hours and Mac closer to thirteen. Each of them helped him as best they could. Mac made a good show of being serious, even earnest, but Jenkins was completely nonchalant. I didn't believe either of them. It was a great responsibility to be a clerk in Whitehall Street and many wanted the position. He might show up hungover, and move slowly at first, but everything that needed to be done was done by five o'clock. Barker never need worry on that score.

Mac desperately wanted to be an enquiry agent. He reveled in situations outside of Barker's home where his services were needed. He thought he needed to impress the Guv with his pluck. Of the three of us, I was the only one whom Barker had not originally helped out of jail. I'd been out a few months when I was hired. I was about to take a long walk over Waterloo Bridge. Barker had rehabilitated all of us, and we were grateful for all he had done.

We came to a stop near the entrance to the *Gazette* and waited. About five minutes later a number of men came out of the alleyway looking rather confused.

"Gentlemen!" I called out. "It just so happens that there is a private party at The Old Bell. All of you are invited!"

The men broke into grins and lifted their cloth caps. There is a certain warm glow which accompanies the words "the drinks are on the house." I noticed no one dawdled. We had the place all to ourselves. I walked up to the back door and grasped the handle.

"It's locked," I said, shocked.

"Of course," Barker purred. "They took every precaution. And yet somehow, we broke in."

He took the skeleton key from his pocket and jiggled it about in the lock for a moment. Like the rest of us, it soon gave up and let the Guv have his way.

"Will Stead get in trouble for this?" I asked.

"Probably, but I happen to know he is starting a new business venture with *The Strand Magazine*. This merely provides him the opportunity to resign."

"How did you know that?"

"I read the newspapers. All of them."

The door opened and we stepped inside. Mac loitered in the alleyway a moment or two to make sure a constable was not wandering the area. Meanwhile, Jenkins hurried to the printing room.

"Marvelous!" he said. "A new linotype and a rotary printer. We'll be in and out in half an hour. Have you got the article to print?"

I pulled it from my pocket and gave it to him. He perused it with a professional's eye.

"I see the rest of the articles are here. Ours should take two columns. The rest we'll take from the planned first page, as well as the entire back of it."

"How does this linotype thing work?" I asked.

"There is a keyboard here, similar to your typewriting machine. I press the key and it lays a letter down, and when it is all typeset, a thin slurry of hot lead goes down, making a solid sheet. After it's done printing, the sheet can be broken up and used again."

"That's ingenious," I said.

"Here, I'll show you."

Despite being reformed, Jeremy seemed to have a strong grasp on the latest inventions in the printing world. He stood at the linotype and began pressing letters into the machine. I am not a mechanical person. If given a watch in pieces I couldn't put it back together if given the whole of time. I had written the letter and Barker liked it. So far as I was concerned, I had already contributed and that was good enough for me.

Within fifteen minutes the front page had been finished, and to be sure, he recopied the back of the page as well.

"They misspelled two words," he said, scandalized.

Once the printing plate had been completed, we carried it over and set it on the machine. He inspected the ink volume and primed the paper, and at his word, the three of us removed our jackets and climbed aboard the huge printer.

"You're to see that the paper doesn't jam, and that the cutter is working properly. It should not take long," he said. "We are only printing fifty copies."

Had it been run on steam I'd have known what I was about, but these modern dynamos flabbergasted me. With a touch of a switch, paper spun by my face and was sliced neatly in two by the cutter, which was inches away. Were I to reach in and touch something, I'd find myself missing a hand.

Barker looked on approvingly while Mac tried to look as if he ran a rotary printer every day. Before I knew it, we were done.

"That's it?" I asked.

"That's it, Mr. L," Jenkins said, and brought over a single large sheet of newsprint, still warm and drying, with my article in print.

"Good work, Jeremy," I said. "My first appearance in print and I didn't get a byline."

"You'll be the envy of your friends," Jenkins said.

Mac looked a little green.

"And back in prison as soon as you can say 'knife' if we're caught," he stated.

"Let's try not to be caught, then," Barker said.

Our next duty was to strip the front page from fifty copies of the *Gazette*. It was the work of only a few minutes. Soon we had a stack of finished newspapers in front of us.

"Mr. Maccabee," Jeremy said.

"Yes, Mr. Jenkins?"

"I've been there when the newspapers are delivered at the Home and Foreign Offices. As I recall, they are bundled in string. First one way, and then the other. Here is the string, but I'm hopeless at wrapping. Would you do the honors?"

"Of course."

Mac soon had the bundle sufficiently tied. He was a bit sulky about it, though. He had hoped to shine, but instead Jenkins had supplied the luminescence.

Armed with the bundle and an armload of other copies, we left the building. Barker inserted his key and locked the door soundly. Mac went out first to see if a constable was coming along on his appointed rounds. We strolled out into Fleet Street while in the distance, Big Ben tolled midnight.

Ten minutes later we were in The Old Bell. The newspaper workers were enjoying themselves, possibly too much.

A man spoke up from a table nearby. It was Henry Cathcart himself, presenting his bloodshot eyes to me.

"So what's all this about, then?" he asked in a voice different from his own.

"Dunno any more than you," he continued in a second voice. "Alls I know is free beer and try not to drink so much that you can't do your job ar'terwords."

He shook his head. "And nobody thought to invite me."

"Sorry, Henry," I said. "I don't know what we were thinking."

He ran a hand down his snowy beard.

"Evening, Young-fella-me-lad. Some doings, eh?"

"Indeed!"

As usual, the Sponge knew where free alcohol was available in London Town. He sucked down a glass of pink gin neat.

Mac and Barker returned from the bar with pints of Whitbread's finest. The foam was frothing over the sides. When the four of us were seated, I nudged Barker with my elbow. He looked over at me. I, in turn, looked at Mac. He was looking very down in the mouth and sipping at his beer. Beer is never meant to be sipped.

"Mac," the Guv said, "that was superior work, as always. Thank you for lending a hand."

Our butler suddenly took on a warm glow.

"Oh, I didn't do much. Thank you all the same. Very good work, Mr. Jenkins."

"Thank you, Mr. M."

Mac frowned. He didn't mind others being called by our last initial, but he drew a line at himself.

Having been deprived of nourishment for most of a night, Jenkins made short work of his pint and went back for another. Meanwhile, Barker took gulps of his pint in measured increments. Years before he'd been a sea captain and was known to put down several bottles of grog at a seating. Now a reformed Baptist, and a good deacon, he imbibed rarely and in moderation. So, too, did Mac, always hoping to impress his employer, usually at my expense. It was all too exhausting. I enjoyed my pint, though I didn't have another.

"What do we do until morning?" I asked.

"I originally planned to have us sleep rough in the offices, but it is not really necessary," Barker said. "We shall have to change into fresh clothing in order to exchange the newspapers."

"What kind of fresh clothing?"

"I haven't decided yet. But I shall by morning."

I finished my pint. Barker's was still half full, while Mac's was near the top. As for Jeremy, he'd finished his second and returned with a third. When we stood to leave, he was sitting with his arm around Henry Cathcart, trying to recall the words to "Loch Lomond."

We left, Mac still clutching his stringed package, and I with an armful of loose *Gazette*s under my arm. Barker split the air with a whistle and a cab came down the street and slowed to a stop in front of us.

"Evenin', gents," he said. "Where to?"

"The wilds of Newington," I told him.

"He's drunk," Mac murmured.

"Not on one measly pint. At least I drank it. I didn't mouth it, like some."

"I'm not fond of beer. I prefer wine."

"But you make ale of your own. Damned good stuff it is, too."

"I make it, but I don't drink it," Mac informed me.

"How do you know you've done it correctly, then, if you don't test it?"

"I follow the recipe stringently."

"Mac's Stringent Ale."

We stopped talking after that. All right, so perhaps I was feeling some slight effects of the ale. Before I knew it we were home, and Barker was shaking me awake.

"I'm tired," I insisted. "I'm not drunk."

We opened the house and stepped inside. Harm waddled forward for our inspection. Barker was approved, as he always is. Mac was not, because he was gone when his sole purpose is to let him in and out of the yard. Constantly.

Harm raised his nose and looked at me accusingly. Sometimes I think he's more of a Baptist than Barker.

"I had a beer," I insisted as he gave a shrill yip. "One! I admit it! Now will you let me alone?"

I went upstairs, took off my shoes, which suddenly weighed as much as cannonballs, and struggled out of my jacket. Then I dropped onto the bed and immediately fell asleep.

CHAPTER THIRTY

We had about four hours' sleep that night. Morning dawned even earlier than usual, if such a thing were possible. We were up and dressed at four A.M. Barker had asked me to wear my country browns, right down to a pair of leather gaiters I almost never wore. No self-respecting Londoner would dare wear such colors. Brown screamed of the country, but then that was the intention.

Our purpose was to switch our newspapers with the real editions to be delivered to the Foreign Office. Barker and I had agreed, after discussing various methods of bait and switch, that the simplest way was generally the best. That is to say, the Guv had decreed it and I had agreed to it, if you take my meaning.

I carried a large ordinance map of the West End, and at the given time, which was around five forty-five, I was to come out of Downing Street with the map fully opened, looking hopelessly lost. I'm good at that. I have one of those faces. Anyway, I was to distract the clerk from the Foreign Office with this oversized map and, in my befuddled way, ask the fellow where the bookselling part of Charing Cross might be. If all went well, I would draw him away from the bundle in time for my employer to step into the spot between the clerk and the newspapers, and consult his watch. Then Mac would switch the real *Gazette* for ours, and stow the originals in his coat and walk away.

Our second objective was much easier. The *Gazette* was also delivered at Lord Diosy's house. Three copies, in fact. They were delivered by a rascally young man who agreed to deliver our newspaper instead, for a not very small fee. The delivery was later than the one in Whitehall, and we had just enough time to arrive with little or no margin for error.

Barker came down in his morning coat and inspected my ensemble: a tweed suit, with breeches and hose, the aforementioned gaiters, and a peaked cap. I had placed the cap rather jauntily on my head, but he set it right. I was to look lost and befuddled.

"Satisfactory," Barker rasped.

Then Mac came in, also in a cap, but in dark gray tweed. He wore no jacket, only a black waistcoat over trousers, and his shirtsleeves were carelessly rolled up to his elbows. His boots were scuffed. I suspect Mac came out of the womb in well-polished boots, wiped down by himself in preparation for his entrance. Having to go about in scuffed boots must have been painful to him.

"How do I look, sir?" he asked.

"Splendid, Mac. Thank you."

Barker's pet. Mac always got the pat on the back, and I the boot in the posterior. I had come to accept this treatment anyway, so it didn't rankle much. After all, Mac wanted more than anything to do enquiry work, whereas I would consider maintaining a house and polishing bannisters all day as nothing less than torture.

We left, and squeezed the three of us into a hansom cab at the Causeway, in front of the Metropolitan Tabernacle. The horse's hooves had to dig into the limestone cobbles below to find purchase and then we were off to our destination. I perched upon about four inches of leather seat, with my arm hanging over the batwings of the cab, looking out at the early dawn and ruminating.

It was a good plan, but not a perfect one. It required theft, subterfuge, bribery, and chicanery. As Christian gentlemen, apart from Mac who was Jewish and a good son of the Torah, we strove to meet our clients' needs without breaking the law. As enquiry agents, one either keeps the law or one doesn't. If one did not, one was no better than a detective, a word which Barker considered pejorative. Sometimes, however, one must break the law if it is for the common good. Whether this was for the common good I was not certain, but I hoped it was. I hoped very much, for you see, it looked to me as if the Guv was double-crossing his client.

"Here we are, lad."

"What o'clock is it?" I asked.

"Half past five."

The vehicle shuddered to a stop at the curb in front of Downing Street. Just a few hundred yards away, the prime minister was snoring into his pillow, dreaming of consolidating his party against those damned muddleheaded savages, the Conservatives. He was welcome to it. We had work to do.

"Are you ready, lad?"

I pulled the ordinance map from my pocket and began opening it.

"Ready."

"Let us rehearse."

I walked toward number 10, the prime minister's residence, while Barker crossed in front of the Home and Foreign Office to the other side. Mac stood in the street, with a bandanna around his neck, carrying the false papers we had made. Oh, yes, I forgot. We must add counterfeiting to the other crimes we were perpetrating. I really hoped this was for the common good, and not Barker trying to settle old scores.

We had worked out that General Mononobe had hired us assuming that we could not discover that he was responsible for

Ambassador Toda's death. If we had, and really, he should have known better, he had diplomatic immunity. He could not be arrested or charged, and even if he could, we hadn't enough evidence to prove that he was the culprit. He even had a bodyguard willing to make the sacrifice of confessing, right before strangling himself. Scotland Yard was satisfied they had their man and had moved on to other things. The Foreign Office was satisfied that selling arms and battleships to Japanese war interests would not reflect badly on them, and our manufacturers were vastly content. The Japanese delegation was pleased that their new embassy was establishing a foothold, in spite of the ambassador's untimely death, as well as that of a few unimportant bodyguards. General Mononobe was satisfied that his plan to purchase armaments for certain wealthy elements in his country would turn his country into an imperial nation like England and America. Everyone was satisfied except Barker. If they were to reap the whirlwind, well, that was their fault, not his.

We blocked out our movements in full view of the Foreign Office building, but then it was mostly empty. Somewhere inside a crew of workmen were finishing their cleaning rounds and a clerk was snatching a hurried cup of tea before starting his duties.

I was back near number 10 when Mac spotted the delivery van coming down the street, and lifted his cap, as if he were wiping the sweat from his forehead. Slowly, I began to move forward, clutching my map. I could feel my heart thumping against the inside of my rib cage. I had to control my breathing, force myself to be calm, and pace my feet. I did not want to arrive one second too early.

The van arrived, the clerk came out to the street, and I arrived at the corner simultaneously. I opened my map and surveyed Whitehall from one end to the other. I scratched my head, and pushed my cap back farther on my head. A country bumpkin in the big city.

"I do beg your pardon, sir. I 'pear to be lost."

The clerk held the newspapers in his hand by the string. I had to get him to drop them.

"To where do you wish to go?" he asked.

"I heard there are some good booksellers in Charing Cross. Beryl will be quite discontented if I don't bring her some of the latest books from London."

"They are to the north. Go past Nelson's Column and they should be on your right."

I scratched my head again and consulted the map.

"So, which way is north?"

The clerk pointed.

"That way. Can't you see Nelson's Column?"

Of course I could. It was right down the street and one hundred and sixty-nine feet high. But I wasn't going to tell him that. I consulted the map again, looking rather desperate.

"Where?"

"Right there. Can't you see the column?"

"Now wait a minute," I drawled. "Beryl and I drove by that yesterday, and the guide told us it was Trafalgar Square."

"It is Trafalgar Square, you—sir," the clerk said. "Nelson's Column is in Trafalgar Square."

I attempted to push half the map into his hand, but he clutched the newspapers tightly by the strings, refusing to surrender them.

"It doesn't say Nelson's Column anywhere on this map," I argued.

"I don't care about your bloody map. I'm telling you, that is Nelson's Column!"

"With the lions."

"Yes!"

"What are the lions called?"

"How should I know?"

"Well, you seem to know everything. I thought you would know the lions' names."

"Look, you—"

"What seems to be the trouble?" a man said, a very helpful man with black lenses and a thick mustache.

"This fellow's lost, and I'm trying to convince him that *that,*" he said, pointing north, "is Nelson's Column."

"I assure you, sir, he is right. Now let us consult your map."

Thunk. The newspapers dropped to the ground.

Barker took one side of the map, and I pulled at it from the other side. The clerk was between us.

"Okay. I get it. The statue is Nelson's Column. The place is Trafalgar Square. Are the bookstores in Trafalgar Square?"

Gradually we moved to the corner, but I was too occupied to see if Mac was making the switch. The clerk had been gnashing his teeth.

"Yes, sir," Barker said, which told me he was playing a role since he generally said "aye" after the Scottish fashion. "They are right here past the church of St. Martin-in-the-Fields."

"Why didn't you say so?" I asked the clerk.

"I did!" the clerk almost bellowed. "The next time you're in London, sir, which I hope is never, I suggest you don't go out anymore without your guide!"

He crossed behind Barker, picked up his newspapers, and headed into the building. Had Mac had time to switch them? It was close. We watched the clerk retreat into the building. Mac came up behind us.

"The cab's waiting. We don't have much time."

"You switched them?" I asked.

"I did."

"I could kiss you!"

"Not if I have any say in the matter."

Time was of the essence. We jumped into the cab and it bowled off.

"Thank you, sir," I told the Guv. "If you hadn't come along, he would never have released the newspapers. He was clutching them like the mortal remains of his sainted mother!"

"By now, the newspapers are being disseminated among all the departments of the Foreign Office. We'll see what sort of chaos your little article will cause there."

A few minutes later we came up to the large residence that housed the Japanese embassy. The young man was standing on the pavement to one side with the bundle by his feet. His arms were crossed and he looked none too happy. We jumped out.

"Are you ready?" Barker asked as Mac exchanged newspapers.

"Not so fast. As I see it, I'm taking all the risks. I don't even know your names."

"Is that so?" Barker asked coolly.

"Yes. I want ten pounds."

"We agreed on five!"

"Ten."

"Seven, then."

"Ten, and not a pence less!"

Barker spit in his hand and extended it. The young man did the same.

"Pay the man."

With reluctance, I tendered a ten-pound note. Of course, we had agreed on ten pounds all along. We'd only offered him five. If he hadn't been so greedy, he'd have received the other five as a bonus. Now they had agreed. He couldn't peach on us now, or defy underworld society.

After pocketing the note, the youth picked up the newspapers and headed toward the embassy door.

"Ta, gents," he said.

Then, and only then, did I relax. I was like a balloon deflating. The youth delivered the newspapers into the hand of one of the last remaining bodyguards. The man shut the door. I waited a moment, as if the entire house were a big dog which might or might not spit out the medicine he was tricked into taking. Waited, waited. Nothing happened.

That is to say, nothing happened outside. I suspected a good deal was happening in the house, once the front-page article had been noticed.

Suddenly, we heard a muffled cry from within.

"It would be best," Barker said, "to not be found in the vicinity. My first visit here proved that."

He raised his stick at a passing cab. We climbed in and were away.

"Will it work?" I asked. "As easy as that?"

"If it doesn't, we must attempt something else."

"Sir, if it's not too much to ask, who killed the ambassador? Was it Kito?"

"It doesn't matter, Thomas. All the guards but Ohara were in his grasp. I mentioned thimblerig, a shell game. The general moved them about until one slipped from the room unnoticed."

CHAPTER THIRTY-ONE

The morning began as if it had no interest in us or our work. In Whitehall the street was full of cabs and dray carts. People were walking to their shops or places of business. Street merchants were calling to the public to look at their wares. In number 7, we'd had no sleep.

I was leaning back in my swivel chair with my eyes closed. The rug beneath Barker's desk looked so comfortable I wanted to lie on it. If I could have an hour, even twenty minutes, I thought, I might get by.

Jenkins looked miserable, but then he had consumed a good deal of free ale; free to him, anyway. Whenever I crossed the chamber, he held his head at the noise as if he were holding the pieces of his skull together.

"Mr. L, could you try not to walk so loudly?"

As far as Barker was concerned, it was an ordinary day and nothing untoward had happened overnight. He looked expectant.

If anything, he was full of nervous energy, as if he'd sucked it up from the rest of us.

"Is something happening?" I asked.

"Possibly, but not yet."

He opened the back door and paced in our back alleyway for half an hour. It occurred to me that we had not broken our fast. That is to say, I'd had no coffee. None. Not one little drop. I could not work under such conditions.

I put my head out into the yard. "Sir. Breakfast."

"Fetch a few buns and some tea."

"Right."

Out in Whitehall Street, I found a stall serving hot Chelsea buns and tea in tin mugs. If one was honorable, one returned the mugs. I found a regular bun, since Barker did not care for sweets. A cup of coffee was nowhere to be found. I purchased three Chelsea buns. Jenkins and I would fight over the third.

When I returned, Barker was reading the morning editions. I set my purchases near the edge of his newspaper. A bite was taken out of the bun. Then a sip. Then a bite.

Jenkins was too debauched to eat, which left two buns for me. After we ate, I totted up the expenses and tried to make a reckoning. I knew when a case was winding down.

They came when I had begun considering lunch. As before, two bodyguards appeared and searched the room, only they were different guards from the first time. Ohara had fled to Newington and Kito was shot. They brought in Mononobe. He wore an elaborate kimono with padded shoulders in place of a Western suit. He looked very grave as he lowered himself into a chair. It somehow looked wrong, him in his robe and getas, sitting in a wooden chair.

"Mr. Barker, I wish to terminate your services."

The Guv put down his pen and sat back in his chair. "Sir, I have done as you asked. I have found the ambassador's killer. He sits in front of me."

"Then you have succeeded. Please present a bill."

I stood and laid it on the table in front of him. He turned and glanced at the new bodyguard. The man came forward and paid the amount from a wallet deep in his pocket. Apparently Barker was not the only one who disdained carrying cash.

"I believe our business is concluded, General," my employer said.

"One last thing, sir. A favor. I would ask a favor."

Cyrus Barker's eyebrow rose over the top of one lens. "I don't generally do favors for murderers. I would think not turning you over to the authorities would be favor enough."

"Nevertheless."

Barker silently faced Mononobe for a few seconds.

"Very well," he finally answered. "I make no promises. What favor would you ask?"

"I require a *kaishakunin*. Would you be willing to perform such a duty?"

I watched my employer run a finger in tiny circles around a glass on top of the desk.

"Alas, sir," he finally said. "I cannot. A long time ago I promised I would never kill you. To go back on my word is unthinkable."

"Ah," Mononobe said. "I would not presume."

It was the voice of a forlorn and totally bereft man. In spite of all he had done, of what he could do in Asia, I felt sorry for him.

"Is there no one else?" the Guv asked.

"None. The admiral is not an honorable man. Both ministers are modern and have no respect for the past. The bodyguards, they are but children. You are the only man in England capable of such a duty."

"I will attend, sir, but I cannot do what you ask. However, there is one man in London capable of performing this service. He is schooled in tradition, highly skilled, and Japanese."

"Of whom do you speak?"

"Ohara."

"He is still in London? I thought he would return to Tokyo to inform the Kempeitai."

"He has been staying in my house."

"Impossible. I have had your house searched."

"Nevertheless."

"You are resourceful, sir."

Barker nodded. "I have needed to be."

Our former client sat for a moment with his head down. "Will you at least oversee it all? Ohara is still rather young. You are of a proper age and I trust you know the old ways."

"As I said, I will be there. I'll make certain protocol is observed."

Mononobe stood and bowed. It was a much deeper bow than I had seen him do before.

"I shall ask him right away, if you will guarantee his safety. If he is harmed, I will see that you are captured, clad in irons, and sent back to Japan for punishment."

"The result is much the same. Very well, I shall promise that Ohara will come and go unmolested. He may be my final hope."

Barker also rose. "I shall speak to him immediately."

We saw him to the door, and without saying anything, Barker hailed a cab for the two of us. I climbed aboard and said nothing. Even I have moments of brilliance.

"General Mononobe was your father-in-law."

"Aye," Barker said.

"He—he killed his only daughter. He beheaded her. Why?"

"He sent her to Hokkaido, where she was safe, or so he thought. The island and the castle on it became a stronghold for the rebel army. I suspect he asked to be in charge of the expedition in order to save his daughter, but she had joined the samurai with me. When his army overran our village, he dispatched me very quickly. I was not yet proficient with a sword. He was surrounded by his own army, watching his every move. She was defiant. There was no other choice. He could not show favoritism."

"What happened after that?"

"I buried her, of course, and then I mourned. One day Ho appeared out of nowhere and took me aboard the *Osprey*. I did my best to try to put what had happened in Japan to rest."

I opened my mouth to speak.

"Enough!" he growled. "I have explained enough for now."

We reached Newington and entered the house. Mac and Harm were overjoyed to see him home early. Barker went to the door to the basement and called down. A minute later, I heard the staircase protesting under Ohara's weight.

"You are safe," Barker told him. "It is nearly over. Come out into the garden. I have something to discuss with you."

I followed them out into the garden. In the shade there was a cool breeze, which disappeared in the sun. I chose to believe it was a harbinger of fall.

This was going to be marvelous, I told myself. Finally, I would learn the solution to everything. They sat in the pagodalike gazebo and began to talk in Japanese. I heard that word again, *kaishakunin*. I could parse almost any Western word. I can read Greek, Latin, French, and most of the so-called Love languages. They were of no use to me here.

Ohara looked troubled. At first he refused, shaking his head. Barker convinced him, however, or so I worked out for myself. It all had to do with favors. Barker traded upon them.

The big man stood and nodded heavily as if it were half a bow. He crossed the bridge over our brook and went inside.

"What?" I began, but my employer raised a finger. There was something almost Japanese about the gesture, as if he were drawing his manner out of a well of memories. Painful ones.

In the hall, Mac was wiping down the telephone set in the alcove by the stairwell. It didn't need it. No self-respecting bit of dust would dare settle in Jacob Maccabee's house.

"What's going on?" he asked in a low voice.

"I wish I knew."

Considering himself safe once more, Ohara took himself to Ho's for some proper food. We were able to keep the fact from Etienne that the Japanese thought his food slop. He'd have quit immediately and I would need two months' worth of pleading to get him back. Two solid months without truffled eggs or pain au chocolat. It was not to be borne.

We were settling down to dinner when Mac came in from the front door.

"Sir!" he cried. "You'll want to see this!"

We rose and went to the front door. The evening edition of the *Pall Mall Gazette* was out. My article was on the front page.

"Stead must have verified the sources and decided to publish," I said. "I have a published article!"

"That is satisfactory," Barker said, and returned to the dining room, as if the point were moot. The laws had not been broken after all, but we had bent a few out of shape.

We did not return to our offices. That evening, we ate a perfectly fine meal, but Barker was almost completely silent. He would not start a conversation, nor would he participate in one. I almost considered going to the Japanese embassy. I'm sure things were more interesting there. Finally he spoke.

"Thomas, I want you to set out your morning coat. Mac, press and brush it. I want him more presentable than he has ever been before. Do you understand?"

"Yes, sir."

"I shall have much more detailed instructions for what I shall wear."

"I'm to wear my morning suit, sir? To where, exactly?"

"Wherever our destination shall be."

"That goes without saying."

"You're not going to catch me out so easily, Mr. Llewelyn. I suggest you forgo your usual frivolities and prepare. We shall be up early in the morning."

I was tired, naturally, but I didn't want to go to sleep without having some questions answered.

"Sir," I said, "could you inform me what is going to occur,

before it happens? I don't want to look a total git when we arrive, and me in a funeral suit."

"Later, Thomas," he said. I suspected his patience was wearing thin.

"I'm going to bed, then."

"I fear not. Go harness Juno."

"What?"

"Do I have to repeat myself, lad? We've got work to do."

"Yes, sir."

"You'll have to catch such sleep as you can tomorrow. Meet us here in half an hour."

I looked at the hall clock. It was about to strike ten.

CHAPTER THIRTY-TWO

I patted Harm on the way out the back door, then crossed to the moon gate at the back of the garden. There I took the alleyway to the Old Kent Road. I strode purposefully, but there was no need to hurry. I'd be back in plenty of time.

I reached the stable and woke up the stable boy. He never complains, knowing he can earn a sovereign or two for a few minutes' work. Once Juno was in her traces I inspected her for any signs of weakness or injury, finding none. Then I climbed into my perch and bowled out into the Kent Road to the steady clop of her hooves.

There was a feeling of foreboding I could not shake. Not a sense of danger, mind you. That tends to go with the work, and is something of an old friend by now. Israel Zangwill has an expression that he uses when something is "not kosher," that is, not according to the rules. Something was going to happen and I could not see what the consequences might be, since I didn't know what was going on. Barker, a taciturn fellow at the best of times, generally tells me what's going on, provided it is not illegal or morally questionable. I began to suspect it might be both.

We cantered into Lion Street and I saw someone standing by the front door. It was Mac, and he had a number of items with him: a bucket and mop, some cleaning rags, a rolled-up straw mat, some sheets, a low table, and several smaller items in a catch-all bag. I drew up to the curb.

"Has Mr. Barker explained what all this is for?" I asked.

"Ours is not to reason why," he answered.

"Ours but to do or die."

"Let us hope it doesn't come to that."

"Is that all of it?" I asked.

"Yes, except for what the Guv is bringing."

"Where is he?"

"He borrowed my whetstone and oil. Didn't say what for."

The door opened and Barker came outside. It was a cloudy night with the moon playing peekaboo.

"Let's get these things loaded into the cab," he ordered.

"Yes, sir," the two of us replied.

Mops and pails are not ideal items to stow in a moving hansom cab, nor are rolled tatami mats that are eight feet long. By the time we were loaded, both Mac and Barker would be holding everything in place while I drove.

"Which bridge?" I called out after slapping the reins.

"Westminster!" he called out.

Westminster. That could mean anything. We could be going to our offices or any one of a thousand buildings nearby. But most of them were occupied and kept clean. Where would we go where Jacob Maccabee's expertise came into play?

Soon we came to the familiar old bridge and crossed over the Thames, our way lit by a necklace of gaslights. When we reached the far shore, my employer indicated we were to turn south, rather than north to our offices. We were on Abingdon Street, on the east side of Westminster Abbey. Surely we were not going there, I thought. We passed it and found ourselves in a maze of old buildings. We were in the center of London, but there wasn't a soul to be seen.

"Here, lad," Barker rumbled.

We pulled up in front of a tall, thin, derelict-looking building. By the architecture it was several centuries old. I tugged on the level and the doors opened. My two passengers got out and stretched. It had been difficult holding everything together as we drove.

Barker approached the building's front doors, which I noted were padlocked with heavy chain. He pulled out a ring of keys from his pocket and began trying them in the lock.

"What is this place?" I asked.

"It is the old Jewel Tower," he answered.

There are few relics of the former fourteenth-century Palace of Westminster, the pride of Edward III. This was perhaps the last survivor, the storehouse of his accumulated treasure. It had been used for various purposes since then, for storing records and even housing the offices of Her Majesty's Weights and Measures. Now it stood vacant. Our employer found the right key and took off the padlock and chains. With a squeal, the doors opened.

We stopped a moment while Barker lit a dark lantern. Then we stepped inside. In the gloom, I saw a vaulted and ribbed ceiling overhead, and an old and dusty parquet floor underfoot. He led us through the room to the next, which I assumed was the actual jewel chamber itself.

"This will be satisfactory. I want this room mopped thoroughly. Wipe away all the dust with wet cloths. This room must be spotless."

"Yes, sir," Mac said.

"Thomas, do whatever Mac needs you to do."

"Of course, sir."

There was a lot of dust and suddenly our tools seemed woefully inadequate. We set to, mopping and wiping with our jackets off and our sleeves rolled. We were soon sooty faced and coated in dust. When Mac sets to something, he is a tartar. Nothing else matters until the job is done. He lit a larger oil lamp so that we could see what we were doing. I hoped the light would not pene-trate to the outside. We had broken in here and, if spotted, we could be arrested.

When we were done, Barker helped roll out the mat. Then we spread a few layers of white linen bedsheets over them. Mac had brought along a small contraption, an oil lamp which heated a small iron when lit. He spent close to half an hour ironing those sheets and tucking them just so around the matting. Barker was relent-less, pointing to the slightest wrinkle on the sheet, or a speck of dust for me to wipe away. He's wound up like a clock, I told myself.

From Mac's bag Barker removed a couple of Oriental trays, and set them both carefully on the mat. Then he removed a small handleless cup and a stoppered bottle. Lastly, he removed a sin-gle sheet of paper. It was not pure white, but resembled vellum. He set it on the other tray, then he walked around several times, glaring at everything, seeing if it met his standards. He moved the cup closer to the bottle. He moved it away again. Even when we were making dynamite for a case I had not seen him so par-ticular or precise. Afterward, we wiped our faces and clothes.

Finally, we met his standards. He asked Mac to mop a final time, removing even any trace of his foot marks when he had circled outside of the pristine mat. When I thought we were almost ready to go, Barker took a box from his pocket. It was only a few inches across, but almost a foot long. He opened it and revealed a small Japanese writing set. There was a block of ink, a brush for writing, folded sheets of paper, and a small tray. Barker went down on his knees on the bare floor and began mixing what water we had left with the ink he ground in the tray. His hands, in fact, his whole body, seemed too large for such a delicate task. Mac looked ready to jump in and take over, but Barker would only do this himself, as the official second. He would not spare himself any pain or labor. He set the writing set on the small table between the two trays.

Then he stood up. It was actually our moment of truth. Barker inspected his trousers, where he had been kneeling. There was no dust on them. He nodded his approval. We exhaled.

"Our work here is done," he pronounced. "Until the morning."

Stepping outside, I was relieved to see that Juno's cab was not encircled by constables. Barker and Mac hung the chains again and attached the padlock. Mac threw out the water in the bucket and began loading the few items we hadn't left into the cab. Then we absconded, rolling along Abingdon Street as Big Ben just ahead of us chimed midnight.

They were talking inside the cab, I noticed, or at least Barker was. Fresh orders to which I was not privy. I lifted the hatch a bit on the top of the cab in time to hear one word: "clothesline."

"Yes, sir," Mac said. He lives for this kind of thing. A task! A job! Something to do in the proper manner! Nothing slipshod. Mac, for all his Jewish soul, would have made a good Japanese.

Eventually, we came to a stop in front of number 3 Lion Street again and they descended. Mac took down his pail and mop while I took Juno on to the stable. Perhaps it was due to what had occurred, but I would not allow the stable boy to deal with her. I curried her mane, brushed her down, checked her hooves, and then fed her a bag of oats myself. Then I went back home.

"Lad," Barker said after I had entered the house. "Your duties are done for the night. You can go to bed."

"I would prefer to stay up for a while, if I may," I said. "I wouldn't feel right sleeping while Mac is working. What is he doing, if I might ask?"

"He is preparing my clothing for the morning. What little Japanese clothing I still own has been packed away. Mac is seeing to it for me."

"I'll find out if he requires an extra hand."

"Thomas, you have done a good night's work. Thank you."

"Not at all, sir."

I went after Mac. Nothing embarrasses a Briton so much as being sincerely thanked for something.

Our butler had the clothes Barker was going to wear spread out upon the dining room table.

"Cor!" I said when I saw them.

"You have been hanging around the East End too long," Mac told me.

To begin with, it looked like enough clothing for four people. There were layers of coats and trousers, most of it made of silk.

"Look at these hose!" Mac marveled.

They were white hose made of silk cloth, with small metal clasps to close them at the heel. They fit the foot a way a pair of gloves fit hands. The large toe was separated from the others.

"What's it for?" I asked.

"The sandal fits in between the first and second here, see?"

"There are a lot of ties and ribbons to hold it together."

"Presumably, Mr. Barker will show us how to dress him. It would be a tragedy if we made that chamber to standards and then Mr. Barker was ill-dressed."

"How do you clean silk?"

"You don't. I'll string them up on a clothesline in the garden and hang them out until morning. Then I'll press them if they require it."

I helped him string the clothesline and hang the clothes. Harm came out into the garden to see what we were doing in his domain without his express permission at one o'clock in the morning. The musty clothes sent him into a sneezing fit.

When we were done I went upstairs. All the way upstairs. Barker was seated in one of his chairs flanking the unlit fireplace, wearing his Oriental dressing gown over his nightshirt. He was smoking one of his meerschaums.

"Shall I sleep in the library, sir, or will you wake me when you get up?"

"That won't be necessary, lad."

"I insist. I must see this through."

"See what through, Thomas?"

"I haven't the foggiest idea," I admitted. "But something is going to happen tomorrow morning."

"Indeed it will," Barker said, puffing out smoke. "I only hope the agency can survive it."

CHAPTER THIRTY-THREE

Half past four is not a civilized hour. I had finally fallen asleep perhaps three hours before. Then I recalled what we were waking so early for. General Mononobe was going to perform some sort of ceremony, whether in protest or in confession, I was not sure. One would think something like that could wait for a time that did not inconvenience everyone.

Mac came in with hot water. At one moment, I came awake to discover I was standing with my face lathered and my razor in hand sound asleep. Somehow I shaved and dressed myself. I'm not saying how well I did it, but it was done.

Going downstairs, I found Mac pressing coffee in the kitchen alone. We would be gone before Etienne Dummolard even arrived. Neither of us was inclined to talk. I looked out into the garden and even the gardeners had not yet arrived. I found some day-old croissants in the pantry and spooned some gooseberry jam on them. Mac and I split the press of coffee between us.

Barker came in then. He had bathed cold in the bathhouse. It takes a good hour to heat properly and we did not have the time. I heard him enter the house and climb the stairs. I sat down in a chair, munched the bread, and allowed the coffee to work its magic in my bloodstream. Vaguely, I recall I heard Barker call for Jacob Maccabee. As soon as he left, I closed my eyes again.

The next I knew, the Guv was beside my chair in his long coat. When I jumped up he turned and I could hear the whisper of several layers of silk. He was wearing the Japanese suit under his coat. From the neck down he looked like an old stereoscopic slide I had of a samurai warrior.

"Shall I bring the cab around?" I asked.

"It might prove inconvenient later," Barker replied. "We'll find one in the Causeway."

As it happened, we did find one in Newington Causeway, but the cabman looked at us a bit dubiously when he slowed to the curb. I had to convince him with a half sovereign. Barker had a long, thin bag with him, which he was cradling carefully.

"What is in the bag, sir?" I asked.

"Nothing that should concern you, Mr. Llewelyn."

"Nevertheless, sir, I am concerned," I argued. "I suspect there are swords in it. Are you and the general going to have a battle?"

"No."

"What, then?"

"Watch and see."

"Is this," I said, as the cab reached Westminster Bridge, "the result of what I wrote for the *Gazette*?"

"Very much so."

"I was afraid of that."

I was fully awake now. "If what I suspect is about to happen is correct, you have to stop it. The general must not die if the newspapers were false."

"They were not false," Barker rumbled.

"Not the facts, perhaps, but the fact that they were reported. It was a trick and I'm glad it stopped him, but I don't want him to die because of it."

"Here," he said, pulling a yellow slip of paper from his pocket. "I hope I will be forgiven for intercepting this."

I opened it. It was a telegraph from Stead himself:

*Thomas Llewelyn stop Cracking good story stop If Barker
ever tosses you into the street come knock on my door
stop end*

"You read it?" I asked.

"I did. If you intend to wed, here is a safe occupation for you."

"You're offering me a way out."

"Aye."

"Don't. I'm able to make my own decisions, thank you. It is flattering that Mr. Stead found my article satisfactory, but I'm an enquiry agent first and foremost."

"A reporter would be more palatable to the Mocattas," Barker argued.

"Oh, bother the Mocattas. It's Rebecca alone I care about. The Mocattas will have to take me as they see me."

"We're here."

We were back in Abingdon Street again behind the Jewel Tower. Another cab was waiting. Two men alighted. One was in all black, the other in white. The second was the general. The first, I was not surprised to see, was Ohara. We all stood as the cabs circled us and bowled away. We were in for it now. Our transportation had left.

"Is everything in order?" Ohara asked. His silk jacket was a deep black, outlined in squares of gold. The general's outfit was the purest white. He looked like a ghost.

Barker nodded solemnly in response and walked up to the entrance. He transferred the bag to the other arm and removed the key from his coat pocket. In a minute or two we stepped inside. My employer lit a vesta and used it to light the solitary lamp.

"Satisfactory," the general murmured, looking about.

Ohara nodded in agreement. Mononobe bowed to Barker and the latter bowed in return.

In a series of slow and precise moves, the general removed his sandals at the edge of the mat, walked across to the small table and lowered himself step by step to his knees. He picked up the small brush there and dipped it in the ink. Then he unfolded a piece of paper with the other hand.

I was beside the bulk of Mr. Ohara.

"What's he doing?" I asked in a low voice.

"He is writing his death poem."

I watched Mononobe begin to write. Japanese calligraphy had always interested me. The symbols, the words, became almost a painting by themselves. I watched him set down each character stroke by stroke. Had the general written this down beforehand or was he composing extemporaneously?

He's going to top himself, I told myself, and these two are fine with his decision. Someone should go for a policeman. This is not all right. It must be illegal.

Men in London blew their brains out every day in gentlemen's clubs. They built up debts they couldn't repay or were caught embezzling at the bank. Collectively, people looked the other way while the poor beggar took "the gentleman's way out." One pulls the trigger. It ignites the gunpowder. There is a buildup of gas, which causes the ball inside to propel down the barrel of the gun and out. It crosses the void until it meets a wall of flesh and hair and thin bone.

The problem was, there was no gun here, only swords. What was going to happen? I hadn't a clue.

With a sigh, the general put down his pen. The poem was complete. Ohara took it up and he and Barker looked it over. Both nodded in approval. Of course, I couldn't read it. It was written in kanji. The general seemed content that both men were satisfied with his poem. He opened the small bottle and poured a little of what was inside into one of the cups and drank.

"What is it?" I asked.

"Sake," Ohara said.

I recalled a bottle in what passed for a wine cellar in our basement. One of the bottles had Chinese characters on it. I always wondered what was in it. Barker had several swords as well as this bottle in the house. Did he imagine such a time when he might need these articles?

Mononobe offered the wine to Barker, who refused. He drank. It was no more than a mouthful. Meanwhile, my employer set out a set of swords in three lengths: the *katana,* which is the longest, the *wakizashi,* and the *tantō.* Mononobe now picked up the last. He slid the sheath from the sword and looked at his own reflection in the polished metal.

The general slipped his hand up into the sleeve of his kimono, until it was at his neck. He peeled back the jacket. His chest was all wiry muscle. Only his neck showed signs of age. Very precisely, he peeled down the jacket to his waist. He tucked the sleeves carefully under his limbs, which were folded under him, the top of one foot resting up on the bottom of the other. It was all incredibly precise.

It was also calm. Knowing what I assumed would happen next, one would expect General Mononobe's hand to shake. Not a bit of it.

Barker said something to him in Japanese, and the man replied. Both nodded. Ohara watched, almost like a referee in a football match, to see that all was in order.

Mononobe picked up the small strip of beige-colored paper, and wrapped it carefully around the blade of the sword, up close to the guard. Then he lifted the naked blade, so that it pressed against his stomach.

It was going to happen. It was really going to happen. I thought Barker would find some way to stop it. Suddenly I didn't want to be in this chamber. The dawn was just coming in through the high windows facing east. It was going to be a beautiful day.

I looked back and saw Mononobe close his eyes and inhale. Such peace. Such calm. He might have been ready to peel an apple or cut a melon.

The blade bit into the flesh of his stomach and plunged in inch by inch. Mononobe's eyes popped open. The exposed part of the blade was close to a foot long, and it continued to go in deeper and deeper. Finally, it reached the paper guard and it stopped. The general's lids fluttered. He breathed in again. Then he began to pull the blade across his abdomen.

Seppuku, they called it in Japan. Or hara-kiri, which means "belly-cutting." The latter name is considered vulgar, I understand, and is spoken, while the first is written.

Mononobe made a growling sound in the throat as he brought the short sword across and through his own flesh. Even a short sword is not meant to cut through ten inches of solid flesh easily, let alone living flesh. Blood began to spill out of the huge wound, but less than I would have thought.

He had nearly bisected his entire stomach now. How long would it be until he died from his wounds? The general was a tough old buzzard, but it could not take much longer.

Then I saw Ohara step up behind him. In his hand he had that length of raw driftwood that I saw in Barker's room. As I watched, the driftwood split in two and a long blade was revealed. He raised the weapon behind him, high over his head.

No, I wanted to call out, but my tongue cleaved to my throat. There would be consequences here. Not to Ohara. To us.

The blade came down and smacked the new ambassador on the back of the neck before coming back into the air again. It was coated in blood now. In fact, I saw an arc of blood spray across the canvas the general sat upon. It was a painting in monochrome.

The general's hands stopped moving. Slowly, the head fell forward into his lap. The spinal column had been severed, killing him instantly. The body sagged, but it did not fall. It was held in place by the sleeves which the general had so carefully tucked under his limbs. Blood bubbled from the neck wound, staining the white kimono and the bedsheets.

Ohara shook out his blade onto the floor with another arc of blood before putting it back in its sheath. Barker made a sound of appreciation, as if someone had just finished a Bach cantata. Outside, I heard horses galloping nearby.

We all sat still for a minute or two, not moving, as if there were four corpses and not one. I heard voices shouting. Someone was giving orders. The outer door was pulled open. It seemed as if everything were moving incredibly slowly. I watched Barker tuck the sword into the sash tied about the waist of his kimono. Ohara puffed out his chest and pulled back his sleeves in order to fold his thick, bare forearms across his chest.

Men came into the room then. It was the Secret Police squad, led by Trelawney Campbell-Ffinch. Their eyes went wide at the carnage they found here. Campbell-Ffinch looked stricken, his head still wrapped in gauze from his shooting.

"Late, as usual," I said.

CHAPTER THIRTY-FOUR

Toss 'em in darbies, lads," Campbell-Ffinch said to his compatriots.

There was no use arguing or struggling. He had us dead to rights. Ohara Kogoro had just killed someone on British soil. The general was near death when he struck the fatal blow, but I'm sure under British law it was murder. This was what the Guv meant when he spoke earlier of the agency itself being in danger.

The Foreign Office man stepped onto the blood-soaked sheets and regarded the victim, bending over for a better view.

"Who did this?" he asked, indicating the sword standing perpendicular from Mononobe's stomach.

"He did," I said, pointing at the kneeling corpse.

"Topped himself, eh? Don't tell me he cut off his own head."

"I did that," Ohara admitted. "I was his second."

"Some sort of ritual?"

"Yes."

"Her Majesty's government won't think so. That's an ambassador to a foreign power there. One we were hoping to impress. This property belongs to the Crown, Barker. How did you get in here?"

"With a very small key."

"Take the key ring from him," Campbell-Ffinch told the men. "Try those coats by the wall. Breaking and entering in addition to murder. Better and better."

"You would prefer that he dispatch himself fully?" my employer asked. "I had no wish to prolong his suffering."

"I'm not sure," I said, "that you can arrest Mr. Ohara here. He is not a British citizen."

"I'll take my chances."

Ohara put on his most stoical face. If anything he had a look of bemusement. I would be willing to bet he would be out of his handcuffs not long after we reached Scotland Yard. We were another matter entirely.

"I'm sending for the Big Brass. They're going to want to see this. Let's try to leave everything as it is until they arrive."

"What about our coats?" I argued.

Campbell-Ffinch smacked me across the face. Being a boxer, he was good at it. I was going to feel that for the rest of the day.

"What in hell was that for?" I demanded.

"I warned you about cheek. Gents, take these three away. I'm tired of looking at them."

Fine thing, striking a fellow when his hands are secured behind him, not to mention that you outweigh him by sixty pounds. We were led out into bright sunshine. So little of it had pierced the gloom of the Jewel Tower that I had assumed it was overcast.

I climbed with some aid into a waiting police van. That meant that they knew ahead of time that they would have someone to arrest. However, they had not known in time to stop what happened. I suspected whatever happened to us, the blame for it would ultimately fall on Campbell-Ffinch's shoulders. Just the thought of it put me in a cheerier mood.

It was a short drive to the New Scotland Yard. The original premises that I was accustomed to using had been locked up and used for storage or boarded over. Part of the buildings housed records and the so-called Black Museum containing evidence from various high-profile cases. Time ticks away and the things we are accustomed to change beyond recognition.

New Scotland Yard was a multitiered wedding cake in alternating layers of red brick and white marble. It looked faintly Dutch. In my opinion, it didn't quite go with the rest of Whitehall Street, but then I don't suppose they took my feelings into account when they built it.

"If you get a chance for a telephone call, call Lord Whatsit," I told Ohara.

"Lord Whosis?" he asked.

"The fellow whose house you've been staying in. Have him come and take you out before you have to answer any questions. This Special Branch crowd is liable to cut up rough."

"Do you mean Lord Diosy?"

"That's the bloke," I said.

"But I must stay and tell them what happened so that Mr. Barker can go free."

"There are men here at Scotland Yard who would like nothing more than to see Cyrus Barker busted down, you see."

"Surely they cannot blame him for meeting the demands of the general. It is a long-held custom of my people."

"They do it here, as well, though not as dramatically. However, it is still illegal."

Ohara heaved a sigh. "Actually, it is illegal in my country as well, but people do it, anyway."

"That's no comfort," I told him.

We were locked away in a cell, the three of us. Ohara sat cross-legged on one of the beds, tucked his hands into his sleeves, and closed his eyes. Meanwhile, my employer sat down in a chair and waited patiently. Apparently, I was the only impatient one. I paced the cell.

"You got what you wanted," I told him.

"How so?" he asked. I suspected his eyes behind the dark lenses were shut as well.

"After what he did to your late wife, you've had your revenge."

"That has been twenty years."

"Best served cold."

"I have long since given up a desire for revenge. I understood his reasons. How was he to know that the samurai class would be outlawed? When he overtook our village, his men knew who she was. He had to make an example of her."

"I'm sure you did not feel that way at the time."

"No. No, I didn't. But we were in the middle of a civil war. It set families against one another."

"What was it about the sixties? Japan had a civil war, China had one; even the United States."

"One must learn to forgive, for one's own sake, if not for others'. Of course, that takes time."

"You're a Scotsman. They don't forgive anything. I'd assume you would have forgiven Culloden before this."

"The treachery of the English at the Battle of Culloden is another matter entirely," he stated.

"But she was your wife."

"Aye, she was. I would rather he hadn't asked me to be his second, but he did. I promised her I would not kill him."

"Why did you invite him to play Go with you?"

"To gather information, of course."

"This is one for the books. You managed to have our client's head cut off."

"You understand hiring us was merely a ruse."

"If by that you mean the general had committed the murders himself, I had worked that out. Or perhaps Kito had done the murders on his orders. I assume that in fact all the bodyguards worked for him."

"No," Ohara objected. He ran a hand up through his kimono

and scratched his neck. "As I said, I work for the Kempeitai, the Secret Police."

"On whose authority?" Barker asked.

"The emperor. You would call him a very canny fellow."

"He might," I said, indicating my employer.

"With the ambassador dead," Ohara continued, "the general made several orders without authority. Now the emperor can punish the families for whom Mononobe worked."

"Conquest," Barker said. "China?"

"Korea first, I suspect. And Formosa. Of course, we have the fine example of the English when it comes to securing territory."

"I would argue," I said, "but nothing springs to mind."

"Mr. Ohara," Barker said. "You say you work for the emperor. How, pray, have you influenced events while you have been here?"

"Not enough to make up for allowing the ambassador to die. Mostly, I collected information for my report and followed people about. Again, I apologize for attacking you in your rooms. The general assured me that you were responsible. I did speak to your Mr. Stead yesterday morning and assured him that all the information in the article was accurate and that if he wished to scoop his competitors, he should publish."

"Scoop?" I asked. "You have a fine grasp of English. Where did you learn?"

"Oxford," he said. "I was the bodyguard of the emperor's nephew when he was educated there."

"I remember him!" I said.

"The general was not the only one making purchases," I said. "The admiral signed contracts for ships, engineering equipment, and manufacturing engines."

"This is true," Ohara said. "But these supplies were ordered by the government, but General Mononobe had associated himself with the most important families, manufacturers and such, and was doing their bidding, which happened to go along with his interests."

"To what end?" I asked.

"The conquest of all Asia. The general believed such a thing was possible. He used all his knowledge gathered over the years and his connections to the government."

"Even China?" I asked. "It's a hundred times Japan's size."

"Especially China! He had a plan for dividing and controlling the country. The old Qing dynasty cannot stand much longer."

"And how do you feel about such imperialism?"

"I am a servant of my government. I'm not entitled to an opinion."

"Nonetheless, you have one."

Ohara shrugged his massive shoulders.

"The West had taken over Hong Kong and Shanghai and even Peking. The Americans streamed into Yokohama harbor forty years ago and began to dictate terms to us. I don't care for conquest, but we must have a way to defend ourselves at the very least. Especially—"

The door to our cell opened and the commissioner of Scotland Yard entered, along with several detective inspectors, including Terence Poole. There was no love lost between Commissioner Munro and Barker.

"You have finally gone too far, Barker. You cannot slice the head off the Japanese ambassador and expect to get away with it."

"Mr. Barker is taking the blame upon himself," Ohara said. "It was I who was General Mononobe's second. I asked him merely to find a room for the ritual to be performed."

"And who the bloody hell are you, sir?" Munro demanded.

"I am the new ambassador, now that the general is dead. He formally handed over his office to me this morning, before we left for the ceremony. I speak for the emperor in this matter."

"It was I who removed the general's head," Barker insisted.

"Nonsense," Ohara said. "Mr. Barker was once married to the

general's daughter. Why, they were playing Go in his garden three days ago."

I wanted to elbow my employer in the ribs and tell him to be quiet. Ohara was spreading diplomatic immunity over us like a mantle, while Barker was kicking against the goads. As for the commissioner, he looked like a child who has had his lolly taken from him.

"There is still the matter of breaking into a government building."

"Guilty as charged," Barker stated. "While I understand the ceremony of seppuku as a means of escaping disgrace, I do not condone it. I would not have it in my back garden, and so I felt I must choose an appropriate locale. I was aware the Jewel Tower was currently vacant."

"You had a key!" Munro cried.

Barker nearly smiled. "A key! It was a common padlock and a fourteenth-century lock. Even the lad could get through it in five seconds."

Even? I thought I would let that one pass.

"How do we know any of what you say is true, Mr. . . . ?"

"Ohara. The coat I was wearing contains all the papers necessary to prove my assertions. I believe Lord Diosy would be willing to translate."

"Your embassy was a failure, sir." Terence Poole spoke for the first time. "Will you be going home in disgrace?"

"Not I. The general in a letter took full blame for all matters that occurred here in London. My duties are merely to facilitate our journey back to Tokyo."

"You still butchered someone on British soil," Munro said. Not able to fix the blame on Barker, he turned to Ohara.

"I am an officer of the Japanese Police. I was working at the request of the emperor himself. If you wish to take this up with my government, pray do so. I've got work to do. I demand to be released in the name of Emperor Meiji himself!"

None but us had even heard of the emperor, but it was spoken with such authority that, in the absence of a higher government entity, Munro kowtowed to the pressure of diplomacy. I shuffled to the door and looked at the commissioner. He could only hold us for trespassing.

"Oh, get out, the lot of you. Quit wasting the Yard's time. And stay out of trouble!"

I didn't need to be coerced on that score.

CHAPTER THIRTY-FIVE

One would think that having been freed from a murder charge, Cyrus Barker would be elated. Not a bit of it, as it turned out. He asked the cabman to take us to our home in Newington. I had assumed we would go to the office. It's the sort of thing he would normally do. There would be no shirking. The fact that we just ended a case did not mean that he would not want his usual eleven-hour workday out of me. I knew he had a change of clothes at the office, so there was no need to cross to the Lambeth side of the river. Not that I was complaining, mind you.

Barker was unusually taciturn the entire way home. He looked grim, which on his rough-hewn face was practically savage. However, we had just witnessed something that would make anyone grim.

Once in the house, Barker did not change clothing. Absently, he scratched Harm's head, then passed through the hall and out the back door into the garden.

Mac looked at me, with a question in his eye.

"Mononobe's dead," I said in a low voice. "Gutted himself. Mr. Ohara cut off his head, then claimed diplomatic immunity."

I know Jacob wanted a longer explanation, but I didn't have time for it. I went outside and crossed over the bridge. First I thought he was taking another bath, then I saw him in the pagoda-roofed gazebo. I crossed to it and found him contemplating the half-finished game in front of him.

There is a time for studious silence while picking up on the subtle signals another gives. Then there is a time for blundering in with the best of intentions because one cares about someone. This was the latter.

"What is it, sir?" I asked.

He sat shaking his head over the Go game they had been playing. He put down a white stone, but there was no one to pick it up again. I did not know how and, besides, I felt it wasn't my place.

He reached into his sleeve and pulled out a faded blue velvet frame, the size of a ring box. He opened it and offered it to me. Inside was a small photograph of a young Asian woman. It was hand-tinted, the kind one sees from the Orient. It was just like the one in Mononobe's office, the one he had shown to Barker. She had been pretty. Delicate features, neat hair, pulled back and pinned, a few shades lighter than the deep black I had seen in photographs of Japanese women. I tried to connect with it, with her, but I couldn't. It was too long ago and too far away. She was dust and bone somewhere now, and her soul at rest. Her spirit, well, I'll leave that to the theologians.

"Very nice," I said.

"A good woman."

"You've got another one now. Mrs. Ashleigh."

"Aye, I do, lad."

"Why don't you take a couple of days off and go down to Sussex," I suggested. "I'll mind the office. If a case is too big, I'll call you."

"Perhaps," he said.

"Please," I insisted. "You should call her now. She should be here, or you should be there. You'd go there if she went through something half as difficult as what you've just been through. You've never taken a holiday before. I'll even teach your antagonistics class for you. We'll go over basic drills."

"Do you think you can manage?"

"Like I said, I'll ring."

"Thomas, I want you to do something for me."

"Yes, sir."

"I have been a poor son-in-law. I will not be a poor father-in-law. Find K'ing. Turn over every opium den in London until you find him."

"What shall I do when I find him?"

Barker shrugged. He had not worked that out yet. Too many things had happened over the last two days.

"Take him to Fu Ying. She is the one who cares and will care for him."

He nodded, but it was as perfunctory as when he had petted Harm. He was far off somewhere in his mind and possibly in pain.

Barker put down the stones in his hand and started toward the back door of the house. I stood and followed after. Mac was standing in the doorway, and we met by the little pebbled sea in the middle of the garden after Barker had gone into the house.

"Where's he going?"

"To call Mrs. Ashleigh. I've convinced him to take a short holiday. Very short, if I know him. You'd best start packing his cases."

"I will. Shall he close the offices?"

"No, I'll run things for a few days. I can call him on the telephone set if something is too big for me."

"Good thinking. Was the general really killed?"

"Ohara sliced his head nearly clean off, but only after the man had disemboweled himself."

Mac made a grunt of disgust, and went off to pack. He had something to do, while in fact, I didn't. I decided to go back to Whitehall, open up the offices, and get on with my day. There would be people in need of an enquiry agent, the best to be had in London, actually, and they shouldn't have to go away disappointed.

I passed Barker who was talking to Philippa on the hall telephone. I passed Mac by his door and told him I was going to work then. I passed Harm and chucked him under the chin. He actually wagged his tail. It had only taken me six years to make a friend of him. Then I went out and hailed a hansom cab. It was one of those moments when one realizes that somehow one had turned into an adult. I suppose it had to happen sooner or later.

I took a cab to work, and as it happened, we went over Westminster Bridge. As we passed Abington Street, I looked south. There was a knot of carriages near the Jewel Tower. It wasn't my problem anymore. The cab turned and we headed north.

When I reached the office, it took half an hour to relate to Jenkins everything that had occurred since he had helped us the night before at the *Gazette*. It was his duty to type all the facts and every suspect of a case for our records.

"The offices are shut down, then," he finally said.

"Why would you say that?"

"Mr. B's gone to Sussex."

"But I haven't."

"You're going to run the office yourself?"

"Stranger things have happened this morning," I pointed out.

"Suppose you need him for advice?"

"He'll be in Seaford within the hour. They actually have a telephone exchange there."

"It's your funeral," he finally decided, shrugging his bony shoulders.

"Thank you. Your confidence overwhelms me. Get those notes typed for me, would you?"

As it turned out, I had a case that morning. It was simple enough and I had it done and ready for my client by five-thirty. I'm afraid I put Jenkins through his paces. I wanted everything typed and perfect, even if it was a simple case of a husband with an overly active imagination. He feared his wife was having a dalliance, and she was, but only with the suffragette movement. Women hoping to vote, *quelle horreur*. Next, we'll all be ironing our own shirts and the empire will go to ruin.

I let Jenkins go to the Rising Sun a half hour early. I also made certain he would be paid extra for the work he had done for us in the middle of the night. He's a lazy rascal, but I suppose Barker said the same about me. The thing was, Jenkins was talented, and we couldn't have found someone who knew how to set type and was willing to work overnight. I wanted him to know we appreciated his efforts.

Mac called me on the telephone set, wanting to know if I would be home and should expect supper. I told him to take the night off. I didn't require a butler, knowing how to light lamps and dress myself, and even to fix my own dinner. Those of us privileged enough to work for Cyrus Barker are paid very well by London standards, but we are required to do an awful lot and often our lives are in danger. I know for a fact that Mac worked sixteen or more hours a day. If he were wise, he'd use the time to sleep or at least go visit his parents.

So, of all things, I was free, except for one matter. I had promised to tell Rebecca how the case had ended, since she had some small connection to it. I called her on the telephone and requested to speak to her, apologizing for the suddenness of my call. Yes, I could come over to her house. She had something to discuss with me. Her maid would act as chaperone. It was not strictly necessary now that she was a widow, but she was careful, being the daughter of a rabbi. I was not to bring flowers or chocolates, which would tell one and all that she was being courted by a Gentile. In fact, we were engaged, but I would not press her and make her uncomfortable.

I had dinner at the Barbados Coffee House, which grills a fine cutlet and chips and serves the best coffee in England, not that that is anything to boast about; most coffee here tastes like it was strained through an old sock. I had a pipeful of tobacco and a second cup and still arrived early at her door for our seven o'clock rendezvous. Strange, I had been seeing her for almost a year and I still had palpitations whenever I approached her door, at the very thought of seeing her. I hoped that feeling never went away.

The door opened and the maid looked at me sourly. I believe she thought enquiry agents should use the servants entrance. When Rebecca and I were wed we would discuss servants. I asked to speak to Mrs. Cowan, and after a deep rolling of the eyes, she complied. Rebecca met me in the hall as if she was glad to see me. I was certainly glad to see her.

"I have a guest in the house," she said. "I wonder if you can tell me who it is."

"I haven't the vaguest," I admitted. "I cannot guess."

"It is Bok Fu Ying. Her husband still has not returned. He was seen a couple of nights ago in an opium den, badly burned from the fire. Fu Ying doesn't know what he will do. She also had no one to help her, since some people I will not mention by name were out chasing Japanese delegates all over town."

"We forgot," I said.

"You forgot?"

"There has been a lot going on. I need the den's address. I promised Barker to track him down."

"Then tell us. Fu Ying is in the parlor."

She led me into the room. Fu Ying was seated in an easy chair in her widow's weeds. In fact, both of them were wearing black.

"Come in. Fu Ying has told me how you two first met. Did you really drop her from an upper window onto a mudflat?"

"Guilty as charged, I'm afraid. I throw myself on the mercy of the court."

"The jury is still considering whether we'll forgive you."

"Thick as thieves now, eh?"

"Indeed."

"My only hope is clemency, then."

"How is Sir?" Fu Ying asked. "Is he well?"

"Ah," I responded. "I need to tell you both about that. It's a bit of a story."

I told them and it took even longer than telling Jenkins. Rebecca had never heard of such a thing, and vacillated between wanting to know the details and not knowing them. Fu Ying, with her knowledge of Asian culture, understood.

"Is he really quite up to traveling alone?" Fu Ying asked when I had finished.

"Oh, yes. He'll get through this. He just needs to see Philippa's face again."

"I'm sure you are right. If anyone can soothe him, it will be her."

"I cannot wait to meet this woman who embodies the Virgin Mary," Rebecca said.

"Look who's talking about the Virgin Mary."

"Just because I'm a Jewess doesn't mean I haven't read widely."

At the same moment we looked at each other. We were squabbling like an old married couple. I hoped it was a sign of good things to come.

"When shall he return?" Fu Ying asked.

"It could be days, I suppose," I said. "Why?"

"I hoped he would find my husband. He has been seen in the lowest of opium dens, trying to stop the pain of his burns. I have awaited his return for three days. I'm very worried about him."

"Mr. Barker has asked me to look for him. He's probably weak as a kitten somewhere and wishing he were home with you."

I couldn't read her expression. It hadn't been an easy time for her these last few weeks.

Rebecca leaned forward and looked at me. "Fu Ying has something else to tell you."

"I need you to find my husband so he will know that he shall become a father."

I glanced at her momentarily, and then away, trying to make sense of her statement. Then, suddenly, an image came into my mind: Cyrus Barker at his most monolithic, towering like a mountain over a tiny morsel of human flesh, just two days old.

"Oh, please," I said. "Let me be the one to break it to him."

Read on for a
Barker & Llewelyn story,
the first time in print

AN AWKWARD WAY TO DIE

The telephone set jangled on the corner of Cyrus Barker's desk, and we both turned our heads to stare at it. I do not like telephones. They rarely bring good news when one is a private enquiry agent. Barker snagged it with his beefy hands and grunted a terse greeting. After half a minute of listening, he sighed, muttered a thank-you, and hung the receiver back on the hook. He pushed the set away from him and then drummed on his blotter in thought.

"Someone has died," I stated.

"Aye," the Guv answered. "It is Vasilios Dimitriadis."

"Your tobacconist?"

"The same."

"Isn't he the one who blends your tobacco for you but won't say what is in it?"

"Not 'isn't,' Mr. Llewelyn. 'Wasn't.' Scotland Yard has requested our presence immediately. Come along."

I found a cab in Whitehall Street and we were quickly on our way. The tobacco shop was found in the Minories, one of those few lanes in London that has no street or road in its name. It is just outside the City of London and was once a convent. Now it lay between the City and Whitechapel, without actually belonging to either.

The tobacconist had a shop on the corner of the Minories and St. Clair Street. It had no hoarding above the door, but a discreet sign beside it, reading: *V. Dimitriadis Fine Tobaccos*. A constable guarded the door from the public, but at our advent nodded the two of us inside.

"Barker!" a man called from the back of the shop.

I waited for a moment as my eyes adjusted to the gloom. As usual, the room was redolent of fresh tobacco and cigars, a homely scent.

"Cleaver," my employer rumbled in response.

I had heard this inspector's name before without actually having met him. "Inspector Clever," his compatriots called him, though I didn't know if it was a term of admiration or irony. He was a stocky fellow, with a small mustache and a forthright manner. It is as if the Criminal Investigation Department stamped out inspectors from a mold, like gingerbread men.

"He's there in the humidor," Cleaver said, gesturing toward a room not much larger than a wardrobe, lined with boxes of cigars. The open door was studded with glass panels.

I peered in upon the mortal remains of Vasilios Dimitriadis. In life he was a jovial fellow approaching forty, olive-skinned and dark-haired, with thick eyelashes and a ready smile. In death he was tragic, no less so because of the small, ornate dagger protruding from his breast.

"He was found this morning by those two gents there," the inspector said, indicating a pair of elderly men sitting at a round table by the front door, who were watching our arrival with some interest. They each wore a cutaway coat and bowler and had a medal pinned to their lapels.

"Sirs, I am Cyrus Barker," my employer intoned. "I was acquainted with Mr. Dimitriadis."

"I'm Alfred Stokes," the bearded one said, shaking his hand. "And this here is Colin MacKellar."

"I'm pleased to meet you both. Which one of you discovered the body?"

"We both did, sir," Stokes replied. "We arrived at the front door, found it locked despite it being working hours, then went 'round the back and saw the door there hanging open."

"Do you gentlemen come here often?"

MacKellar nudged his partner, then spoke in a high, reedy voice. "Come here often? Sir, we practically live here. This is the most convivial spot in all of London, or it was until this morning. It topped every public house. Sometimes Mr. Dimitriadis would allow us to try his wares for free. He showed the proper respect for veterans."

Barker turned to Cleaver, who was behind the counter opening random drawers.

"Was the store robbed?" he asked.

"The cash box is empty."

"A common robbery, then," the Guv said, with a look of disappointment.

"Strange knife," Cleaver remarked, as if it justified calling us out there.

He held up the brass knife for our inspection, having removed it from the corpse. It was shaped like a scimitar with an ornate handle, but was no longer than my hand.

Barker paced along the counter, past large glass jars of various blends and ingredients. Reaching over them, he lifted a pencil cup and began digging through it with his thick fingers. He retrieved a flattened cylinder of brass. It was a sheath.

"Your murder weapon is a letter opener, Inspector."

"Damn!" Cleaver cried. "I was hoping for an Arab secret society, at least!"

"There appears to be a small quantity of white powder underfoot," the Guv remarked.

"Yes, we'd noted that. I think it is chalk."

"Tell me, gentlemen," Barker said, addressing the elderly men at the table. "Was the door to the humidor as wide open as the back door?"

"That is how we found it, sir," MacKellar replied.

Cyrus Barker stepped gingerly into the humidor, though the chamber barely fit his outsized shoulders. He lowered himself to the floor and examined the corpse, even going so far as to open the stiffened jaw with his thumb. Finally, he rose to his feet, staring at the array of tobacco. His mustache tugged at the corners of his mouth. My employer was smiling.

"What?" I asked. "What is it?"

He shook his head and lifted one of the cigars to his nose, inhaling the aroma. Choosing a box, he lifted it and carried it out of the humidor.

"I believe Mr. Dimitriadis would not mind if we sample his wares."

"Here, now!" Cleaver warned. "That's evidence!"

"Come, Inspector, allow us to at least smoke a cigar in his honor," the Guv said, already offering the box to the old pensioners.

The latter had no objection to a free sample. There was a cup of vestas in the center of the table, and we all lit a cigar. Immediately, we began to choke.

"Worst cigar I've ever had!" the inspector said. "It tastes like seaweed. How did this man stay in business?"

"The odor you smell is chloroform," my employer replied. "Vasilios's tongue is blue from cyanosis. He has been asphyxiated. Someone coaxed him into the chamber and blocked the door until he succumbed. He was stabbed as an afterthought to put Scotland Yard off the scent, then the killer threw open this door as well as the one at the back to air the room. However, the chloroform gas leached into the cigars. He removed the bottle of the anesthetic and took it away with him."

"That's an awkward way to die," Cleaver said. "Why not just stab him here and have done with it?"

"Why, indeed?" Barker muttered.

"So, not a robbery at all, then."

"Decidedly not, Inspector. Thank you for calling. I assume there was some particular reason you thought of me?"

Clever Cleaver shrugged his shoulders. "The Greek kept a box with the names and addresses of his clientele, as well as a record of every sale. You were in the box."

"Did he by chance keep a record of his blends?" Barker asked, more interested in his supply of tobacco than the fact that he might be under suspicion by Scotland Yard in a murder enquiry.

MacKellar cleared his throat. "He always kept them in his head. Best blender in London."

My employer didn't care for that answer, but he pressed on.

"You gentlemen knew him better than I. What was he like?"

"Very nice, but bit of a dog where women are concerned, our Mr. Dimitriadis."

"Oh? Did a woman come into the shop yesterday?"

"No, sir," MacKellar answered.

"Hold on, Colin, yes there was," Stokes said, sitting forward in his chair. "But you was in the humidor when she come in. Mrs. Hornby fetched a box of cigars for her husband."

"Isn't it unusual for a woman to purchase cigars for her husband?" Barker asked, looking up from the list of customers Cleaver had shown him.

"Heard her say she took them to him and he'd take her to lunch. Not a bad trade."

"Who else came yesterday?"

"There was that Syrian. Khalif, his name is," Stokes said. "A pipe carver. Bit of an artiste. They argued, but not in English. Almost came to blows. Passionate sort of fellow was Mr. Dimitriadis."

MacKellar nodded. "There was also a fellow I saw speaking in low tones. Very mysterious gentleman, I thought. Thin chap, dressed in a long cloak and a glossy top hat."

"What did he purchase, if you can recall?" Barker asked.

"A pound of the house brand, Mr. Barker. 'Blender's Best.'"

The Guv ran a stubby finger down the list of customers. "'J. Welling, one pound B.B.' The box has a card giving an address in Kilburn.

"Inspector, I feel we owe something to our victim for his good service these last ten years. May we come along? If I find the murderer before you, you may have the credit for his capture."

Cleaver frowned, coming to a decision. "I'll tolerate the two of you, but I reserve the freedom to toss you out if you become a nuisance."

"Perish the thought," I said, raising my hands.

"There! Like that. None of that sarcasm. Sorry, gentlemen," he said to the elderly men at the table. "You'll have to clear out and find a new roost to nest in. Leave your addresses with the constable."

The Guv inspected their medals as they stood.

"Are you gentlemen out-pensioners?" he asked.

"Yes, sir," Stokes and MacKellar said in unison.

"Crimean campaign. Where did you serve, Mr. Stokes?"

The little man puffed out his chest like a bantam. He looked like he was about to salute. "Sevastopol, sir. Royal Artillery."

Barker shook his hand with a nod. "And you, Mr. MacKellar?"

"Balaclava, attached to the 4th Light Dragoon."

The three of us, including Cleaver, stopped and looked at him.

"Attached?" my employer asked.

"Orderly, sir. Medical unit. I was the one who carried the poor souls wounded and dying from the field. I sawed many a shattered limb that day."

"'Into the Valley of Death rode the Six Hundred,'" I quoted.

The old man shivered as if I'd poured water down his back.

"Where do you live, if I may ask?" Barker asked them both.

"The City," Stokes said.

"Houndsditch," MacKellar answered.

Barker nodded, as if answering his own question. "Inspector Cleaver, the case is yours. How shall we proceed?"

"Let us visit Mr. Welling of Kilburn."

The mystery of the patron clad in black was solved as soon as our cab arrived at the address on his card. Welling's Funeral Services, Ltd. was in Springfield Lane. I could hear Cleaver laughing to his constable in the next cab.

"So much for our killer draped in black," he called as we alighted at the curb. "But while we are here, let us see if he has any information germane to the case."

We entered the establishment. A clerk led us to the manager in an office at the back. There the owner stood and gestured toward some chairs. The constable and I remained standing.

Welling was over six foot and rakishly thin. He was perhaps in his fifties, but his hair and beard were dyed black to compensate for the inevitable passage of time. His short beard had been carefully and precisely shaved. I could see why someone might consider him sinister. He looked like a stage actor.

"Scotland Yard?" he asked after Cleaver had introduced us. "What would bring you here?"

"A Mr. Dimitriadis was found dead in his humidor this morning. I believe he is an acquaintance of yours."

"Dimitriadis?" the man asked. "Dead? I have bought my tobacco there, but I would hardly call him an acquaintance."

"You were there yesterday, I understand," Cleaver went on. "'Blender's Best'?"

"The best in town," Welling agreed. "Now, where I am going to get my mixture?"

Barker sighed. No doubt he was pondering the same question.

"Sir, can you establish your whereabouts last night and this morning?"

"Certainly, Inspector. I've a wife, children, and servants who can vouch for my presence. I left at six that morning by cab and arrived here by the quarter hour. My clerk arrived shortly thereafter."

"Had you developed an impression of the victim, or heard anything of him, apart from his abilities as a blender?" Barker asked.

"I don't mean to speak ill of the dead, but I've heard he was a rogue. He was a good-looking chap, I suppose, and he had a gift for jollying customers, so why not try those qualities on the fair sex?"

"Was there anything else?" the inspector asked.

"I've recommended him to various chaps. He had a way with a tobacco leaf. Am I a suspect in this crime?"

"The opposite, in fact, sir," Cleaver assured him. "We merely wish to establish your whereabouts in order to eliminate you from suspicion. There must be hundreds of customers, so we are starting with those who were at the shop yesterday. Could you give us your home address, sir?"

"Certainly."

"Then we'll take up no more of your time or ours. P. C. Fields," he said, turning to his constable, "take down the gentleman's address. Good day, Mr. Welling."

When Barker and I returned to the cab, the Guv sat back and frowned.

"The inspector is no piker. Welling is indeed a suspect, but Cleaver made himself appear sympathetic to his situation."

The cab bowled forward into Springfield Lane. Our next destination was an office in the City. Mr. Daniel Hornby had not been in the shop the previous day, but his wife had. No sooner had we been seated in his office than he offered us one of the new cigars. After having had one laced with chloroform that morning, we each declined.

"What's this about, then, gentlemen?" Hornby demanded.

He was in his late thirties, as well built as a rugby player, with blond hair that was nearly ginger and steel-blue eyes. He was a stockbroker, and a good one, I should imagine. I hated him on sight. He was the kind of aggressive, mean-spirited fellow I avoided in grammar school.

"Are you acquainted with a man named Vasilios Dimitriadis?" Cleaver asked.

"Of course. He's my tobacconist. He sold me these very cigars."

"So you purchased them yourself?"

"No, my wife did."

"Why is that, sir?" Barker asked. "I understand he delivered cigars. Why send your wife to a questionable neighborhood?"

"First of all, she's my wife, and I can send her wherever in hell I like. As it happens, she bought a box for me one day when I ran out, and in appreciation, I took her out for tea. We've been doing it every month since. It helps her to avoid several calls and to get some air. I'd prefer a whiskey and soda, but Pearl requires some handling, so I take her to an A.B.C. She can't say I'm ignoring her if I take her to tea, can she?"

Hornby fell further in my estimation than before, telling a group of perfect strangers that his wife needed special handling.

"Had you visited the shop before?"

"Yes, but the task has fallen to my wife. She is always eager to please me."

Barker pushed himself to his feet.

"Obviously, sir, you were not there yesterday to add any information to our investigation," the Guv said. "Nevertheless, we would prefer to have your private address if we should have another question."

"I say, is that necessary?" Hornby asked. "Merely because some foreigner died?"

My employer turned to the inspector, as if deferring to him.

"If you have any objections," Cleaver said, "you are welcome to come to 'A' Division to enumerate them for us."

"That's not necessary, gentlemen. I'll give it to you."

Barker nodded and left. Even Cleaver would not shake his hand. I followed after as Constable Fields took down the address.

"Where shall we go next?" I asked the inspector when we were out on the street.

"The sculptor, Khalif."

Uri Khalif's studio was hard by the Docks of Wapping, a little garret covered in gritty white dust. It crunched under our boots and we dared not sit anywhere or a cloud of it would waft across the room. Khalif himself was covered in the powder. It speckled his curling black hair and beard and his gutta-percha apron. The cuffs of his trousers were filled with it. In fact, it was sepiolite, which is to say meerschaum.

Khalif was jittering, perhaps due to the cup of Turkish coffee I saw on the table. He had a block of the mineral in his hand and was carving as he worked, his sleeves rolled to his elbows. His English was better than I expected, given his exotic appearance.

"What were you doing in Mr. Dimitriadis's shop yesterday?" Cleaver asked.

"I was collecting my orders for the coming month. He had commissioned several pipes for me to carve."

"Aren't such pipes generally carved in Turkey and shipped here?" Barker asked.

"Generally, yes, but my pipes are works of art. I try to capture not only likenesses but movement as well."

He opened a drawer and retrieved a random pipe from among many. It was carved in the likeness of Napoleon. The curl on his forehead seemed to stand out from his brow and he was frowning as if in a fit of pique, perhaps at just losing Waterloo. I saw what Khalif meant by movement. The face was so realistic, I expected it to change expression.

Barker was taking in all sides of the chamber and I believed I understood why. The chances were good that this artist had carved a pipe I saw my employer smoke during our first case, with the Guv's own visage carved in it. The pipe had since been destroyed. I assumed he'd like a duplicate.

"Very nice," Cleaver said, retrieving his notebook, oblivious to the artistry of the pipes or our reactions to them. "A witness saw you involved in an argument with the late Mr. Dimitriadis yesterday afternoon."

"No worse than usual. Vasilios was a passionate person, always ready to argue or bargain. He was an artist himself, of sorts, but he was also a canny businessman. We argued over how many pieces I should finish by the end of the month. If I met all his orders, I would have no time to eat or sleep, or to visit my girl in Poplar."

"You have a girl in Poplar, then?" Cleaver asked. "What's her name?"

"Annie Sanders."

"An English girl, eh?"

The inspector said no more than this, but the scorn he put into the words at the thought that a Musselman should be accompanying a bloom of English womanhood was unmistakable. Khalif did not react. I'm certain he was accustomed to such comments.

"So, you argued with the deceased over the number of orders he wanted you to do," Cleaver stated.

"Yes, sir, but we always argued. We were bargaining, you see. He quoted too high a number, I too low a number, and—"

"I'm familiar with the concept of bargaining, thank you, Mr. Khalif. You claim these arguments were habitual and not heated?"

"No doubt the argument might appear heated to someone else, but I assure you, I might buy the man dinner some evening and play chess with him after."

"Did you notice anyone in the shop while you were there?" Barker asked.

"A couple of old men at a table nearby. There was a woman in the shop, too, I think. What is the English word for when a horse looks ready to bolt?"

"Skittish?" I supplied.

"Exactly. She looked skittish."

"Thank you, sir," Barker rumbled.

Inspector Cleaver stood and nodded to the constable.

"All right, I've seen enough. Mr. Khalif, or whatever your name is, I arrest you in connection to the murder of Vasilios Dimitriadis. Anything you say may be used in court. Fields, clap the darbies on him."

So much for Inspector Clever, I thought. Obviously, Scotland Yard made quick decisions due to their heavy caseload. It was always easier to blame a foreigner, as if England had no criminal class of its own. We watched him loaded into a Black Mariah. As the vehicle began to move, Barker shook his head.

"Let's go back to the offices. I think we need to do further thinking on this case on our own."

Once there, Barker smoked one of his cigars from the box on his desk, a rare occurrence. He sat back and blew a smoke ring into the air and stared out over the courtyard.

"I knew a Chelsea pensioner when I first came to London," he said. "We met on a park bench, of all places. We fell into conversation and I told him I intended to be a detective."

"Private enquiry agent," I corrected.

"No, nothing as grand as that. I still hadn't made my plans. Anyway, he encouraged me to study the streets of London, and possibly even take the test for cabmen. He took me about the city, street by street. The old man was quite an ambulist. Morrison, his name was. I always called him Mr. Morrison, out of respect."

"You never introduced him to me," I said.

"Oh, he passed away, not a few months after I passed the test. I attended his funeral. I still miss him at times. It's good to know a man or two ahead of you in the walk of life."

This was a red letter day. I realized Cyrus Barker was revealing a part of his past without being asked.

"All the same," he said. "Go to the Chelsea hospital and get the addresses for our pensioners."

"Why their addresses, sir?"

He gave one of his wintery looks.

"I'll be on my way, then," I said, donning my hat and stepping into the street.

The Royal Hospital Chelsea, being over fifty acres in the heart of the West End, was not difficult to find. When seeking information from a public source, it is best to tell the absolute truth or to create a plausible lie. This time, I chose to go with the first. I was passed from the clerk at the front desk to his superior. In his office, I lay my card upon his desk.

He glared at it for a moment, trying to take it in.

"How can I help you?"

"Two of your out-pensioners were very helpful during one of our investigations recently. It was my employer's wish to send each a card of thanks, along with a small remuneration. Are out-pensioners' addresses private?"

"They are," he told me.

"Oh, blast. I was hoping to give the lads a small treat. They really were instrumental in our investigations."

"What are their names?"

"Alfred Stokes and Colin MacKellar."

"I suppose I could break the rules this once."

"Oh, I wouldn't want to get you in any kind of trouble."

"No trouble. It is up to my discretion. Let me get those addresses for you. Actually, I don't have to look at MacKellar's file. He's one of ours, an inpatient."

I took both addresses, but when I delivered them to Barker, he stuffed them absently in his pocket. He's like that. He'll praise me for the smallest thing, then take something which required a bit of effort in its stride. But then, I was used to it by now.

"Take a letter, Mr. Llewelyn," he said.

I drew my notebook from my rolltop desk.

"Dear Mrs. Hornby,

I wish to ask you a few questions regarding the death of Mr. Vasilios Dimitriadis. We are not from the official police. Please meet me at our offices tomorrow morning at ten o'clock, or I shall have no concern for your reputation.

Sincerely,
Cyrus Barker.'

Type that for me and give it to a messenger. You should have Mr. Hornby's private address in your notes."

Promptly the next morning, Mrs. Hornby arrived on our

doorstep, looking as nervous as a cat with a long tail. She was an attractive young woman with blond hair and blue eyes, approaching thirty. I helped her to the client's chair.

"How can I help you, sir?" she asked Barker, clutching her reticule.

He stood at the side of his desk and looked down at her. The sheer size of him had to be intimidating to a skittish young woman.

"Tell us, Madam, how long has Mr. Dimitriadis been blackmailing you."

Mrs. Hornby looked stricken. There was no way now for her to deny that such an event had occurred. The Guv raised an eyebrow, and his roughhewn face softened a little.

"I—I don't know what you're talking about," she said.

Barker sighed. "There's no use for it, Mrs. Hornby. Besides, no doubt you could use someone willing to listen and to help you in any way he can."

"At what price, Mr. Barker?"

"My interest is merely to end my investigation, not to bilk you for more money. I'm certain you have given enough. I don't intend to go into the unsavory relationship between yourself and Mr. Dimitriadis. I understand he was . . . Mr. Llewelyn, what was the term?"

"A bit of a dog, sir?" I supplied from my notes.

"Precisely. What evidence did he have in his possession?"

"A letter, Mr. Barker," she said, looking ashen.

"No doubt in answer to one of his own. You were unwise to set your feelings down on paper."

"I realize that now, sir," she said, squirming in her chair. She began twisting a small lace handkerchief in her hand.

"Could you provide definitive proof of where you were yesterday morning between five a.m. and noon?"

"Of course. I saw my husband, Daniel, out the door, and then worked upon the family accounts. Our nanny was in the house, seeing to little Nicholas."

Barker tsked. "A child, Mrs. Hornby? Really."

Her face fell. She was almost in tears. Barker generally does not encourage the expressing of emotion among female witnesses—or male, for that matter—but in this case, he provoked it.

"You knew about the death of Mr. Dimitriadis, I assume."

"Yes, Mr. Barker. It was in the late edition. I'm afraid I was relieved."

"How much did he demand you to pay, Mrs. Hornby?"

"Twenty-five pounds a month, sir. It was a good portion of my household expenses. I had to be careful in my accounting to keep every pence."

"Do you suspect that your husband might have discovered your affair and killed your lover?"

"Oh, don't call him that, sir! We only talked and exchanged letters. I had not realized he was such a cad, but that is no excuse for my behavior. Did he? Do you think my husband killed Vasilios?"

"No, Mrs. Hornby, he did not. Under such conditions, a jealous husband prefers to strangle his wife's seducer face-to-face, but locking a man in a chloroform-filled cabinet requires no physical strength. It is a woman's method."

"But, sir, as I said, our nanny was with me the entire time."

Barker sat back in his tall, green leather chair.

"A nanny in your home would be willing to provide an alibi, lest she break up the home and lose her situation."

"No, sir," she replied. "You are wrong. In fact, she would like nothing more than to prove I had gone out. My husband has been having a dalliance with her for over a year, under my very nose. Dan thinks I don't know."

"That explains why you should have fallen to Mr. Dimitriadis's charms that first time you bought a box of cigars for your husband."

"That explains it, Mr. Barker, but it does not excuse it."

The Guv nodded, but not unkindly.

"Did the tobacconist seem different in any way when you saw him yesterday?"

"No. He was loathsome, as always. He continued to press me for more money. He threatened to send the letter to my husband. Do you have it? Does Scotland Yard?"

"I haven't," the Guv replied. "And I suspect Scotland Yard does not know about it, either."

Barker scratched under his chin, a gesture that occurs when he is pondering something.

"Very well, Madam. I have no more questions at present. Thank you for your frankness. Good day."

Our visitor blinked. She made no attempt to rise.

"But who killed him, Mr. Barker? Who killed Vasilios?"

"Not you, apparently. I assume you have no acquaintance with the uses of chloroform."

"No, sir, of course not."

"Then I have no further need to trouble you."

He waved her away and reached for the morning post. She looked at me, nonplussed. I saw her to the door and returned to my chair near his desk.

"That was a bit ungallant, sir," I dared say.

"I have no time to soothe ruffled feathers. I have an investigation to conclude. Speaking of which, let's go, Thomas. We don't have time to dawdle all morning."

A minute later, we were in a cab, heading who knows where.

"Do you remember the uniforms of the Yeomen Warders at the Tower?" the Guv asked.

"Of course, sir. Dress red on important days, dress blue on days without ceremony."

"The Chelsea Pensioners have a similar dress, both red and blue, but it has to do with distance from the Chelsea Hospital. Nearby they wear dress blue. Two miles or more away, they wear red."

"How does that help us, sir?"

"According to the addresses you procured from the hospital, Mr. Stokes lives in the City, but Mr. MacKellar is an inpatient. He tried to make us believe that he was a long time habitué of

Mr. Dimitriadis's establishment, like Stokes, when in fact, I suspect he wasn't."

"That's right," I answered. "He said Houndsditch. But why? Why go to the trouble of appearing as if he were from one area of London and not another?"

"That's the wrong question, lad," he rumbled. "We should ask why he should frequent a tobacconist so far from his residence. And why go in civilian dress when he is permitted to wear the scarlet coat?"

The hansom pulled to the curb at the hospital as I was contemplating his words. My first thought as we stepped inside the building was that it was rather fine for old soldiers on a fixed budget. They were almost like gentlemen's lodgings. The porter questioned us severely before leading us to the pensioner's door. When Mr. MacKellar answered, he was in his dress red with a row of medals on his chest.

"Ah," he said. "Yes. Let them in, Smithers. They are my guests. Come in, gentlemen."

We entered and I looked about. He had a small spartan but well-furnished flat, dominated by a large painting over the fireplace. I gravitated to it. It was a military scene, soldiers on horseback in battle. I read the legend at the bottom. *Sevastopol.*

The old fellow eased himself into a chair, cane at his elbow, and waved us to our chairs.

"Let us get this over with, gentlemen, if you don't mind."

"Very well, sir," Barker said, frowning. "At some time in the past month or two you began to frequent Mr. Dimitriadis's shop. You must have passed several tobacconists in order to reach that one. Why did you travel so far?"

The old gentleman seemed reluctant to speak, but my employer was adamant.

"We must get to the truth, sir. We do not wish to expose the young woman to a public trial."

"Trial?" MacKellar asked, looking stricken.

"Yes. With a sympathetic jury, her sentence will be commuted.

No sense in hanging a young woman over a cad who was black-mailing her."

"Hanging!"

Barker turned to me. Not only did I know that Mrs. Hornby hadn't been arrested, I knew Khalif had. I wondered what card the Guv was playing.

"Lad, you might not be aware that chloroform was first used during the Crimean War, as a way to sedate patients prior to am-putation. Sometimes the dosage, given inadequately, would cause the patient to wake in the middle of the surgery. Too potent, and the patient would die, as Mr. Dimitriadis did, asphyxiated by fumes."

"I could not overpower a man as young and strong as he!" MacKellar said.

"No, but you could place a canister of chloroform into the humidor, then request the owner to select a cigar for you. When he entered, you slammed the door behind him and wedged your cane underneath the knob. Then you had the pleasure of watch-ing the man die. Afterward, you removed the canister, and opened the doors, then hid around the corner of the alley until Mr. Stokes came to the front door."

"And why should I do all this?" MacKellar demanded.

"While Mr. Llewelyn went to the Chelsea Hospital this morn-ing, I spent a little time at the Public Records Office. It appears Mrs. Hornby's maiden name was MacKellar. You are protecting your granddaughter. Perhaps she could not confess what she had done to her parents, but a beloved grandfather would be like a father confessor."

I turned to look at MacKellar and his cheeks were damp.

"And your granddaughter was blackmailed by Dimitriadis."

"There was no question he needed to be stopped. I am a feeble old man, but I am skilled with the use of chloroform. I entered the establishment one day and saw the benefits of the humidor to lock the man into. I befriended Mr. Stokes to have a reason to come regularly. On that day, I arrived early and convinced my granddaughter's seducer to let me in. After I opened the canister, he stepped in to choose a cigar for me and when he died, I opened the door and stabbed him with the letter opener as a *coup de grace*. I had no sympathy for the blighter. Then I searched his papers behind the desk until I found her letter, took the money, and left."

"What did you do with the letter?"

"I destroyed it."

"And the money?" my employer asked.

"I would not profit by this. I gave it to the Salvation Army. It was no more than ten pounds."

"Mr. MacKellar, I have no client, and as it turned out my to-bacconist was a disreputable fellow. However, you had no right to take a life."

"Agreed. What shall you do now?"

"You shall put your affairs in order, tell your granddaughter what you have done, and turn yourself in at a constabulary."

"And if I escape instead?"

"I was a member of Her Majesty's army in Shanghai. You know as well as I that it is a matter of honor. If you run, it would blacken the name of your regiment."

"I see. Thank you, Mr. Barker."

We stood and bowed to the old gentleman and took our leave. Outside, the Guv pulled his pipe and sealskin pouch from his pocket. He stuffed his pipe in his mouth with the last of his to-bacco and patted his pockets for a pack of lucifers.

"Why didn't we escort him to Scotland Yard, sir?" I asked.

"The man is seventy-four," Barker replied. "Either he will do the honorable thing or time will inevitably be his judge and jury."

"He'll turn himself in," I remarked.

"Of course. He's a soldier of Her Majesty's army. It's a matter of honor."

He struck the match against the wall of the hospital and brought it to the bowl of the pipe.

"Wait!" I cried.

"What is it, lad?"

"Why not take that tobacco to another blender and see what he can make of it?"

The Guv chuckled.

"Thank you, Thomas. A capital suggestion. I knew there had to be a reason I keep you about."